P9-DSZ-885

carly
phillips

hot number

HQN™

Recycling programs
for this product may
not exist in your area.

ISBN-13: 978-0-373-77473-9

HOT NUMBER

This edition published by arrangement with Harlequin Books S.A.

For questions and comments about the quality of this book please contact us at Customer_eCare@Harlequin.ca.

® and TM are trademarks of the publisher. Trademarks indicated with ® are registered in the United States Patent and Trademark Office, the Canadian Trade Marks Office and in other countries.

www.HQNBooks.com

Printed in U.S.A.

This book is dedicated
to the most important people in my life:

My husband Phil, *my* number 22 and the sexiest guy
in a baseball uniform. Didn't you know
that's what kept me coming back for more?

My mother for raising me to be independent and to
believe in myself and for renewing my love of
baseball—even if she is a Yankees fan, I'm a Mets fan
and my husband, from Boston, is a Red Sox fan.
At least our family life is interesting and fun!

My father, who has no interest in sports but survives
the bickering with a smile and who is my most loyal fan.

And as always my girls, Jackie and Jennifer,
for just being you!

And an extra-special thank-you to Janelle Denison,
who saved me midway through yet again.
Where would I be without you?

I love you all.

hot number

PROLOGUE

THANKS TO A FATAL plane crash in the Andes, Yank Morgan had been raising his sister's children for the past two years, and as a result, even his chest hair had turned prematurely gray. Ages fourteen, twelve and ten, the girls were independent little scrappers and didn't hesitate to tell him exactly what they thought. Which was why Annabelle, the oldest, stood before him, hands on her hips, her breasts pushing against the cotton of her too-tight shirt. When the hell had she developed boobs? he wondered and ran a hand through his wiry hair.

At the moment though, his niece's face concerned him more than her chest. Black eyeliner was smudged around her bright blue eyes and though normally he didn't mind letting the girls make their own mistakes, her raccoon-like appearance was too humiliating to allow, so he'd decided to step in.

Keeping Lola's words in mind, he opted to tread gently with the girl. "Dang it, Annie, you look like Jim McMahon getting ready to throw a pass."

Her blue eyes filled with tears and she ran from the room. He raised his gaze toward the ceiling. "What the hell did I do wrong now?"

"Way to go, Uncle Yack." He glanced over to see the youngest, Micki, standing in the doorway glaring at him.

"It's Yank," he muttered, though they both knew that the nickname she'd started to use the day she'd come to live with him gave them a special bond.

"You insulted Annie," said Sophie, the middle one, joining them.

Figures they'd gang up on him. "You think so?"

He turned toward them for the first time and his gaze immediately zeroed in on ten-year-old Micki. Or rather his gaze zeroed in on her tits.

"What the hell are those?" he asked, pointing to the overly round, out of proportion, different-size melons poking from beneath her shirt.

"Like 'em?" She squared her shoulders.

Yank winced.

Lola, his assistant at the agency and one-time lover, strode into the room. She showed up on weekends to do the girls' laundry along with her own. Although having her around aroused him and forced him to remember their short-lived affair, Yank was grateful for her help and couldn't imagine life without her. Not that he'd ever admit as much. The woman and his feelings for her scared him worse than raising the girls.

"Who's been stealing things out of the laundry basket?" Lola asked.

Sophie snickered. "Ask Micki."

"Michelle?" Lola strode over and glanced down at Micki's protruding chest. "Do you have my bra?"

Yank groaned.

"Nope. No bra." Micki chewed on her lower lip, a sure sign the kid was lying.

"Yes you do too have it! You see?" Sophie reached a hand down the front of her sister's shirt, pulling out the padding. Then she glanced down at her hand and frowned. "Hey, those are *my* socks you stuffed your boobies with!"

"Are not!" Micki said, crossing her arms over her now flat chest.

"Are too!" Sophie retorted.

Yank felt a headache coming on.

"Well, you gave them to me," Micki shouted, tears filling her eyes.

"Did not!"

"Did too!"

"Did not!"

"You know the rules. Once you give, you can't take back!" Micki cried and darted out of the room, following Annabelle's earlier lead.

Sophie took off after her.

Yank met Lola's amused gaze and desire flared between them. A strong yearning flickered in her deep-set eyes, an echo of the spark he'd spent the past two years working hard to suppress. Though they'd once had a hot affair going between them, the girls' arrival had put everything on hold. Now, knowing he was a father for life scared the pants off him. No way would he add a wife, as well.

"Micki's something else," he said and gestured to the doorway his nieces had stormed through.

"All three girls are something else. They need guidance."

What she meant was a *woman's* guidance. But Yank had no problem deliberately misinterpreting her words if it helped him put distance between them. "I think you got a point. Micki does need guidance. So maybe you'd better go give the young one a few pointers on being *one of the guys.* You'd probably be good at that." He let that sink in. "She's obviously trying way too hard to be a woman."

She scowled at him and stormed out of the room, probably ticked off that he'd insulted her femininity. He let out a groan. Well, she'd steer clear of him for a while, which was exactly what he wanted.

And with those words, Yank sealed both Micki's upbringing and his own fate for the next sixteen years.

CHAPTER ONE

PUBLICIST MICKI JORDAN strode into the locker room of the New York Renegades, the sports world's best prospects to win the World Series, and looked for her client. In her hand, she held a copy of today's *New York Post,* which she'd folded open to the head-line Nails, Nails, Nails. Will John Roper's Manicure Interfere with his Willingness to Catch Fly Balls?

Most days she loved her job as the publicist for the Hot Zone, an offshoot of her uncle's sports agency that she copartnered with her sisters. And then there were days like these when she wondered why she always ended up handling the more high-maintenance players instead of turning them over to one of her sisters. Even if *this* high-maintenance player had ended up being her best guy friend.

Micki already knew the reason Annie and Sophie delegated the tougher athletes to her. *You're like one of the guys, Micki, and they respect you for it.* She shook her head in frustration that had been building for a while, but she'd have to worry about her own image later. Right now she was worried about her client's.

"Hey, Micki," one of the players called as she passed the first row of half-naked men and their open lockers.

She waved and kept walking, keeping her gaze straight ahead. When people asked how Micki could be so at ease around a men's locker room, she always countered with how could she not be comfortable since it was the atmosphere in which she'd grown up?

Micki had been eight, Annabelle twelve and Sophie ten when their parents had passed away. From then on, their uncle had provided them with the only stability they'd known. As the oldest, Annabelle had taken over as the mother figure and mediator whenever Micki and Sophie bickered, which had been often.

In an effort to keep their small family together, Annabelle had kept them both in line and attended to everyone's needs, often at the expense of her own. As a result, Annie had been close with both of her siblings but Micki and Sophie's relationship had always been more distant.

While Annabelle and Sophie had been girlie girls, Micki had latched onto Uncle Yank, tailing after him everywhere he went. Locker rooms included. Growing up with her sisters, Micki had been the odd girl out, a pattern that had continued in school, where she found herself trying to keep up with the boys, playing sports and challenging them with her knowledge of all games. In fact her comfort level never faltered with the opposite sex—as long as dating wasn't involved. Then Micki became out of her element all over again.

"Hi, Mick," Juan Sierra said, flicking her playfully with a towel and reminding her of her mission to find her client.

"Where's Roper?" she asked him.

"Holding court at his locker." Ricky Carter, the backup center fielder jerked a finger toward the back of the room, answering a question she hadn't directed his way.

Micki and Carter had never been formally introduced but she'd heard plenty about his cocky personality. She'd also caught wind of his certainty that he'd replace Damian Fuller by the end of the season. Micki held back a snort. She'd pay good money to see Ricky Carter try to take on the team captain and come out whole. If Carter was lucky, he'd only be knocked down a few pegs. If he pushed too hard, he'd probably end up back in Triple-A.

That's how much his teammates respected Damian Fuller. That's how much his fans loved him, as did most women, Micki thought wryly. Herself included.

Especially since their New Year's Eve kiss six months ago. She closed her eyes and could almost feel the star center fielder's lips on hers. It had begun as Micki's attempt to take him outside and sober him up before he made a scene destined to hit the papers. And it had ended up a kiss that had shaken her world and shown her what she was missing in her all-work, no-play life. Unfortunately, he'd either been too drunk to remember Micki's magic moment, or the kiss had meant so little to him he'd put it out of his mind. Worse, maybe he *wanted* to forget.

And why wouldn't he? The man was only seen with gorgeous women. The models, actresses, and even *Playboy* bunnies he dated were all well-endowed arm candy. All unlike every guy's pal, Micki Jordan. And so she'd been tiptoeing around the secret kiss and its effect on her ever since. Because that kiss had shifted Micki's perception of her world and forced her to face the unfulfilled feeling she had about her life.

Even Uncle Yank sensed she'd grown more edgy and restless lately and had begun to ask why. She didn't want to hurt him and so she refused to admit the truth. That Damian Fuller was the one man who made her wish she'd spent less time with her uncle and his friends and more time with her sisters as they'd locked themselves in the bathroom, laughing, giggling, putting on makeup and talking about boys.

Hanging out with Uncle Yank hadn't prepped Micki for flirting with men nor had it taught her how to be one of those females who automatically caught a man's attention in the ways that counted. Damian was drawn to overtly feminine women and his reaction to Micki, or lack thereof, reduced her to feeling worse than an awkward teenager.

She tried to hide her frustration with herself and her lack of feminine abilities, and as long as she didn't deal directly with Damian face-to-face, she'd be successful. It helped that the Renegades players were generally Annabelle's clients and Micki could avoid the sexy center fielder.

Leave it to John Roper to misbehave and put her directly in temptation's path. So far though, she hadn't seen any signs of Damian and since she hadn't tripped or fallen over a bench, Micki figured he wasn't anywhere around.

She followed Carter's direction and found Roper freshly showered and joking around with reporters. She halted behind them and waited, not wanting to read him the riot act in front of the press and cause any more problematic headlines.

The New York press was an entity unto itself, creating celebrities out of athletes and saving headlines for the players' personal lives. Like their crosstown rivals, the New York Yankees, the Renegades players knew how to work the media and enjoyed keeping their names in the papers. None more than Damian Fuller, who frequently graced not only the

sports sections but the gossip columns. His headlines kept him alive and vibrant in the public eye. If
Damian had a slump, the fans came to cheer him out
of it. He was a huge stadium draw and a necessary
commodity to team management. Noting which
woman he had on his arm, how often he'd dated her
and when he'd move on was every New York colum-
nist's favorite pastime. The difference between
Roper and Damian was that Damian's press was always flattering.

As a friend, Roper was the best. As a client, the
man was the ultimate pain in the butt. He'd hired her
to help him maintain a masculine image yet he did
everything possible to screw with her plan. He obviously liked the attention he received when he did
something metrosexual and outrageous, but they'd
been over and over the need for him to keep a low-
maintenance profile, and keep the media's focus on
his baseball game.

"We're meeting in ten minutes, so wrap up the in-
terviews." Coach Donovan's voice boomed throughout the locker room and Micki knew she had a short
time to knock some sense into Roper's head.

She cleared her throat and stepped into the crowd.
"I think Roper's finished answering questions for today," she said, asserting her authority.

He scowled. "But I was just—"

"Shutting the hell up," a familiar masculine voice

drawled. "Unless you want your publicist to kick your ass," Damian Fuller said, laughing.

His deep tenor sent Micki's body into sensory overload—her skin suddenly grew hot and prickly, her breath became heavy and her stomach churned with excitement. It might have been easy to ignore the other half-dressed men in the room, but not *this* man.

She tensed as Damian strode forward, sexy and sure. Freshly showered, he wore a towel hung low on his hips, revealing a tanned, muscular chest. His coarse hair had just the right sprinkling of gray.

Her breath caught and her throat grew dry. She was totally aware of all six foot three inches, 215 pounds of him. In a weak moment the day after she'd kissed those sculpted lips, threaded her fingers through that thick brown hair and scraped her cheeks against his short, scruffy beard, she'd read the stats Annie had in her press folder on number twenty-two.

Just thinking about that moonlit New Year's Eve turned her on all over again. She cleared her throat and glanced into Damian's chocolate-brown eyes but he barely acknowledged her presence. Her stomach plummeted and her heart squeezed painfully in her chest, yet somehow she maintained her composure. Micki schooled her expression so that nobody would view her disappointment or realize she'd been hurt.

"Sorry, people. No more questions for today." Roper's voice drew her attention as he deferred to his captain and called an end to the impromptu press conference.

Before the media took off, Ricky Carter sauntered up to Roper and slung an arm over his shoulder. "I guess good old Fuller's right about you, Roper. You're afraid your publicist will string you up by your—"

"Shut up," Damian said, abruptly cutting Carter off. "We're in mixed company." He and the rest of the guys stared beyond her to the newest person in the room, Veronica Butler from Esports Network.

The gorgeous redhead in the cream-colored suit with gold stitching coanchored the cable network's most popular prime-time show. She was also a friend of Micki's and a colleague who booked many of the Hot Zone's clients. Like Micki, as a woman in a man's world, she demanded respect and received it. Unlike Micki, she also received the deference due a lady, at least where Damian Fuller was concerned. In his eyes, Veronica wasn't *one of the guys*.

Micki swallowed hard. Considering her upbringing, foul language wasn't a shock to Micki and yet she might have been grateful for Damian's sensitivity anyway—had he been worried about *her*.

Unwilling to stand around a minute longer, Micki jabbed Roper in the arm. "Private talk. *Now*."

Her client followed and Micki finished their meeting with a threat that if he didn't cooperate with the PR plan they'd agreed upon and lay off the day spas and back waxes during the season, she was through as his publicist. She then escaped the locker room, including its accompanying male testosterone and humiliation, as soon as humanly possible.

THAT NIGHT, MICKI SAT in her apartment's small kitchen across from Roper. His eyes gleamed as he devoured the meal she'd cooked for them both.

"Micki, you make the meanest omelet I've ever had the pleasure of eating," he said between the fork-fuls of food he shoveled into his mouth.

"No need to suck up, John. I've already cooked for you."

He grinned. "And I thank you for inviting me."

"You invited yourself," she reminded him, recalling his phone message about how he'd be over around seven for some good food.

She knew he meant they'd go out for a bite. She and John often caught a late meal together if they were both free. He was one of the guys she felt completely comfortable around because she could be herself and he didn't care how she looked or dressed. He accepted her in her after-work sweats or old faded jeans. Which was why she didn't mind cooking for them so they could really relax instead of eating in a restaurant surrounded by people.

She glanced down at the Spanish omelet she'd prepared, frowned and pushed her plate aside.

"No appetite?" he asked.

She shrugged. "Not really."

He switched his empty dish for her full one. "Do you mind?"

She shook her head.

He dug into her portion with equal gusto. "If you want him to notice you then you need to step up," Roper said between bites.

At his words, Micki froze in her seat. "If I want *who* to notice me?" she asked, feigning ignorance and buying herself some thinking time, she hoped.

She and John clicked on many levels and he was a close enough friend that she'd confided in him about many of her deepest insecurities, but she'd avoided discussing Damian Fuller and *that kiss*. Roper was Damian's teammate and Micki knew the propensity for guy talk in the locker room. Still, unlike most men, John had a sensitive side and she didn't think he'd deliberately betray her confidence if she decided to fill him in.

She pursed her lips in thought, still undecided about how much to reveal.

"Hey, babe, you should know by now you can't put anything over on me. You obviously have the hots for Fuller."

She swallowed and choked on her own saliva, grabbing for a glass of water.

"Easy," he said, laughing. "It's just me, so before

you try and argue, remember I'm the one who knows how you always felt left out when your sisters would start with the girl talk growing up. And I also know how hard it is for you to date or open yourself up to guys on any level other than friendship. So why wouldn't I notice your reaction when Fuller rolled out the red carpet for Veronica but ignored you?"

"Way to watch out for my feelings, Roper." She glanced down at her hands, unwilling to meet his gaze or admit he was right.

"Hey, you've been dancing around those feelings, which hasn't helped you any, so I decided it was time to bring things out into the open." He raised his eyebrow, challenging her to talk openly with him.

"I had no idea I was so transparent," she muttered.

"Only to those who love you best." He treated her to his trademark grin and the dimples women loved. Thank God she wasn't into him *that way,* Micki thought wryly. She had enough trying to handle her attraction for Damian Fuller.

"So what are you suggesting? That I step up… how?"

"Why hasn't Damian noticed you as anything other than my publicist up until now?" John countered her question with one of his own.

"Because…" Her voice trailed off. She *really* didn't want to tread these painful waters, Micki thought. Didn't want to dig into the differences between herself and her sisters, the girlie girls versus the tomboy.

Not that her sisters had ever criticized or belittled her choice to be more like Uncle Yank. In fact Annabelle had coddled and babied Micki. She'd looked out for her little sister and made sure Micki felt safe and loved. And though Sophie had been more reserved, that was her personality. Annabelle reached Sophie more easily because they had more in common. Still, when all was said and done, there was a loyalty between the sisters that ran deep. In their hearts, the Jordan sisters remembered being left alone in the world by their parents with the knowledge that they only had each other to count on. Each other, Uncle Yank and Lola, their surrogate mother.

"I'm going to tell you why Fuller hasn't noticed you yet," John said, intruding on her thoughts.

His soft tone indicated she wasn't going to like what she heard. "I don't suppose you can spare me the details?"

Roper shook his head. "Fuller hasn't looked twice because you blend into the woodwork, doll."

She winced at his too-accurate assessment.

He patted her hand. "That's not to say there's anything wrong with who you are. I happen to adore you. It's just that you've fallen for a guy who likes frills. Now take me for example."

"At the moment, I wish someone would."

He shook his head and laughed. "We're hanging out and I'm wearing what?"

Micki didn't have the foggiest notion what he was talking about. "Clothing?" she asked.

He groaned. "A Hugo Boss shirt, Polo pants and Cole Haan loafers. I've gelled my hair and—"

"Waxed your back and painted your nails with clear polish. I get it. You've done all the things I'm trying to break you of doing until the season's over!"

"Exactly." John leaned back in his seat and smiled contentedly. "If you would put in half the effort, Damian couldn't help but notice that gorgeous face, perfect complexion and those darling curls you hide in a ponytail." He gave a fake shudder at the last word.

She glanced at the ceiling, thinking about the validity of his point. The insecurities she'd experienced growing up around her beautiful sisters and the self-doubt she'd felt with Veronica in the locker room today surfaced again now.

He leaned forward. "So what's going on in there?" He tapped on her forehead.

"It's just that if I change who I am on the outside, then I wouldn't be me. Don't I deserve to find someone who appreciates me for who I am?"

"Of course you do." John placed a comforting hand over hers. "And if you did what I just suggested, you would still be you—only more obvious. Once you catch the right man's interest, he'd be a fool not to see all you have to offer him."

"You're a great guy," she told him, then gave him a sideways look. "I notice you didn't say that Damian Fuller is that right man."

John shrugged, conceding the point, then leaned back again in his chair. "Fuller's my captain and teammate. I admire him. But he's still living the life of an athlete who just made his first million. He may have the potential to grow up, he may not. I don't want you to get hurt but…"

"But what?"

"Maybe Fuller has potential. That's up to you to discover."

Micki shivered at the prospect.

Meanwhile Roper fidgeted in his chair, glancing at his watch when he didn't think she was looking. "Hot date?" she asked.

"Would you be insulted if I said I had to eat and run?"

She rolled her eyes. A free night during the season didn't happen often. "Of course not but you need to promise me you'll behave. No more antics or giving the press cause to speculate on anything, okay?"

"You drive a hard bargain," he said, as he cocked his head to the side. "How about we make a deal? I won't get the earring I wanted if you promise to consider my advice—you step up a little and see if

Fuller notices you." He winked, then rose, collecting their plates and placing them in the sink.

The man was a true find. "Some woman's going to be lucky to land you, Roper."

"I'm nowhere finished sowing my wild oats."

She stood and walked him to the door. "I'm afraid Damian isn't either."

"You'll never know until you try." John wrapped a friendly arm around her shoulders. "Remember Roper's word to the wise—life is nothing without risks."

She laughed. "I'll remember."

He kissed her head and took off.

Alone in her apartment, Micki rinsed their plates and dried them, her mind preoccupied with Roper's words. He was right about a lot of things but most importantly about her feelings for Damian. She did have the hots for him and had since this past New Year's Eve. Damian's kiss, planted on her in a drunken stupor, had been a prelude. One taste hadn't been enough and he'd whetted her appetite for more. When his full lips had been on hers, and his hard body against hers had warmed her in the cold winter air, she'd realized how much she desired the man.

Micki wanted to feel the excitement of a home run with Damian. Unfortunately he didn't even remember reaching first base.

THE NEXT MORNING, Micki stood in front of the mirror in the restroom of the Hot Zone. She eyed her standard look—her blond curls hastily pulled into a ponytail and her white button-down shirt tucked into a pair of black slacks—and frowned at the lackluster sight. Was it any wonder that when she strode into a locker room full of naked men, none of them "stood at attention"?

She was sick and tired of being considered one of the guys, especially by Damian, and Roper had made it perfectly clear why the man failed to notice Micki. Last night's conversation was fresh in her mind and she couldn't help but be frustrated with the status quo. Though her practical side understood that being treated as an equal was what female reporters and publicists had been fighting for for years, the female side of her had been ignored too long and demanded recognition.

"Micki? It's meeting time." Her middle sister, Sophie, called from the hall.

"I'm coming, I'm coming." Micki turned away from the mirror just as Sophie stepped into the ladies' room.

Her gaze scanned Micki's face. "Okay, what's wrong?" Sophie nailed Micki with the knowing stare she'd perfected as a child.

The desire to reveal all was strong until Micki's gaze raked over her beautifully dressed sister. Not a stray hair fell from Sophie's sleek chignon, and her purple tweed suit was the height of fashion. Probably Chanel. No quick, off-the-rack shopping run for Sophie or Annabelle, Micki thought.

Her insecurities rose full force and any thoughts Micki had of admitting her recent bout of uncertainty fled in the face of Sophie's perfection. "What makes you think anything's wrong?" Micki asked, lifting her chin a notch.

Sophie turned the lock on the company restroom door, shutting them in the small lounge area alone. "You're my sister and I know you. Since Annabelle married Vaughn and got pregnant, you haven't been your usual spunky self."

Micki placed a hand on the white sink, aware of the cold porcelain beneath her hand and the intensity of her grip. "I'm not jealous."

Sophie raised an eyebrow. "Did I say you were? Listen," she said, approaching Micki slowly. "I know that Annie's marriage and move has changed the dynamic of your relationship."

Micki acknowledged that truth with a nod. Annabelle used to live across the hall from both Micki and Sophie until she and Vaughn had relocated to his lodge in Greenlawn, a small town in upstate New York. Though the couple had kept Annabelle's apartment, they didn't spend much time there. Even Sophie's presence and Roper's visits didn't ease that loss.

"I know we've never been as tight as you and Annie, but I miss her, too," Sophie admitted, the uptight armor she normally kept around her softening as she spoke. "And maybe this is a good time for us to…" Her voice trailed off.

Could confident Sophie be hesitant, too? Micki wondered.

"Maybe we could get closer?" Micki met her sister halfway and hoped she hadn't misread her intent.

Sophie nodded and relief filled Micki. Apparently, despite their very different personalities, she and Sophie really *had* formed a bond, even if they'd drifted for a while. Annabelle's life change offered the perfect excuse for them to forge a new beginning of their own.

Micki knew just where to begin. "Soph?" Micki asked tentatively.

"Yes?" Her sister sounded just as wary.

With Roper's suggestion that she "step up" and capture Damian's attention ringing in her ears, she turned to her feminine, perfect-looking sister. "Can you teach me how to be more of a…girl?"

Sophie's eyes sparkled with surprise and excitement at Micki's words. "It's about time!" she said, practically salivating at the idea of making Micki over.

Together they headed to the conference room to meet with Uncle Yank and tried not to rush him too obviously through the weekly meeting. They didn't have

to worry since their uncle was overly grumpy thanks
to Lola's appearance last night at a charity event.

Lola had been a surrogate mother to the girls.
She'd also been Yank's assistant until she'd finally
taken a stand. She'd told Uncle Yank to admit his feelings for her or else she was walking away for good.
He hadn't believed her—why would he when she'd
spent the better part of her fifty-eight years at the
man's beck and call?

She'd sacrificed her youth and deserved more
from her life and the man in it. So Lola had quit and
gone to work for Spencer Atkins, Yank's biggest
business rival and ironically his closest friend. She'd
also begun dating him while Uncle Yank gnashed his
teeth—and did nothing about it.

Everyone from her sisters to the office staff knew
all Uncle Yank had to do was admit he was ready for
a committed relationship and Lola would willingly
return. At least they thought she'd come back, but
lately she and Spencer seemed to be spending more
and more time together while Uncle Yank grew ever
more stubborn.

With Annabelle at a doctor's appointment and Uncle Yank in a surly mood, he'd dismissed their meeting early and demanded they all show up again the
next morning. With the afternoon free, Micki and Sophie left the office for the day with the shared goal
of making Micki over.

Now Micki sat on Sophie's bed, her knees curled under her, while Sophie made frequent trips to her bathroom and closet, creating separate piles on her dresser.

"Ready?"

"Ready as I'll ever be."

"Then let's get started." Sophie handed Micki a pad and pen to take notes on what she would need to purchase to put Sophie's lessons into action. "This," she said, picking something up from behind her, "is a blow-dryer."

Micki rolled her eyes. "Tell me something I don't know."

"Okay, this red thing is the on/off switch. You have gorgeous hair but you hide it like you did when you used to pitch Little League." Sophie pulled out the elastic holding Micki's hair in place and yanked out a few strands in the process.

"Ouch." Micki rubbed her scalp.

Sophie ignored her. "A little light gel and some blow-drying and your hair will fall around your face in soft waves."

As she spoke, Sophie played with Micki's hair like she'd seen her do to Annabelle when they were younger.

"Are you getting all this down?" Sophie, the organized one, asked. "Blow-dryer, hair gel, soft styling spray. Write," she ordered.

Micki laughed and did as her sister instructed. "Okay. Hair is done."

"Then on to clothing and makeup. The key is to accentuate your already beautiful qualities to make them pop more." Sophie excitedly went through some simple makeup tips with Micki and offered her the spare jars and tubes she had in her make-up cabinet.

"Good thing you're anal and afraid of running out of things," Micki said.

"It's even better that we have the same hair, eye color and complexion. Otherwise I'd drag you to Bendels for a full makeover. But that can wait until the weekend."

Sophie applied as she explained and soon Micki wore a full face of makeup. She'd expected it to feel like armor but instead it was light and made her look…sexy, she thought glancing quickly in the mirror. Heart pounding with excitement, she let Sophie lend her clothing, too.

Transformation complete, when she finally turned around before the full-length mirror, Micki stared at a woman she no longer recognized but one she definitely wanted to get to know better. She couldn't help wondering if Damian would feel the same way.

"Now remember, you can't just rely on the outer dressing," Sophie said, oblivious to Micki's thoughts. Her sister was obviously just pleased Micki was showing an interest in all things feminine, for once. She hadn't asked why.

"Attitude is everything," Sophie continued. "Fortunately for you, you're comfortable with guys, so that's one hurdle down. Now just flirt a little and you'll be all set."

Micki squared her shoulders and shimmied a bit, intentionally shaking her boobs. "Like this?"

Sophie laughed. "That's it. Work on the voice, too. A little breathy is sexy, you know?"

"Next thing I know you're going to ask me to sing 'Happy Birthday, Mr. President.'"

Her sister grinned.

Micki glanced at her watch and groaned. "It's nearly midnight. Do you realize how early I'm going to have to get up in the morning to duplicate this look?"

"That's the price of beauty," Sophie said way too cheerfully.

"I might as well just sleep standing."

"Whatever works for you." Sophie shrugged, but couldn't stifle a yawn. "I don't know who you're doing this transformation for, but I hope you'll tell me one day."

Micki didn't know how to reply. She wasn't ready to admit the truth aloud. She could barely admit it to herself.

"I also hope he deserves you."

"I do, too," Micki said and hugged her sister. The only consolation she had was that regardless of Damian Fuller, this step in Micki's life was long overdue.

CHAPTER TWO

THANKS TO A CLUMPY mascara wand and a distinct lack of ability, Micki was late for work the next morning. Normally they didn't keep specific office hours but today Uncle Yank had insisted on his weekly meeting. With his obnoxious mood, Micki didn't want to draw attention to herself, especially not when she was dressed so out of character. However, with his vision problems and refusal to discuss the diagnosis of macular degeneration, Micki could only hope he wouldn't notice the changes she'd made.

She passed by the main desk, planning to head directly for the conference room, but the ringing of the telephone stopped her. Raine, the very new and young receptionist, wasn't sitting at her desk. Voice mail could take care of the caller but Micki hated to let one of their clients wait for no reason.

She grabbed for the phone. "The Hot Zone, may I help you?"

"This is Damian Fuller. I need to speak to Annabelle."

The deep, masculine voice reverberated through the telephone lines and Micki shivered, her reaction a jumble of emotions. She didn't know what affected her more, the rumbling baritone, the sound of his name, or the lingering memory of the degrading feelings she'd experienced in the locker room yesterday.

"Hello?" Damian asked, drawing Micki back to the present. "Is anyone there?"

She cleared her throat. "Sorry. I was distracted. Someone just stopped by the desk," she lied. "What can I do for you?"

"I already told you I'd like to speak to Annabelle."

"Oh right." She heard the annoyance in his voice and she quickly glanced down at the check-in sheet Raine was instructed to keep. "Annabelle isn't in yet. Can I—" She was about to ask if she could take a message when an idea dawned.

Here was the man who'd prompted her transformation in the first place. Why not start flirting over the telephone? It would be good practice. Her heart rate picked up speed at the prospect.

"I haven't much time to talk," Damian said.

Before he could hang up, Micki pulled herself together. "Hold on, Mr. Fuller. I'll put someone on the line who can help you."

Micki pushed the hold button, then drew a deep gulp of air. *Think sexy, think sultry,* she told herself and settled into the oversize chair. She crossed her legs in an ultrafeminine pose and slowly lifted the phone. "The Hot Zone, Micki Jordan speaking. What's your pleasure this morning?" she asked in the huskiest voice she could muster.

"Micki?" He sounded as if he didn't quite believe it. "It's Damian Fuller. I needed to speak to Annabelle about the schedule she's got lined up for the team this coming weekend."

"I'm sure it's nothing a guy like you can't handle," Micki said, infusing her breathless words with subtle meaning.

Damian Fuller could nail anything on the field *and* off. Micki just wished he wanted to nail her.

He coughed into the phone. "I realize Annabelle's just doing her job and the autism camp's a yearly thing, but I don't want her overbooking the team's PR appearances. We're in first place going into August. I don't want the guys to blow it by being too exhausted to play well."

"Are you sure you aren't just looking for more time to pursue *other* off-the-field activities?" Micki cringed as the question toppled off her tongue, especially since both Joe Gordon, the Renegades owner, and Coach Donovan had called with the same request.

He let out a laugh that set her nerve endings tingling. "Let Annabelle know I called, okay?"

"I'll be sure to convey your concerns when she gets in," she assured him.

"Thanks, and Micki?"

"Yes?"

"Take care of that cold. You sound really hoarse."

She hung up, completely mortified, and glanced up.

The clock on the wall caught her attention and she cursed just like the gamblers who'd come to her uncle's house every Thursday night while she was growing up. Micki scribbled a note for Annabelle, who was late, or Raine just hadn't checked her in as she was supposed to.

Micki rose and made a mad dash for the conference room. Tripping on her borrowed heels as she turned a corner, she saved herself by hugging the nearest wall. She waved at a startled Gert, the new office manager, a burly-looking woman who'd lasted a full three months so far in comparison to the others, whom Uncle Yank had sent home in tears—men included.

"That's it. I'm finished waiting. The meeting will come to order." Micki heard her uncle slam the gavel against the rubber plate, calling the Hot Zone's second meeting this week to order.

Micki yanked off the shoes she'd borrowed from Sophie, determined to make an unnoticed entrance. But if she'd botched her physical transformation as much as she'd messed up flirting with Damian, she wouldn't have to worry about her uncle realizing she'd done anything different.

She strode into the conference room and slipped quietly into her seat.

"You're late," her uncle grumbled without looking up.

"Good morning to you, too," Micki said and blew him a kiss.

Sophie met her gaze and gave her a thumbs-up sign. Relief swelled inside her and she grinned back.

"Where's Annabelle?" Micki asked, glancing around. Apparently Raine hadn't botched attendance and once again they were one sister short.

"That's what I'd like to know," Uncle Yank said. "Ever since she married that no-good, low-down snake Vaughn, she's become a typical, unpredictable female."

Micki laughed at his not-so-veiled reference to Lola. "You adore Vaughn, so lay off him or I'll tell Annabelle you're at it again," she said, referring to his past rocky history with Annabelle's husband.

"Actually, I have a message from Annabelle," Sophie said. "I was just waiting for Micki to get here so I could tell you both at the same time."

"What's wrong?" Micki recognized the serious note in her sister's voice and her stomach plummeted. Annabelle was just a little over three months pregnant and Micki crossed her fingers that all was well.

"Nothing that can't be fixed with a little bed rest," Sophie said quickly. "Annabelle tried to call you this morning, but nobody answered."

"I must've been blow-drying my hair," Micki muttered.

"Well, apparently she's spotting and the doctor wants her off her feet." Sophie, true to her analytical nature, proceeded to describe the graphic details of Annabelle's problem in terms of color and amount until Uncle Yank cut her off with the swing of his gavel.

"I don't want to hear the gory details about female problems." His skin had turned green. "I just want Annie and her baby to be okay."

"And they will be," Micki said, placing her hand over his. "Right, Soph?"

"Right."

"Speaking of doctors—"

"Next subject," Uncle Yank said, his tone leaving no room for argument.

Micki sighed. Sophie had been begging him to let her take him for an evaluation with a doctor who was performing a new procedure on patients with macular degeneration. But the big man who put the fear of God in everyone he knew—except his nieces and Lola—was afraid. Not that he'd admitted as much.

"Okay, with Annie out, our biggest problem is now the New York Renegades PR blitz she was scheduled to handle in Tampa this weekend," Sophie said, tapping her pen against her yellow notepad.

"Well there's a simple solution to that problem,"

Uncle Yank said, his gaze darting between Micki and Sophie.

Micki wasn't about to let him hand this assignment over to her. "There sure is a simple solution," Micki agreed. "Sophie, you head on down to Tampa instead."

Uncle Yank glanced from Micki to Sophie, seemingly torn as to whom he should push to go to south Florida.

Before he could choose a niece, Sophie shook her head. "Tsk, tsk, Uncle Yank. You can run but you can't hide and you *know* I made you a doctor's appointment next week with that specialist and I intend to be by your side to make sure you keep it."

Which explained why he would want to get Sophie out of town, Micki thought.

He scowled. "I don't need another doctor looking into my peepers." He slammed the gavel hard for emphasis, stunning them all into silence.

At that moment, an electronic voice spoke. "Nine thirty, a.m." Uncle Yank cursed and pressed a button on his newly purchased watch, designed so that the visually impaired didn't have to try to decipher small numbers.

"Divine providence?" Sophie asked sweetly.

"I was just testing the thing by wearing it," he muttered. "It doesn't mean I need it yet."

He might be telling the truth. Micki wasn't sure she understood what her uncle could or could not see, just that there had been some worsening since he was diagnosed a year ago. For all his denials about needing a specialist, he'd gone ahead and begun acclimatizing himself to the accessories and implements made for the visually impaired. It was almost as if he'd resigned himself to the inevitable without a fight, and *that* was so unlike her feisty uncle, it hurt her heart.

Despite how close Micki and Uncle Yank were, Sophie was the sister who understood clinical things best and the sisters all agreed Sophie could handle him *and* his specialists.

Still, Micki could definitely stand in for Sophie this once. "If you go to Florida, I'll make sure he keeps that appointment," Micki assured her sister.

"I know you would, but I've done the research and I'd feel much better hearing everything the doctor had to say." Not to mention that after all her research, she'd better be able to understand the diagnosis and explain it to the rest of them, Micki thought.

The noose was tightening as she came closer and closer to becoming the chosen one to replace Annabelle in Tampa. Micki's heart began to pound harder in her chest at the thought of spending up-close-and-personal time with Damian, which would mean facing her inadequacies firsthand.

"I think Peter or Jamie can handle Tampa," Micki said, referring to the newest publicists who'd recently joined the firm.

Though the Jordan sisters prided themselves on their family-oriented agency, their client list had grown to the point where they'd had no choice but to expand. Regardless, they kept the weekly meetings limited to family only so the partners kept up to date on both the sports and PR aspects of the business. Micki and her sisters held separate meetings with their staff, which was why even as she'd suggested one of the new publicists take over the Florida gig, Micki knew she was just acting out of desperation. There were many reasons why the other publicists couldn't handle this job.

Sophie shuffled her papers, evening them on one side. "Even if Peter or Jamie could go to Florida, you know Joe Gordon insists one of the partners handle his team's PR. It's you or me."

"I know. I'd just forgotten," Micki said.

"Conveniently forgotten," Uncle Yank said.

"What's that supposed to mean?" Micki asked.

Her uncle shook his head. "Nothin' important. You can handle the team, Micki. There's nothing you can't handle, remember that."

If only he knew, Micki thought and sighed in resignation. "When do I have to leave?"

"*After* you get that painted gook off your face," her uncle said. "If Sophie hadn't been sitting next to me I'd have thought that was her running in late."

So Uncle Yank *had* noticed. "Why, thank you. I'll

take that as a compliment." Micki deliberately fluttered her lashes at him.

"Compliment, my... Never mind. Just quit looking like a floozy, else I'll think you're taking lessons from Lola."

He'd noticed Micki's clothing overhaul, too. Maybe the eye specialist still could help him, Micki thought and met Sophie's knowing gaze.

And maybe they could get Uncle Yank to make an overture toward the woman he missed so badly. "Speaking of Lola," Micki began.

He slammed the gavel hard. "Meeting adjourned."

Micki rolled her eyes. The man could be as stubborn as a mule and she didn't envy Sophie's trip to the doctor with him. Still she'd rather deal with her surly uncle than cope with being around Damian Fuller in hot, steamy Florida. And *that* was saying a lot.

INTERLEAGUE PLAY. The fans loved it, Damian Fuller thought as he crouched in center field and waited for Manny Ramirez, one of the Red Sox's best hitters, to swing on a three-two pitch. Ramirez cleanly tackled a fastball and it sailed toward center. Damian ran back, back, and jumped high, snagging the ball at the same time he hit the wall. Regaining his footing, he immediately threw to his cutoff man, preventing the runner on base from tagging and running home, but the second he released the ball, a burning pain seared through his left wrist and he grabbed his hand in agony.

An hour later, Damian sat in a hospital room because, as luck was scarce at the moment, the X-ray machine at the stadium had broken. While waiting for the test results, he forced a smile and flirted with Darla, the attractive nurse who lingered in his room. She provided a nice distraction but he preferred to be alone.

Today wasn't the first time his wrist had given him trouble. Hell, every body part ached now and then, but it was the first time the burning numbness in his fingertips had lingered. And that couldn't be a good sign.

"Hungry?" Darla asked, obviously content to hang around and cater to needs he didn't have.

"Not for food, darlin'." He shot her a wolfish grin and she blushed a deep red.

"You really do live up to your reputation as a ladies' man," she said, laughing.

What choice did he have? Perception was everything. And in New York especially, the media shaped that perception, helping him reach the fan base that turned out to see the Renegades play. Damian needed them to want to see him play. And they would—as long as they had no idea that age was catching up with him.

His eligible-bachelor status and photographs of him partying with beautiful women cemented the impression that, at thirty-five, Damian Fuller was still going strong. That was a vision Damian needed his teammates and coaches to buy into as well. Throughout his career, the perception had helped him survive record-setting years and major slumps, making him an icon to the fans—untouchable, un-tradeable, a marquee player in a damn tough market.

Damian lived to play ball. He loved the game and after devoting his life to his career, the game was all he had. Hell, he knew he was in the twilight of his playing years, but damned if he wouldn't extend it as long as he was able.

Darla batted dark lashes over her blue eyes. "It's been fun treating you," she told him as the team physician strode into the room, chart in hand.

"Life's too short not to enjoy." He repeated the mantra he'd lived by all his life, although lately living up to his reputation had become more of a job than playing center field. He wouldn't admit it to a breathing soul, but Damian was beginning to feel every one of his thirty-five years.

"So what's up, doc? I'll be back swinging tomorrow, right?"

The older man shook his head, but the minute the guy used the term disabled list, Damian tuned out the rest. There was never a good time for the DL, yet he wondered why the hell fate had chosen *now* to piss on him. Now, when Ricky Carter, the rookie with an attitude, was angling for a chance to prove he could outdo Damian on the field and at bat. It looked like Carter was about to get the opportunity.

Damian walked out of the emergency room and, within minutes, his sister Rhonda pulled up in her Honda minivan. He could have called a car service, but with three sisters and parents within a half hour's drive, and all of them probably aware of his injury by now, *not* calling them wasn't worth the hassle. Besides, he liked how his sisters pampered him.

"Hi, Ronnie," he said, climbing into the passenger seat. A loud farting sound greeted him and he winced. After reaching beneath him, he pulled a rubber duck from under his ass.

She cringed. "Sorry. The kids were throwing the baby's toys around and I forgot to put that one away."

He laughed. "Anything my nieces do is fine by me." He shifted and finally got comfortable surrounded by the mess in the car.

Each sister was married. Being the youngest sibling, Ronnie had three girls under the age of ten, all of whom adored their uncle Damian. His other sisters also had girls, continuing the tradition only Damian's birth had broken. Growing up around females had taught Damian how to treat a lady and more importantly how to have patience with one, too—the constant questions, the prying into his feelings, the way they invaded his personal space in general.

All of which explained why he never brought the

women he took out home with him. Why should he bother? He never dated anyone he could get serious about; he couldn't risk losing the focus he needed for his career.

"Want to spend the night at my place?" Ronnie asked. "The guest room's yours if you want it. Dave'll keep the girls out of your hair," she said as added incentive.

He shook his head. "Much as I appreciate the offer, I think I'll just go home."

"How long are you out for?" she asked, correctly reading the source of his mood.

"Fifteen days. Longer if the tendinitis doesn't clear up."

She didn't turn his way. "Not so bad."

"Oh really?" He snorted. "It's July, we're in first by three and a half games. Atlanta's breathing down our necks and Carter's aiming for my position on the field and in the lineup. Now he's got a solid two weeks to make an impression. You're right. It's not so bad."

"I'm sorry."

He flexed and unflexed his good hand. "Don't be. It's *my* headache." Just like his age was his headache, as was the way his body didn't always cooperate the way it used to.

All he'd done was catch a damn fly ball and he'd overextended his wrist. He supposed there was a lesson to be learned here but he wasn't ready to heed it.

Damian was convinced he still had a few good years left and he wasn't about to quit.

"Are you going with the team on your next road trip?" Ronnie asked.

"Yep." He had to keep an eye on Carter and an ear out for his big mouth. Besides, he never missed a game unless he had no choice. "This Tampa trip is the one where Gordon sponsors the one-day camp for autistic children. The kids spend a day with their favorite player," he said of the Renegades owner's pet cause.

Because Joe Gordon's son had been diagnosed with the disorder, he did all he could to brighten the lives of kids with the same ailment. All players were required to show up, but none minded. Beginning with his nieces, Damian loved kids, and each year he participated in the camp, he learned something from the determination and guts of the children involved.

"Maybe the publicity and PR will help take your mind off not being able to play," Ronnie said, as his Gramercy Park building came into view.

Publicity and PR immediately brought his thoughts to the one person he'd been unsuccessfully trying to avoid thinking about since he'd last seen her.

Micki Jordan. Before his injury, she'd definitely been his biggest problem—a woman who invaded his thoughts when he ought to be focusing solely on the game. Even in clothes that covered up her curves, she stood out in a crowd, never mind a locker room. Pretending not to notice her took more energy than ignoring Carter and his big mouth.

With those unruly blond curls, baby-blue eyes and soft skin, Micki had an innocence that made her an unmistakable contrast to the women who came in and out of his personal life. Women who knew the score. Women who wanted a fast lay and who wouldn't get hurt when he walked out later that same night. But most importantly, women who didn't linger in his mind after he'd taken them to bed.

One drunken kiss wasn't supposed to have knocked him on his ass, Damian thought. He clearly remembered her dragging him outside, insisting he needed to sober up before his agent or the media noticed his condition. One minute he'd been insisting he wasn't drunk, defending himself to the one niece of Yank's wearing pants not a skirt, and the next he was kissing her senseless.

Micki had aroused more than just desire and left him wondering if alcohol *had* heightened his perception of the night or if she was really the hot little number he remembered.

Every time he'd seen her since, she'd piqued his interest more and more. And the last time he'd spoken with her on the phone, he'd realized he was talking to the woman he remembered—a husky-voiced Micki who teased him and made him want to get his hands on her again. Which wouldn't and couldn't happen with a woman who distracted him so strongly. At this stage of his life and career, he couldn't let anything or anyone distract him from the game.

"Hello?" Ronnie said, waving her hand in front of his face. "We're here. Are you sure you're okay? I can come in if you need me."

He leaned over and kissed his worrywart sister on the cheek. "I'm fine."

"You wouldn't tell me if you weren't," she grumbled.

"Go home to the kids before poor Dave is taken away in a straitjacket." He forced a grin to relieve her anxiety and let himself out of the van.

"I'll call and check on you later," Ronnie yelled as he shut the door.

To prove she didn't have to worry, he waved with his injured, braced hand before heading inside, Micki Jordan still on his mind. Nothing about Yank's niece should appeal to him and yet everything did, which was why he had no choice but to continue to ignore the attraction and deny her appeal. The distraction was too dangerous. In exchange for keeping his focus, he knew he came across as a first-class, womanizing jackass, which at times he probably was. As long as Micki kept that negative view of him, it'd make it easier for him to keep his distance. Thank God, her sister Annabelle was the publicist in charge of Joe Gordon's camp next week.

YANK PACED HIS OFFICE, a room he'd learned by sense of feel and touch. He knew how many paces from the door to his desk and where the sunlight hit during the day. For now, he could see most things just fine. It was the peripheral that did him in. But he knew his days of complete independence were numbered, no matter what Sophie or those so-called specialists claimed.

While he still had his vision, he intended to make sure his girls' futures were taken care of. It was the least he could do for the little women who'd come in and changed his life. All for the better, though he couldn't have known it back then.

Annabelle was settled down with Vaughn, who'd turned into a decent man despite his uppity folks. As for the baby, Yank knew it'd be fine. He refused to think any other way. By rights Sophie should come next but she didn't want to focus on anything except his eyesight, so he'd decided it was Micki's turn at bat.

Perfect analogy since Yank had the right man lined up already. He'd seen her watching Fuller at the New Year's party and when the man had begun flirting with every woman in sight, Yank had stepped in. Damian was a damn fine man who didn't know when it was time to quit. He needed a decent woman to show him what he could have *after* his career on the field ended. Yank would get him all the broadcasting and commercials his good-looking mug could handle, but first the man needed to realize he was through playing the field.

Playing the field. Yank chuckled at his own joke. Yank represented many players in many sports and only a select few did he treat like his own son. Vaughn was one. Fuller another. Which was why Yank trusted his gut. Micki liked the center fielder and he needed a decent woman. They'd suit each other just fine, Yank thought. Case closed.

So Micki was going to Tampa instead of Sophie, though it'd have been nice to have a chance to bail on that damn doctor's appointment—which was why he'd tried to push Sophie out of New York next week. He didn't have the stomach to go through tests and build up hope only to find out he'd been right all along and he'd need assistance for the rest of his life.

Just as soon as Yank knew little Michelle, the one who'd latched onto his calf and never let go, was settled and happy, Sophie would have her turn. Then Yank would feel like he'd done right by his sister and her girls. Done his job as the parent, though he'd never planned to be one.

"And then what, old man?" he asked aloud.

You'll be alone, a voice in his head told him. Darned but that voice sounded a lot like Lola's.

For someone who'd abandoned him in favor of his best friend, the woman seemed to be talking to him a lot lately. He smacked at his noggin, annoyed he was hearing things.

It was enough he'd be going blind. He didn't need to add insanity to his list of ailments. And dealing with Lola and his feelings for her didn't make a dang bit of sense when the woman deserved better than a blind old bat like him.

CHAPTER THREE

A FEW DAYS AFTER RECEIVING Annabelle's assignment by default, Micki took a late Sunday morning flight to Tampa. Before leaving, she'd spent time with both of her sisters and felt better about Annie and her unborn baby's health. She had also fit in a Saturday lunch with Lola, but the other woman had refused to discuss Yank, just as he always avoided talking about her. Micki doubted there were two more frustrating people on this earth but there was nothing she could do to change the status quo.

Micki checked in to the hotel after dinnertime and headed for the bar where the team had decided to hang out after their late-day win. With the autism fundraiser scheduled tomorrow, an off day, the guys could afford to relax and let loose. Micki decided to join them for a quick bite to eat instead of sitting in her room alone. She had every intention of turning in early so she'd be up and functioning tomorrow morning.

Within seconds of stepping into the outdoor bar, the typical Florida humidity wafted around her and destroyed whatever soft waves she'd managed to create in her hair.

She pulled up a chair and joined a group of players sitting at a rectangular table. "Hey, guys."

"Micki," they all chimed in at once.

She smiled at their welcome. "At least you're not disappointed you got me instead of Annabelle."

"We'll miss her," Ricky Carter said raising his glass, tipping it her way, "but I hear you're single."

Micki didn't take his cocky attitude or his interest seriously but he earned an A for sheer arrogance alone. She pierced him with a scowl. "Doesn't mean you're getting any action, hotshot."

He just smiled and took a slug of his beer.

"With Annabelle married to Vaughn, he would kick our asses if he caught us drinking and hanging out like this with his wife," said Joe Caruso, the third baseman.

"He might kick your ass for giving his sister-in-law a hard time," Micki replied.

"Micki, Micki, that's what I love about you. Your sense of humor." Roper grinned, his gaze zeroing in on her made-up face.

She had no doubt he'd also noticed she was wearing a dress, a definite change from her normal black-and-white uniform. At least he hadn't said anything aloud. Uncomfortable beneath his scrutiny, she was glad Damian wasn't here to make her discomfort even worse.

"I live to amuse," she said wryly. "Someone want to buy me a drink or at least call the waitress over?"

Roper gestured for the nearest waitress.

She walked over, tray in hand. "What can I get for you?" she asked.

"An iced tea would be great, thanks." Micki wasn't much of a drinker. College had taught her she didn't hold her liquor well, and the hangover the next day, even from one glass of alcohol, wasn't worth whatever fun she might have while intoxicated.

"Lightweight," Roper said, but she heard the joking affection in his voice.

She glanced at his highball glass with the cherry floating in it and rolled her eyes. "You're hardly one to talk. What's that you're drinking, a Shirley Temple?"

He leaned back and laughed, then smoothed his neatly cut blond hair. "It's a mai tai."

"Anything for anyone else?" the waitress asked.

The rest of the guys called out their orders and the waitress left to fill them. A minute later, Ricky Carter excused himself and sidled up to the waitress, obviously flirting as the woman worked.

Micki ignored him and made small talk with the players who took turns coming by and getting to know the publicist for the Renegades. By the time the waitress returned with their drinks, almost all of the team was present and accounted for—except for Damian.

Her uncle had let her know about his wrist injury

and extended stay on the DL, asking Micki to keep an eye on him while she was in Florida. Uncle Yank worried about Damian's frame of mind and Micki understood. His absence told her he'd either wanted time alone or he'd found comfort elsewhere. She wasn't sure she wanted to know with whom and she knew better than to ask and call attention to any interest she had in Damian Fuller.

Instead she focused on food. The waitress arrived a second time carrying buffalo wings and nachos with jalapeño peppers. Since Micki hadn't eaten anything except airline food all day, she indulged immediately.

Next to the jalapeño nachos, the wings were the spiciest things she'd ever eaten and she burned her tongue badly. Her mouth was on fire and before she knew it, she'd finished her whole large iced tea in an effort to cool it off. Nothing worked and eventually her tongue grew numb.

"Hey, Roper—" As she looked around the table for her friend, who she thought was sitting next to her, the guys appeared blurry and a sudden rush of dizziness assaulted her. She blinked and put a hand on the nearest arm.

"What's wrong?" John asked.

"Oh, you *are* sitting there."

"Have been all night. What's wrong?" he asked again, narrowing his gaze. "You don't look so hot."

"What a rude thing to say to the woman paid to

make you look good." Was it her imagination or was her speech slurred? She tried to move her lips but they felt rubbery. "Actually I'm not feeling like myself." If she didn't know better, she'd think she was drunk.

"I'd think not after consuming two Long Island iced teas in the span of ten minutes," Carter said.

She shook her head. Big mistake, she realized immediately when the room began to swim. "Long Island iced teas? Impossible. I don't drink alcohol." To prove him wrong, she took a final sip from the second glass, but between the way she'd killed her taste buds with the hot food and the complete fuzziness wrapped around her brain, she couldn't tell what she was drinking.

"I ordered a regular iced tea," she insisted.

"I asked them to spice it up for you a bit. And I made sure you got another one when you finished the first, doll." Carter wedged his lean body between her chair and Roper's and placed an arm around her shoulder.

When Micki had begun her transformation, attracting a man like Carter had never been on her agenda. She shook him off, annoyed. "Watch what you call me or you'll find my fist in your mouth," she said, disliking the man even more than her initial impression had warranted.

"Anyone want to hit Lacie's?" Joe Caruso asked.

Roper slid his chair back and rose from his seat. "Hell, yeah. I'm not gonna waste a night off."

The rest of the guys were equally enthusiastic, ready to head off to their next stop.

"What's Lacie's?" Micki stood along with them and immediately grabbed the back of her chair in order to steady herself. "Whoa," she said, laughing. Giggling really, but she hated to admit that the alcohol had dulled her inhibitions *that* much.

"Easy," Roper said.

"I got her." Carter remained by her side, trying again to slip his arm around her waist. "I like my women feisty."

"I'm not your woman." She jabbed him in the side. "And I like my personal space."

"You heard the lady. Back off," a masculine voice said, coming to her defense.

Damian. Oh hell, Micki thought.

Carter scowled at his captain but surprisingly he listened, keeping his mouth shut before he turned and walked away.

Micki glanced at Damian who'd unexpectedly joined them. In faded jeans and a black silk T-shirt that clung to his gorgeous body and defined his muscles and physique, he looked sexy as hell.

On a good, sober day it would take all of Micki's energy to hide her desire for the man. On a drunken night, she didn't stand a chance. Better to get away fast.

She took one step and tripped, falling toward him.

Roper caught her first. Embarrassed, she steadied herself and as she did, she got her first look at the bimbo on Damian's arm. Even in the Florida humidity, she sported silky smooth hair, perfect makeup and impossibly large boobs.

Micki tried to swallow but thanks to the unrequested alcohol, her mouth had grown dry.

"So, where are you off to?" Damian asked.

"Lacie's." The word fell from Micki's lips before she could stop it.

He let loose a loud laugh. The woman beside him stared at Micki with a pitying expression and chuckled as well. It wasn't just a laugh at Micki's expense, but one with a perfect lilt no man could resist.

"What's so funny?" Micki asked, defensively.

"Someone needs to look after her," the big-breasted woman said about Micki as if she were a child in need of a babysitter.

"Quiet," Damian said when he took in Micki's glassy eyes and heard her slurred speech. He would never have pegged her for a drinker, but separated from her uncle and sisters, who knew?

Still, Lacie's? He'd bet his entire savings that Micki was clueless about their destination.

"You didn't tell her?" he asked his teammates.

"Tell me what?"

His companion squeezed his arm. "Excuse me, sweetie, but I need the little girls' room," she said, obviously bored by Micki and a conversation that didn't revolve around her.

To Damian's relief, Carole, the legal secretary he called whenever he was in town, excused herself.

He'd seen her on and off during spring training and again over a month ago. By then his interest had already died out. She'd been distracted as well, as if she'd already mentally moved on. He hadn't intended to call her again, but between his injury and Carter's mouth on the flight over, Damian had needed a diversion and had picked up the phone. Now he wished he hadn't. With Micki here, he was definitely sorry he hadn't just joined up with the team instead.

From the moment he'd seen Micki's reaction to Carole, the flicker of surprise followed by dismay in her expressive face, he'd felt an unfamiliar pang of guilt and self-loathing. Micki managed to work his emotions as well as his sisters did, which merely pissed him off and reminded him of all the reasons Micki wasn't good for him when he needed to focus on his career plan.

A plan he'd been working on successfully for years. He'd party with the team tonight and when he still showed up first for the camp stint tomorrow, he'd prove to everyone that not even an injury could get him down. End result, nobody would wonder whether age was catching up with Damian Fuller, nor would they worry too much about whether this injury would sideline him from the postseason and the playoffs. They would merely speculate on how soon he'd manage to return.

But where Micki was concerned, Damian was torn. As much as he resented Micki's emotional pull, he also desired to let things play out between them. Frustrated, he ran a hand through his hair. Man, he thought, if he ever let himself get tangled up with Micki Jordan, she'd tie him up in knots so tight he'd never get them undone.

For all his mixed emotions about this attraction, Damian knew he had no choice but to follow his cardinal rule: There'd be *no* screwing around with Micki no matter how much he desired her, and the best way to keep that vow was to distance himself.

"Lacie's is a strip club," he said to Micki. "And I can't see you hanging out at a place like that." He figured she'd blush and make a quick getaway.

Instead she stepped around Roper and faced Damian head-on, treating him to a shocking sight he hadn't noticed before. Micki wasn't Micki, at least not in appearance. Instead of her buttoned-up shirt and dark pants, she was dressed in a bright pink strapless sundress, exposing bronzed skin and sexy thin tan lines that made a man want to devour her. Starting at her shoulders, he imagined licking her soft flesh, heading downward until he discovered just where those tan lines led. With a groan, Damian shifted to accommodate the growing ache in his pants.

"Are you saying I don't belong in that club?" Indignant, Micki perched her hands on her hips, thrusting her breasts out. "That I can't compete with the other women there? Is *that* what's making you laugh at the thought of my going to a strip club?" she asked.

He blinked, sensing there was a wealth of information in that statement. Obviously he'd touched a nerve. Knowing women as he did, he also realized anything he said now could get him into trouble.

In this case, trouble was a good thing if it kept her away from him. "Micki, I'm sure you can hold your own anywhere you go," he said in a deliberately placating tone he often used to tick off his sisters.

"Even among *naked* women?" Micki blushed red, but to her credit she didn't run away.

He figured he had the alcohol to thank for her lack of inhibition and muttered a curse. Meanwhile his teammates looked on in amusement at their exchange.

"Hey, if you can handle yourself with these guys, you can handle yourself anywhere," he said as if he didn't believe his own words.

"Because I'm one of them? Good old Micki, one of the guys," she spat, the disdain in her voice clear.

Now, where had that come from? He hardly viewed her as one of the team, but he wasn't about to alter the impression she believed he had of her when it suited his purpose of creating distance.

"If you say so," he muttered instead.

She nailed him with a vicious glare. "Come on, let's get going," she said to the rest of the men.

Damian shot Roper a warning look. *Do not take her to a strip club.*

Before Roper or Damian could react, the rest of the guys seemed to take her up on her suggestion and, with Micki in tow, headed toward the exit.

"Oh hell." He started after them, pulling Carter aside on his way.

He and the rookie had an obvious hate-thing going, but as the captain, Damian had done his best only to pick on the kid for real mistakes, and there'd been plenty.

Now Damian needed Carter's help. As long as Carole was on his arm, Micki wouldn't listen to a word Damian had to say. He needed to rid himself of Carole and he had to do it fast because he didn't trust anyone else to watch out for a drunken Micki except himself.

"How 'bout a peace gesture," Damian offered the rookie.

Carter shrugged. "Sorry, man but I don't really give a crap whether or not we get along." His cocky demeanor and smirk told Damian he meant what he said.

Okay, so he wasn't going to do this the easy way. "Well I'm going to do you a favor despite your sorry-ass attitude. Instead of the strip club, how about you take my date out?"

"You serious?" The young kid's eyes narrowed in thought, probably at the idea of Carole's huge, surgery-induced breasts.

"Deadly serious."

The difference between Carole and Micki beyond the obvious was that Carole knew the score. Yeah, she'd be pissed at Damian for pawning her off on Carter, but she'd get over it. It wasn't like they were exclusive; she dated other guys when Damian was out of town, which was most of the time. Not to mention that he'd had to coax her to go out with him tonight. He'd wondered if she was waiting for someone else to call.

Damian wouldn't hear from her after this stunt nor would he call her next time he was in town. No loss for either of them, really. Moving on was long overdue. Yeah, Damian wanted to look out for her feelings, but she could handle being passed off to Carter. Weighing who needed him more, Carole or Micki, there was no contest. Besides, Carole would probably enjoy Carter, who'd give her the kind of good time she was looking for.

Damian dug into his pocket and peeled off a couple of hundreds. "I'll even pay for your dinner and drinks."

From the corner of his eye, Damian saw Carole looking around for him in the bar while the guys were loading into cabs. "Well?"

Carter shrugged. "Why not? She looks like a good

time and the little publicist turned out to be a prude even after I plied her with alcohol."

Damian clenched his jaw. He had no time now to deal with Carter and what he'd done to Micki, but he definitely would later.

An eager Carter snatched the bills and swaggered toward Carole while Damian caught the last cab with his teammates. Damian didn't miss the irony. He was headed for Lacie's Lounge, a strip joint he used to frequent in his younger days, so he could watch out for a woman destined to be his downfall in his declining years.

Once at the club, Damian thought things would get worse, but he was wrong. Micki sat quietly by Roper, taking in the women gyrating around the poles on stage. She hadn't ordered a drink, which Damian took as a good sign and he relaxed in his seat.

For the first time, he noticed the tight bond between Micki and Roper. Was there a thing between them he didn't know about? Damian's gut twisted in uncomfortable knots.

Suddenly the music shifted. The beat picked up. The women on stage altered their movements to the more sensual and seductive rhythm. Micki rose from her seat, mesmerized.

Damian started to stand, too, but Roper put a hand on his arm. "Let her go."

Damian glanced at the other man.

"She needs this," his teammate explained.

The words were cryptic yet sincere. Damian lowered himself back into his seat, wary and uncomfortable.

As if aware he was staring, Micki turned and met his gaze. Their eyes held. The music pulsed around them in an erotic beat, increasing the awareness simmering between them that he still didn't understand. She was the opposite of everything he normally desired and yet...

She broke the connection as she slowly gravitated toward the stage, seemingly fascinated by the women and their moves. Or maybe it was their skimpy clothing she wanted a better look at. Either way, she made her way forward, staggering a little as she walked.

Damian clenched his fists but forced himself to trust Roper's judgment. Since Micki had been subdued since they'd entered Lacie's, Damian didn't see any harm in letting her watch from up close.

ONE MINUTE Micki had been watching the women spinning onstage and the next minute she was up and striding closer. She knew she was drunk. She also knew that something about these uninhibited women fascinated her. What made them so bold? So daring? What caused the other women to strut and flaunt their assets while Micki withdrew into herself?

The rhythmic sounds of the music drew her and,

wanting a closer view, she stepped toward the stage, looking for…what? Answers to her own insecurity, perhaps?

The tempo changed and Micki swayed her hips in time to the music, which she realized had picked up. The girls on stage were shimmying their breasts at the men in the front row.

Things in front of Micki blurred as she wondered what it would feel like to dance as if she were a woman every man wanted to look at and touch. To call his own. God, she thought, she really must be drunk.

One of the dancers held out a hand. Micki knew she wasn't beckoning to her and yet she reacted as if she'd been lured onto the stage. This was her chance to find out what it would be like to be anyone other than every guy's pal.

DAMIAN BOLTED FOR MICKI, but she'd already joined a dancer on the stage. Her hips swayed and she shimmied to the beat of the music in an exact imitation of the other woman's expert moves. Damian's mouth grew parched.

"We have to get her out of there," Roper said from behind him.

"No shit."

Damian placed a hand on the stage, intending to haul himself up, but Micki's next movement stopped him. Eyes closed, she pulled down the top of her sundress, revealing a sexy lace strapless bra, one transparent enough that her full breasts were exposed for the world to see.

"Oh shit." Damian jumped up to pull her off the stage but another patron was already there.

The big bull of a guy obviously knew it was hands off when it came to the women who were performing but had decided the house rules didn't apply to a regular customer like Micki. The guy didn't bother tucking cash into Micki's strapless lace bra, he just groped her breast instead.

Without warning, possessive anger and fury surged through Damian, along with one thought: *No one touches her but me.*

Micki's expression reflected delayed horror as she suddenly realized what was going on. She screamed and slapped the guy groping her but he didn't seem bothered at all. Damian intervened, grabbing the drunk by his collar and hauling him away from Micki. While his teammates held the man down, Damian lifted Micki into his arms, doing his best to protect his wrist, and headed for the door.

Straight into the glaring lights of the paparazzi.

SAFE AND SECURE IN THE CAB, Damian finally caught his breath. Looking back he realized Micki hadn't fought his rescue attempt. On the contrary, she'd wrapped her arms around his neck and let him whisk her away. She'd even appeared oblivious to the flash-bulbs that followed them to the taxi door.

Damian didn't know how the press had been privy to where the team would be. He'd done his best to get Micki out of there quickly and anonymously. He could only hope the photographers hadn't caught anything more than a shot of the back of a woman's head, but Micki had been squirming, so who knew?

Now inside the taxi, instead of sitting on her own side of the cab, Micki draped herself across Damian. Hard as he tried to ignore her, he couldn't avoid noticing how nicely her soft body and lush curves curled against him. Her full breasts pressed enticingly against his chest, making him painfully aware that she was every inch a woman he desired.

"What do you say you move over?" he suggested.

Her warm breath fanned his neck and tickled his ear and she curled her fingertips into his shirt collar. "I'm comfortable here."

"But it's safer over there." He tipped his head to the side.

"Since when do you play it safe?" she asked in a husky purr.

He told himself it was the alcohol talking, but she'd kissed him that last time and she'd been perfectly sober. He shook his head to clear those thoughts. He wasn't going to take advantage of her now.

"What's the matter? Cat got your tongue?" Micki tipped her head back and looked at him.

In her eyes he saw a mixture of innocence and seductiveness in one tempting package.

"Mmm-hmm," he murmured, unable to think or focus on anything except the woman in his arms.

She shook her head and her curls fell around her face. "Wouldn't you rather *I* have your tongue?" she said and then, without giving him a chance to answer, she leaned close and sealed her lips over his.

He wanted to do the right thing, the chivalrous thing, and stop her before things got out of control. But the minute her mouth touched his, he was lost, unable to do anything except succumb to her will, and she had plenty. Her mouth pressed hard on his and her tongue slipped between his parted lips. She teased with her eager tongue and nipped with her teeth, proving exactly how much she desired him.

As she worked magic with her mouth, her body reacted, too. Her nipples tightened and pressed against his chest, the flimsy bra he'd seen earlier doing nothing to protect him against the hot sensations she'd aroused.

Yet somehow he kept his hands on her small waist. Somehow he resisted the urge to cup her breasts in his palms. And somehow he refused to allow his hands to explore the rest of her soft flesh and supple curves.

But over time his body tightened, overloaded by sensations that had him teetering on the brink of losing control. Unable to restrain himself anymore, he threaded his hands into her hair, slanted her head and kissed her back, hard and hot, holding nothing back. His mouth fit perfectly with hers and her warm heat settled over his groin, showing him a prelude of what could be, if only he gave in to desire.

Without warning, the taxi hit a bump in the road, jarring Damian back to unwelcome reality. The woman in his lap needed rescuing not ravishing.

He wasn't happy but he broke the kiss, letting them both come up for air. Though it was dark in the cab, he could see her tangled hair and moist lips and the sight made him want to start kissing her all over again. Resisting was the most difficult thing he'd ever done. Because he'd just learned that Micki was the one thing he feared: the hot number he just couldn't resist.

She sighed and leaned her cheek against his, a soft, sweet gesture that hit him like a punch in the gut. Damn, he wished they'd get to the hotel soon. He smoothed the back of her hair and she slowly slipped downward until her head lay in his lap and her eyelids drifted shut.

"Sweet heaven." No doubt about it, she was put on this earth to test him, Damian thought.

He leaned his head against the old seats and gritted his teeth, trying not to imagine her head in his lap for reasons other than drunken exhaustion. A futile effort since the images still came—her curly hair brushing his stomach and bare thighs and her warm, moist, lush mouth closing over his aching member. He exhaled a slow, loud groan, not caring if the cabdriver heard.

From her place in his lap, Micki muttered something he couldn't make out, nor did he care. He couldn't focus on anything except the vibration of the car beneath him and Micki's lips an inch away from his cock. With the next pothole and bump in the road, Damian decided chivalry was way overrated. He wasn't a guy used to denying himself basic needs. Hell, he'd never had a reason.

But he did now, he reminded himself. Because no way did he plan on doing anything more. He'd bring Micki safely upstairs and watch over her until the stupor passed.

They finally reached the hotel. He carried her from the cab up to her room, not an easy feat with both late-night guests and bellmen staring at the sight.

Once in the room, he focused on the necessities. With jaw clenched, he changed her clothes, managing to do no more than skim her curves with his hands, and look through half-shut eyes as he pulled off the dress and replaced it with a shirt he found in her drawer. Micki was so exhausted, she didn't attempt another seduction and he was grateful. He was even more pleased when he finally laid her beneath the covers for the night.

By the time Damian poured himself a glass of whiskey from the minibar and eased into a club chair next to the double bed, he was exhausted. The chair wouldn't be comfortable, but he settled in for a long night.

He knew better than to crawl into that bed. Lying beside Micki on the small mattress would provide too much temptation for a saint. And despite his restraint tonight, Damian had never claimed to be one of those.

CHAPTER FOUR

MICKI AWOKE, painfully aware she wanted to die but not until after she killed Ricky Carter. The last thing she remembered about her night was Carter telling her he'd turned her iced teas into the more potent Long Island kind. The first thing she recalled this morning was a mouth full of cotton and a headache the likes of which she'd never felt before. Drums beat in her skull and she lay in bed unable to move, let alone rise and get a glass of water or Tylenol.

"Here. Take this."

She forced her dry, heavy eyelids open and saw a glass of water and two pills in a large masculine hand. "Damian."

Just like that, highlights of last night came back to her in mortifying, vivid detail. She'd stripped in the bar, been carried out in Damian's arms and, as thanks, she'd attempted to seduce him in the cab.

Oh my God. She would have rolled over and hid in embarrassment except she needed that water desperately. When she sat up too quickly, dizziness hit her hard and she fell back against the pillow, each movement causing pain of a different kind.

"Easy." He helped her to an upright position and she gratefully swallowed the pills, gulping the liquid fast.

"Thank you." She kept her eyelids shut tight, more out of mortification than need. "I'm guessing you brought me back to…where are we anyway?"

"We're in your hotel room. I figured you wouldn't mind me invading your privacy to find your key card if it meant you didn't have to spend the night in my room. And you're welcome."

"You're quite the gentleman," she said wryly. "What time is it anyway?"

"A little after noon."

The camp. Her job. Panic assaulted her. Her eyes shot open and she bolted up, or at least she tried to, but Damian had anticipated her reaction and placed his hands on her shoulders to hold her down.

Her eyes darted around the room. "I'm late for work, you're late for the camp. We have to get moving." But even as she argued, her pounding head and the waves of nausea clearly told her she wasn't going anywhere at the moment.

"Sophie's handling everything," he said, as he loosened his grip on her shoulders.

Sophie had flown down to Florida? She eased

back against the pillows and finally turned her heavy-lidded gaze to Damian.

Even in a rumpled, razor-stubbled state he was the most handsome man she'd ever laid eyes on, while she probably looked worse than roadkill. So much for all of Sophie's lessons and hard work.

"How did Sophie get here in time?" Micki asked.

He rose and walked barefoot across the carpet to the window where he'd thoughtfully kept the shades drawn. "I called her late last night. And before you say another word, how much of last night do you remember?"

Micki narrowed her gaze. If she claimed not to remember the kiss, would he continue to pretend it had never happened? Could that be what *he'd* done the last time, when he'd been the one drunk and out of control? If so, she could definitely understand his perspective better now that she'd walked in his shoes. But she had no intention of handling the situation the same way. Denial wasn't Micki's style but since it apparently was Damian's, she wouldn't rush into dealing with what had happened last night.

Besides she needed some time to clear her own head as well. She carefully wiggled farther up in bed, keeping her pounding head braced against pillows. "I remember going downstairs to join the team for a bite to eat. I hadn't had anything much all day and my stomach was pretty empty. I ordered iced tea and ate the spicy appetizers and guzzled my drink. I found out later Carter had them spiked and ordered two of them."

A muscle ticked in Damian's jaw, his anger barely concealed.

"There's no love lost between you two, huh?" Micki asked.

"Forget me." He slashed his hand through the air. "What I want to know is who the hell raised him to treat women that way?"

So much for a slow lead-in, Micki thought. Impossible when he'd just given her the perfect opening. "Such chivalry from a man who arrived with one woman on his arm and left with another?" She laced her words with teasing innuendo.

"It wasn't intentional," he said, his tone surprisingly serious.

She couldn't argue with his comment and flushed hot, recalling exactly how she'd come on to him after he'd carried her out.

He tipped his head to one side, studying her with too much intense scrutiny for her comfort.

"You need to know that any woman I've ever been with knows the score and agrees to play by my rules."

She swallowed hard and decided to face the consequences. "Is that why you didn't close the deal last night? Because I was too drunk to agree to your rules, whatever they are?"

He shoved his hands into his pockets and stepped closer to the bed. "You remember it all, huh?"

She nodded. "Just like I'm now sure *you* remember New Year's Eve."

He exhaled hard and shut his eyes.

She was struck by the thick fringe of lashes, so sexy on a man. She also realized she was right. He did recall kissing her and had been avoiding and ignoring the fact ever since. Because he didn't find her attractive and didn't want to admit his mistake in the sobering light of day?

Whatever the reason, whatever his feelings toward her, she had to know and put this crazy attraction behind her once and for all.

"Look," he said, sitting down by her side.

She ignored the rocking movement his big body caused and forced a steady gaze.

"You and I couldn't be more different," he explained.

She lifted her eyebrows in surprise. "And you have so much in common with the other women in your life."

To her shock, he burst out laughing. "Touché." Reaching out, he tenderly stroked her cheek. "You're better than the rest of them," he said gruffly. "You deserve more than I could ever give. Especially while I'm still focused on keeping this career of mine alive."

The intimate gesture and honest words took her off guard and her heart did a funny leap in her chest.

And she finally understood. When it came to women, Damian lived by what he considered a gentleman's code. Get involved with easy women and don't worry about the damage left behind.

She didn't consider herself better than anyone else, but he was right about one thing. She wasn't the kind of woman up for a no-strings affair. Especially not when the dynamic was already complicated by emotion, the way it was for her.

"I understand," she said, letting him off the hook.

He shook his head. "I don't think you do. I have three sisters. If anyone spiked their drink intending to take advantage of them, I'd string them up by their—" He cut himself off. "Well, you get the picture. I wasn't about to take advantage of you."

But had he wanted to? They had broached sensitive topics this morning. She wasn't ready to touch that one. "I appreciate you looking out for me. You didn't just take care of me last night but you protected my business by calling Sophie."

"It was the right thing to do." He shifted on the bed, obviously uncomfortable with her gratitude.

For Damian, chivalry was inbred. Just because he'd come to her aid when she needed him, it didn't mean his views on women, relationships or *her* had changed, and she cautioned herself against softening her heart.

An awkward silence surrounded them and Micki

struggled for something to say when a loud banging on the door sounded.

Damian was startled by the interruption but grateful, too. He hadn't expected such a private, intimate conversation between them. He also hadn't anticipated the warm feelings as he'd watched over her last night, then had seen her struggle to face her actions—and call him on his.

The knocking on the door continued and Damian glanced at Micki. "Any idea who it could be?"

She shook her head, then shut her eyes tight against what must still be pain. "I have no idea," she said.

The banging grew louder. "Micki Jordan, open the door or I'll kick it open myself!" a familiar voice yelled.

"Oh God, it's Uncle Yank." Micki groaned and wiggled back under the covers, pulling the blankets over her head. "He's going to kill me," she said in a muffled voice.

Damian cursed. More like Yank was going to murder the man in Micki's room.

He headed for the door, drew a deep breath and let her uncle inside. "Hi, Yank."

"What the hell are you doing in here? Never mind, I don't want to know. I do want an answer to who's responsible for *this*." He shoved a newspaper beneath Damian's nose.

The press. Damian had pushed Micki past the flashing bulbs last night without pausing or stopping. For her sake he'd hoped they hadn't gotten a good shot of her face and he thought the two of them had made a semi-decent getaway.

Obviously not. And though they were both used to the media, he as an athlete, she as a publicist, Micki certainly wouldn't have ever expected to be photographed in such a compromising position. And she didn't deserve to be. Or to have her hard-earned reputation in the business world trashed.

Damian recognized the New York daily and pulled the paper out of the older man's hand. On opening the page, he groaned at the full-color shot of himself carrying a half-dressed Micki out of Lacie's Lounge, Tampa's most notorious strip joint.

"Shit."

Yank slammed the door shut behind him. "Now what do you have to say for yourself, big shot?"

"Hey, keep it down," Micki said from across the room.

"Get up, young lady, and explain this. What the devil are you doing with your dress hiked down, the twins on display and this clown carrying you out of a strip club?"

Micki pulled the covers off her head and faced her uncle. "Damian saved me from being even more of an idiot," she said, defending him at her own expense.

Everything this woman said or did surprised him.

She'd been blindsided, given alcohol she hadn't asked for, and Damian never should have let her set foot in Lacie's in the first place.

"Let me see the paper," Micki demanded.

He didn't see any point in arguing. Reluctantly, Damian walked over and held out the news.

She took in the picture and her skin turned paler, if such a thing were possible. "Those *are* my twins."

Yank let out a disgusted sound. "Since you're obviously hungover now and you normally don't drink, what gives?"

She pushed her curls off her face. "A lot of it's still fuzzy but Carter spiked my drinks and I couldn't taste the added alcohol because of the spicy food." She shut her eyes, obviously trying to remember more.

Damian found himself touched by her fragile vulnerability, making him want to protect her even more.

"I'm going to rip his nuts off," her uncle growled, breaking any tender moment Damian had been experiencing.

"Get in line," Damian muttered.

"If Atkins represented him, Carter would be dog shit. Unfortunately he's a Cambias client," he said, referring to one of the newer, younger, money-hungry agents.

Damian knew both Yank and Atkins Associates were losing clients to men like Cambias. The older players possessed agent loyalty but the younger ones, like Carter, only cared about contracts, perks and cold, hard cash.

"Eventually he'll bury himself." Micki rose from her bed, glanced down at her T-shirt and shot Damian a questioning glance.

He wasn't about to explain how he'd undressed her and changed her clothes. A smart girl would figure it out on her own.

Her cheeks stained red in embarrassment. Nothing wrong with her intelligence, he thought wryly. Her modesty was another unique aspect to her personality, since most women he'd been with willingly bared their assets.

Ignoring him, Micki turned to her uncle. "How's this story playing in New York? Because we've got to spin it somehow."

"Well, the AP's got ahold of it. With Fuller's injury just a month shy of the postseason, his carrying you out of there has the reporters speculatin' that he'll be back on the field in no time. He's being portrayed as a hero."

"That's just great," she said, frustrated.

Damian said nothing, knowing it wasn't the best time to pat himself on the back for gaining positive media exposure at her expense.

"I need to issue a statement." She paced the floor, mentally planning her next move.

"The hell you do. You need to lay low!" Yank countered.

She strode up to her uncle, no longer the fragile, defenseless woman Damian had protected last night. "I'm an adult and I'm responsible for my actions. I made this mess, I'll get myself out of it." Micki paused in thought. "Though for the sake of the agency, I do agree I should keep my face—and twins—out of the papers."

"Attagirl," Yank said.

"*After* I issue some sort of explanation."

Damian admired her guts. Not many men he knew would willingly get into the old man's face. Their family dynamic obviously consisted of love and respect, both things Damian had grown up with and appreciated.

"I hate to take sides—" Damian began.

"Then don't," Micki said.

"Unless it's mine," Yank added.

Damian suppressed a grin. "I think your uncle's got a point. You ought to take time off before going back to New York or issuing any kind of statement. By then the media will have found other bait."

She pursed those lips he wanted to kiss again.

"I don't run away from problems," she insisted.

"But like you said, it's in the best interest of the agency." Yank was obviously hitting on the one thing he thought would change her mind. "And Sophie said to remind you that anything you say will only come out sounding defensive, so take a breath and suck this one up."

Micki shook her head, her displeasure apparent. "I want everyone to know that the Hot Zone publicists don't run away. That'll kill our business for sure." Shoulders back, chin at a determined tilt, she stomped away from her uncle. She headed for the bathroom and slammed the door behind her.

Yank turned toward Damian. The lines around his eyes seemed more pronounced, his expression more concerned than he'd let on in front of his niece. "She'll calm down. Now tell me how the press knew where the team was hanging out."

The same question had been lingering in the back of Damian's mind since he'd seen the photograph. "The paparazzi knows which clubs the Renegades frequent. Lacie's isn't one of them. I have no idea how they found out."

But Damian's mind was already working all the angles and possibilities. Who besides his teammates knew about their spur-of-the-moment decision to hit Lacie's? There were the cab drivers and any waiters and waitresses from the hotel bar who'd heard them talking, but a trip to Lacie's wasn't much of a scoop and so Damian couldn't fathom anyone having any interest in calling the press. There was no money to be made in a story about where the team was going clubbing.

Unless the person who'd leaked the information

hadn't want the money but rather the possibility of an ugly exposé—but still, there had been no guarantee they would even have a story to tell.

Damian shook his head. Who had an agenda? There was Carter, who'd spiked Micki's drink and hated Damian's guts, and Carole, who was probably pissed off enough at Damian to want to cause trouble. But those two had been together and had probably been keeping each other too busy to think about Damian, at least until this morning. He didn't discount them completely but he didn't want to give Yank an unfounded target for his anger.

Damian glanced at the older man and shrugged. "I can't imagine who'd snitch."

Yank snorted. "Micki needs to get away until this blows over," he said, his mind shifting gears.

On this Damian agreed. "Got any ideas?"

The other man rubbed his hand over his wiry beard. "She won't go willingly which means she'll need someone to take her away in secret." He pinned Damian with a determined gaze. "And you can't play ball anyway."

"Thanks for reminding me."

"Yeah well, it's true. That wrist needs some rest."

"I still need to be with the team," Damian countered.

"Under ordinary circumstances, you would. But this ain't ordinary. You need to take care of Micki. You also need to have that wrist looked at by the best.

So I covered your ass at the camp today. I had Sophie tell Gordon and Coach Donovan you were seeing a rehab specialist privately so you could return sooner than anticipated. That's true by the way. I found some hotshot who'll fly in tomorrow and take a look. I already put your test results in his hands."

Damian wasn't sure whether to thank Yank for the help and the positive spin with the team, or to strangle him for interfering and dragging him further into Micki's life.

"No thanks necessary," Yank said. "I was just doing my job. Now you're going to do yours. You got that big resort off the Florida Keys courtesy of that twenty-million-dollar contract I negotiated for you. I suggest you use it to help my niece get some R & R."

Take Micki to his island retreat? "Give me a break."

"The guys told me how you goaded Micki, telling her you couldn't see her hanging out at a strip club."

"I still can't." But he knew Yank was baiting him and as Damian waited for the old man to reel him in, he stiffened, clenching and unclenching his fists.

Yank cleared his throat. "Well, any idiot would know my Micki's pride would push her to do exactly what you insinuated she couldn't do. Add to that you played on her weakness." Yank poked him in the chest accusingly.

Damian frowned at that accusation. "What weakness? What the hell are you talking about?" he asked.

But even as he spoke, Micki's self-deprecating words came back to him. *Good old Micki, one of the guys,* she'd said. And how had he replied? *If you say so.*

"Holy hell." How had his life gotten so complicated in less than twenty-four hours?

"I see you get it now." Yank nodded, pleased.

And Damian resigned himself to the inevitable. "I have a full staff on the island. They'll take good care of her."

"*You'll* take good care of her. No way will you dump her on the island and take off. You understand?"

Damian understood all right. Him, Micki, a luxurious house, a staff, a beach and time alone. He was so screwed.

"I'll tell her you arranged for your private plane to take her back to New York. You can deal with her from there." Yank let out a laugh. "I don't envy you when she realizes she's been had, but I'm sure it'll build you some character."

"I didn't know I needed any." Damian shoved his hands into his jeans pocket.

Just then, Micki walked out of the bathroom, her face freshly washed and her hair pulled back into a ponytail. She'd put on sweats in addition to the large shirt he'd chosen last night but her eyes were still glassy and red.

"I want to go home," she said. "I promise to lay

low once I'm there. There's a difference between running away and being cautious about the agency's reputation."

"We were just discussing that," Damian said.

"I'm not in any shape to argue with you two—"

"And we're not going to fight you. You obviously know what's best." Damian hated lying to her, especially when he'd be the one to face her anger later, but Yank counted on him to get her away from emotional harm. He only hoped she'd thank him and not throttle him when they reached his island retreat.

He sighed. He'd bought the place for himself and had never before taken a woman there. He didn't have a good feeling about doing so now.

YANK GLANCED AROUND the hotel room he'd booked for the night. Sophie would be staying next door, probably so she could keep an ear out for him. But he couldn't be pissed. Sophie was a good girl. When she'd gotten the call about her sister being in trouble, she'd contacted him and they'd hightailed it to Florida pronto. Yank was proud of the girls and how they stuck together.

At this point he was proud of himself, too. He couldn't have planned a better way to get Micki and Damian together. Micki had tried to fight it, of course. She'd wanted Damian to attend the autism event, but under Yank's glare, Damian had insisted on accompanying her on her flight home instead.

If Yank had had any qualms about Damian, they'd been erased last night when he'd taken care of Micki. Yes, those two would be a dang good fit—as long as Damian could handle her when she found out they'd lied and shipped her off to a remote island.

With Micki settled, hopefully soon, he could turn his sights to Sophie. *His sights.* Now that was a good joke.

If you listen to Sophie, you might have a chance to save your eyesight. There was that voice again.

Yank cursed aloud. "Yeah well and then what'll I have? My eyesight and a lonely life." Though he had no trouble fixing up his nieces, when it came to himself, Yank had concluded he was more afraid of commitment than he was of his condition. If he avoided fixing his eyesight, he had an excuse not to fix his relationship with Lola.

He smacked his hand against the wall and an electronic voice said, "Twelve fifty-five p.m." He'd lied when he'd told the girls he didn't need the watch. It was so much easier than squinting into the fog to try and read the numbers on the tiny face.

Never thought you were a coward. He didn't know if the voice was referring to his eyesight or letting Lola go. Either way, that voice was right. But at least as far as his eyes went, he'd made a big decision, one all three girls would agree with.

He decided he'd been acting like a pansy. Sophie had made him a doctor's appointment first thing Monday morning. He intended to keep it. It was time for him to deal with his health because he couldn't make any decisions about his personal life until that issue had been resolved.

No woman will wait around that long.

Maybe, Yank thought, but that was a risk he'd have to take.

MICKI TAPPED HER FINGERS against the armrest and stared out the window of Damian's private jet, waiting for takeoff. He brought her a drink, Coke with lots of ice, and settled in beside her.

"I don't mean to sound ungrateful because I really do appreciate you getting me home quickly, but why didn't you go over to the camp and salvage what was left of the day? I could have gotten home myself."

He tipped his head to the side and met her gaze. "You said yourself, I'm a gentleman."

"And my uncle's playing on that particular quality to get you to look out for me." She let out a huff of breath. "I'm perfectly capable of taking myself home, you know. I certainly won't make the same mistake twice." Especially since most of last night was coming back to her—piece by humiliating piece.

"Nobody blames you for what happened," he assured her. "Now shut your eyes and get some sleep." He patted her hand and the warmth caused her heart to skip a beat.

She still wasn't operating at one hundred percent and decided a nap was a good idea. When she woke, they were landing, the jarring noise of the engines and the atmospheric shift rousing her from sleep.

Her head still ached as did her muscles. She stretched and glanced at Damian. "I feel like I've only been out about an hour." She looked down at her watch. "I *have* only been sleeping for an hour. Why are we landing?" She gripped the armrests and her stomach flipped in sheer panic. "What's wrong with the plane?"

"Nothing," he said in a soothing voice that would have worked if she believed him.

Micki glanced out the window at the landscape below. "There are palm trees down there so either we're making an emergency landing or we turned back to Florida or—"

"We're landing on a semi-private island," he said, obviously telling her the truth.

Micki stared first at the blue sky and southern landscape and then into Damian's deep eyes. "I'm going to kill you *and* my uncle." But right now, Damian was the only one within spitting distance. *"How could you?"*

She shot him a scathing glare, not seeing the sexy man or the guy who'd been her savior. Instead she saw the man who'd betrayed her trust and discounted her ability to decide what was best for herself.

"Micki—"

"Turn the plane around," she ordered.

"I can't. I promised your uncle I'd get you away for a while."

"What about what *I* want?"

He shook his head. In his eyes, she saw true regret but in the set of his jaw she read a determination to stay the course.

"Then I'll just leave on the next flight." The plane, which had been taxiing, slowed to a stop.

"There is no next flight unless I schedule one." He rose from his seat and extended his arm toward her. "Come on. Let's make the best of this."

She smacked his hand away and strode ahead of him, furious beyond words.

"Welcome to paradise," he said as he followed her out of the small plane.

She ignored him and planned to do so for the foreseeable future.

Once on the ground, Damian steered her directly to the hunter-green Jeep Wrangler waiting for them on the runway. He excused himself to see about the luggage but returned five minutes later with an annoyed scowl on his face and no bags in his hands.

"Where's our luggage?" she asked.

"Apparently it's still in Florida. Someone claiming to be me called and told the people at the terminal to hold on to it there."

Now Micki frowned. "And they didn't find it odd that you didn't want your suitcase on board along with you?"

He shrugged. "Sometimes I bring a bag, other times I don't since I have clothing down here. It was a misunderstanding and there's nothing we can do about it until the bags are flown in tomorrow."

"I don't plan on being here long enough for that. As soon as you can arrange it, I want to go back to New York."

He ran a hand through his hair, obviously at his wits' end. "How about we go back to my place and you can call your uncle and sister from there? Then you can figure out what you want to do. If it makes you happy, you can leave first thing tomorrow. You must be wiped out, so as long as you're already here, use the time to get some rest."

She tapped her foot against the blacktop, the desire to head home warring with the temptation he offered. She might be furious but that didn't mean she wasn't exhausted, too. Besides, she had to admit she was curious about this gorgeous retreat.

"Okay, that's fine," she said, trying to sound grateful when all she really wanted was to strangle him and her uncle for manipulating her this way. "But I want you to arrange a flight out tomorrow."

"We'll see."

As she climbed into his Jeep Wrangler she growled.

CHAPTER FIVE

DAMIAN'S TROPICAL RETREAT literally took Micki's breath away. Tall palm trees and lush plants dotted the landscape made more beautiful by the expanse of blue sky above them. Despite her anger, he kept up a steady flow of one-sided conversation she couldn't help but listen to with rapt interest.

So far she'd learned that there was one small town and five major estates on the entire island, none within walking distance of the others. The wealthy neighbors rarely crossed paths, while in the town—which supplied the necessities for the visiting inhabitants—the neighbors hung out, gossiped and treated each other like family. That, she discovered, was why Damian loved the place.

He could find either privacy or a sense of small-town kinsmanship, whichever he desired at the moment. On first glance at the island, Micki completely understood his reasoning, but she wasn't about to tell him so. Because she wasn't speaking to him unless she absolutely had to.

"My sisters and their families use the house on their vacations," he said as he continued to drive.

"I'm not in the mood for idle chitchat."

"There's not much else to do to pass the time during the ride."

He wanted to talk? She'd talk. "You brought me here against my will. I think that's called kidnapping."

"So sue me." He laughed. "Your uncle wanted you to have some peace until this blew over and there's nowhere more peaceful than Casa de Fuller."

She didn't know who she was more upset with, her family for treating her like a baby or Damian for buying into it. "It was one picture in a New York newspaper. I can handle the fallout."

"I'm sure you can," he said in a soothing voice.

"If you believe that, then why bring me here?"

"Your uncle asked me to. Since the photo showed you out of control, the publicist who can't practice what she preaches, Yank's worried. And since I had a role in last night's mess, he holds me responsible. The least I could do was help fix things."

Damian's gentlemanly side was rearing its head again. "What role are you referring to?" she asked. "That of savior?"

He gripped the wheel more tightly. "Instigator. I got the definite feeling that when you saw me with Carole, it set you off somehow."

"Who's Carole?" she asked, deliberately playing dumb.

The corner of his mouth lifted in a knowing grin. "My date last night."

"Date? Is that what you call her?" Micki asked and immediately could have bitten her tongue in two.

She might not want to reveal her insecurities, but she didn't have to insult another woman just because she was jealous of Damian's interest in someone so feminine.

"It wasn't you or your date that set me off. Not exactly." As she glanced down at her unpainted fingernails, the words she kept inside of her spilled free. "I've always been the tomboy in the family, I guess because of how close I was to Uncle Yank. When my parents died I trailed after my uncle like he was a god." From the day she'd gone to live with him, Uncle Yank had always been there, the most dominant presence in her life.

Damian nodded in understanding. "He took you and your sisters in. Idolizing him wouldn't be all that unusual."

"It was beyond idolizing. I never felt like myself around my sisters, but it was different with Uncle Yank. He just understood me from the beginning."

"So you were into sports, but somehow I doubt you were an ordinary tomboy." He turned toward her, his gaze meeting hers. "Because there's nothing ordinary about you," he said in a husky voice, taking her off guard.

She swallowed hard, fighting the sexual and emotional effect his words had on her. "I definitely had the most masculine role models you can imagine." Still, she rarely regretted her choices. She not only idolized her uncle, she adored him. "It's just that there are times I wish I'd chosen Sophie or Annabelle to worship because maybe then I—"

She clamped her mouth shut before she said more, realizing how much insight into her soul she'd nearly given a man who definitely wouldn't plan on returning the favor. He'd told her as much, admitting the women he chose to be with were the ones who knew the score. Women who'd let him easily walk away.

They both knew she didn't fit the mold.

Damian gripped the steering wheel tightly and spared a quick glance at Micki. The wind had blown her blond curls around her face in an adorable tangled mess, but it was her silence that caught his attention.

"You okay?" he asked.

She nodded, but whatever she'd been about to reveal remained locked inside her.

Not for the first time, he wondered what made this enigmatic woman tick. A tomboy who was comfortable in a locker room full of naked men, yet a female who was uncomfortable in her own skin. What an interesting mix of contradictions she presented.

At least she was speaking to him again. He hoped his next comment wouldn't put the barrier right back up. "My guess is that you wish you'd spent more time with your sisters and then maybe you wouldn't be thought of as one of the boys."

"What makes you say that?" she asked, her voice tight with tension.

"Something you said last night."

"I wouldn't remember."

She was lying, he thought. She remembered everything about last night as clearly as he did.

Suddenly his estate loomed ahead and he pulled onto the private paved road that led to his home. When he hit the remote he kept in his car, two large iron gates slowly opened before them. He pulled up the circular driveway and parked in front. Before he could say anything else, Micki hopped out of the Jeep ahead of him.

He'd have liked to continue their talk, but there would be more than enough time to ask her questions later. Unless she bailed and headed back for New York. A thought he suddenly didn't find all that appealing.

MICKI STOOD in Damian's large kitchen, which seemed to be the center of the first floor. On one side there was a functional working area and on the other, a long counter surrounded by bar stools. In the middle stretched a large table that seated six. Attached to that was a family room with a flat-screen TV, visible from all angles of the kitchen.

Damian dropped his keys and walked straight to an answering machine, which he noticed was blinking red. He hit a button and an electronic voice informed him there were seven messages.

"Hi, it's Ronnie. Just wanted to make sure you got down there safely. Call me."

Damian glanced at Micki. "That's my youngest sister," he explained without being asked.

"Hi, Damian. It's Brenda. We're worried about you and that wrist. Call us."

Micki shot him a questioning look.

"The middle one." He rolled his eyes, but the gesture was purely indulgent.

"It's Dad. Your mother's driving me crazy. She's been calling every hour and hanging up no matter how many times I explain you won't get home until later. Check in before she drives me batty. *Oww.* Damn woman pinched me. Call—" His message was cut off by the beep signaling the end of his allotted time.

Micki laughed.

"Uncle Damian, I *need* you. Mom won't let me go to the movies with a boy. How ancient is that? You have to talk to her. Puhleeze!" The young girlish voice whined into the phone.

Damian shook his head. "Melanie. She's sixteen going on twenty-six."

"Hi, baby brother, it's Marissa. The girls are making me insane. One wants to date, the other won't leave her room. We're home for the night. Call and let us know how the wrist is doing."

He ran a hand through his hair and turned away, obviously growing embarrassed by the train of phone calls. Embarrassed but not annoyed, Micki noted, as another female voice chimed in next.

"It's Ronnie again. I didn't buy your *I'm fine* act. I know you're upset and worried about not being able to play ball. Call me."

A beep and then a voice said, "Hi, honey. You could call your mother every once in a while."

Micki swallowed a laugh.

And finally, the electronic voice chimed in next saying, "End of messages."

"You're lucky to have them, you know. All of them," Micki said, keenly aware of the importance of her sisters, uncle and Lola in her life. None made up for the absence of her parents but she'd be adrift without them and was grateful for them all.

Damian glanced over his shoulder and met her gaze. "I know. But it's a wonder I turned out straight. I mean, what man in his right mind grows up around all those women and wants to be with more?" He shot her his most charming grin.

Micki nearly melted on the spot. She wished she could dislike everything about him, but the more she learned, the more impressed she became.

His home appealed to her as well. The decor exuded as much warmth as the man. Based on the combination of neutral colors and obviously personal touches, Micki guessed that his sisters and not a professional stranger had decorated. That he allowed the women in his life to dominate in such an intimate way told her much about the kind of man he was inside.

He was obviously indulgent with his sisters even now. To continue to have patience for a bunch of women after growing up around them was a miracle in Micki's opinion. No wonder he connected with Uncle Yank in a way that transcended the agent-client relationship. Otherwise he wouldn't have stepped in and brought Micki down here at Yank's request.

With her new understanding, Micki couldn't stay angry at Damian any longer. Though he'd violated her wishes and sense of independence, he'd more than made up for it in other ways. He'd put her needs before his date's last night and ahead of his professional obligations to the Renegades today. She knew he'd be meeting with a specialist while on this trip, but in Micki's mind that didn't negate all he'd done on her behalf.

In two short days, she'd learned he was more than the successful athlete that New York adored and he possessed so much more substance than he let on to the press. What else would she learn if she stayed for a while at this island getaway?

She bit the inside of her cheek. Why not experience the fantasies she'd been suppressing since New Year's Eve? The idea popped into her head unbidden and, once there, took hold. She could not allow herself to fall harder for the man. And she wouldn't, not as long as she escaped the island before her feelings got any more complicated. A short stay couldn't hurt. A brief indulgence wouldn't jeopardize her heart.

Hadn't Roper suggested she step up to the plate if she wanted Damian? And hadn't she undergone a lesson in being more feminine in order to attract his attention? She'd be a coward if she ran away now.

She could stay and take advantage or she could take a flight out tomorrow and probably spend the rest of her life wondering *what if.*

Micki decided immediately. She wasn't into regrets.

DAMIAN SHOWED MICKI to the room his sisters usually used, figuring she would be most comfortable there. It helped his peace of mind knowing she had her own bathroom, which lessened the chance of him running into her in the middle of the night, half-dressed and utterly desirable.

"Help yourself to any clothes you find in the closet." He wasn't ready to tell her that their suitcases had been accidentally redirected to New York and wouldn't be arriving anytime soon.

She raised an eyebrow. "Left behind by all your women?" she asked, with a challenge in her voice he'd never heard before and he immediately went on alert.

Knowing he'd regret the admission, he replied truthfully anyway. "Except for my sisters, I don't bring women down here."

"What does that make me?" she asked, stepping closer. And closer still.

He inhaled, breathing in her fragrant shampoo, an arousing, tantalizing scent that gave him a damn hard-on every time she was nearby. "I think you already understand what I meant."

He wasn't about to enlighten her further or force himself to think about what bringing her here signified. "I need to go into town to fill the fridge. If you want to come along, be downstairs in half an hour."

She nodded. "I can't go out looking like this." She gestured to the sweats she'd chosen to fly down in because they were comfortable. "I guess that'll give me enough time to check out your sisters' tastes in clothes."

Damian nodded, unable to suppress a grin. He knew his sisters' tastes all right. Nice and conservative. Mom-type clothing. Nonthreatening outfits that wouldn't have him drooling over Micki however long they remained on his island.

Half an hour later, she walked down the stairs wearing slacks and a camisole. A sexy curve-hugging getup. Damian clenched his jaw shut tight.

The black pants *had* to be part spandex, what with the way they began at her waist, then molded to her butt and thighs, falling in a long silhouette over her legs. And her top, if he could call it that, was a turquoise tank in a silky, stretchy material with a subtle flower pattern hidden in the fabric. It ended at her midriff, leaving an open expanse of skin for him to see. And want to touch. Then there was the belt tied in a perfect bow over her flat stomach. All he could do was imagine her as a gift he couldn't wait to unwrap.

"You really have to thank your sisters for me," she said as she jumped down the last two steps.

He grumbled in reply. If these sexy pieces were his sisters' clothes, Damian sure as hell had never seen them wearing anything like them. He'd been blindsided and it pissed him off.

If Micki noticed his foul mood, she didn't mention it. Instead she happily bounced out to the Jeep. On the ride there, she chatted about the blue skies, the gorgeous trees and how fortunate he was to have a retreat on the island. She was no longer upset to be here and damned if he knew why.

This time he was silent as they drove in the Wrangler. He was preoccupied, his thoughts on how he'd deal with her seductive look and her sex appeal, which she seemed suddenly determined to turn his way.

Micki glanced out of the corner of her eye at Damian's tense expression. She'd thrown him off guard but that was her plan. He didn't need to know that she had seduction on her mind or that she'd called her sister Sophie for advice.

His contained feelings told Micki he'd yet to figure out how he wanted to handle her. The attraction between them was real, but so was his fear of the kind of woman Micki was. A woman who knew her mind, understood what she wanted, and one he feared wouldn't accept a one-night stand.

Tonight he'd discover she'd accept whatever he was willing to offer. She'd also accept the possibility that they'd leave the island and never acknowledge what had transpired between them again. But she was even more willing to accept the possibility that, just maybe, she'd touch Damian in a way no woman had before.

For Micki, it was a win-win situation. A hot affair that was long overdue or a longer relationship if Damian was interested. *She could handle either,* she promised herself. She had no choice if she was going to follow through with her plan of no regrets.

In town, the streets were small, the facades bright. Quaint storefronts popped in bright pastel colors with basic names, like Pops Grocery and Your Neighborhood Drug Store. An ice-cream cart was propped between the two stores and outside the front of each she noticed empty benches where she imagined friendly townsfolk sat and passed time.

Damian pulled the Jeep to the curb outside the grocery store. Micki hopped out and went in ahead of him. She wanted to help out by buying some of the food and wanted to give him some space. She shopped quickly, picking some of her favorite staple items, assuming she'd be here for a couple of days before heading home to New York.

She rounded the aisle near the register when she heard Damian's voice.

"How are you doing, Pops?" he asked.

"Good, good. Summer's generally rough, what with the snowbirds sticking close to home, but we're getting by."

"Glad to hear it. How's the missus?"

The man named Pops made a snorting noise. "How do you think? Giving me a hard time over nothing which means she's the same and just fine."

Damian laughed, a sexy sound that rippled along Micki's nerve endings. "I'll take that to mean you're misbehaving. Smoking, drinking, giving her reason to worry."

"She's not happy unless she's nagging."

"And you love her." Damian's voice held a warmth she'd only heard when he'd spoken of his family.

"Tell her and I strangle you. How's the wrist?"

Pops asked. "I saw the game. That was a fantastic catch. Made me damn proud to know you."

Damian slapped the older man on the back. "Thanks. The wrist will be just fine and I'll be playing in October," he promised.

Micki whispered a silent prayer he was right. Not because of the bonus clause negotiated by her uncle that promised Damian big money if the Renegades made each successive play-off, but because he so obviously loved the game.

"Eavesdropping?" Damian had silently come up beside her.

She yelped and dropped the container of yogurt she was holding. "No," she lied, caught in the act. "I was just checking the expiration date."

"Uh-huh." A disbelieving grin tipped his lips.

She studied him, noticing a more relaxed expression on his face. Less tension, fewer stress lines. "You seem to be in a better mood."

He shrugged. "Appearances can be deceiving. I'm still trying to figure you out."

"I had you so confused it affected your mood? I'm flattered." She couldn't help but grin.

"Don't be. You're a female, hence you were put on this earth to perplex men."

Micki was oddly flattered by his comment. After all, he'd called her a female and she'd worked hard for him to notice her in that way.

She glanced at her half-full cart. "I've gotten what I need for the next few days." She kept her eyes focused on him, watching for his reaction.

"Next *few* days?" His gaze darted to hers. "When did that happen?"

She attempted a casual shrug. "You and my uncle thought I should stay here until the scandal blew over. I decided you both had a valid point."

"The hell you did. For some reason I can't begin to understand, *you* decided you want to stay. What we think has nothing to do with it."

So he already knew her that well, did he? Telling him the truth wouldn't hurt. "I decided I'd be a fool to leave paradise too soon." She just didn't intend to define paradise, which wasn't just this island but anywhere Damian Fuller happened to be.

"I might buy that excuse if you hadn't been champing at the bit to leave here, if not today then first thing tomorrow. What changed?"

"Everything." She shot him a big smile. "So did you pick up what you needed or do you have to do more shopping?" she asked, deliberately changing the subject.

"I have to shop," he said through gritted teeth.

"Okay I'll just wait up front." She started to push her cart forward but he stuck a foot out, stopping her.

"Don't get too friendly with the locals," he warned her.

"Why not? Do they bite?"

"Funny," he muttered, grabbing her cart, and then took off down the aisle.

She didn't know how or when, but the teasing and flirting with Damian had suddenly become second nature. It came easily in a way it hadn't before.

She wondered what had changed beyond her dress, and realized it was her perspective. Not just of herself as a woman capable of attracting this man, but of Damian himself. He was no longer an icon she feared or a guy with no substance who wouldn't give her a second glance. Now that she viewed him as a man with thoughts and feelings, she could treat him the same way she did the other men in her world, like Roper or her clients. Except for that added attraction, of course.

She could easily become addicted to the sensations taking over her body. She'd seen his reaction to her as she'd come down the stairs. Seen it in his eyes and seen it in his pants. As much as she blushed at the thought, she reveled in the attention so long denied.

She'd already been fortunate in his sisters' choice of clothing. Obviously the items in the closets and drawers were chosen with their husbands in mind. Micki doubted they brought those pieces for trips with their kids in tow. Especially the brand new lingerie with tags still attached. She planned to wear one tonight and would be happy to leave payment and a note of thanks, she thought wryly. No way would she give

Damian advance notice of her intent. Micki was counting on the heat of the moment to carry them away.

Since she was already driving Damian insane, she decided to listen to him and not talk to anyone in the store. Instead she walked outside, purchased a snow cone and settled onto one of the benches she'd seen earlier.

On her first lick, the frozen ice reminded her of the days she and her sisters would buy this kind of treat when they were young. She curled her legs beneath her and sucked the juice from the cone, letting the cold refreshment ease the humidity and heat clinging to her skin. She shut her eyes and just enjoyed, hoping this was the first of many more pleasurable activities to come.

DAMIAN HEADED for the grocery store exit. His bags weren't in hand since Pops never allowed him to load his own car and Damian had long since stopped arguing. The older man thought that since baseball was America's favorite pastime, it was somehow his duty to serve Damian. Pops was a stubborn cuss and Damian had no choice but to give in. Unfortunately that meant it would be a little while before Pops got all the bags into the Jeep.

Damian stepped out into the heat of a sticky summer afternoon that was quickly turning to evening and immediately saw Micki. She sat on one of the benches he'd never paid much attention to until now and enjoyed a basic summer pleasure, one usually reserved for kids. But the woman eating the snow cone wasn't a child and the images she evoked as her tongue worked at the rounded head of the cone were for adults only.

Her eyes shut tight, her tongue covered the ice as she delicately licked the treat, then followed with her lips as she drew the snow cone into her mouth. Sucking. Pulling. Drawing every last drop inside her mouth and down her throat.

His groin tightened at the sight and the erotic visions that filled his mind weren't a huge leap. Not for a man on the edge of sanity.

A jarring, noisy sound broke his concentration and he looked up to see Pops walk out, pushing the shopping cart filled with his bags of groceries. At least he wasn't planning to carry the load to the Jeep one bag at a time.

"I noticed she's with you." Pops angled his head Micki's way.

Damian cleared his throat. "My agent's daughter."

"That's what I call mixin' business with pleasure."

Damian couldn't tell if Pops was issuing condemnation or just statement of fact. "What makes you think it's more than just business?"

"I saw the *Post*," Pops said. "And the *News*. You know we get it flown in late."

"Yeah." Damian knew. He'd just pushed the article out of his mind, hoping his island retreat was far enough away to forget things for a little while.

"You never brought anyone down here before." Pops pierced Damian with his best silvery-eyed stare.

"Never had to, but she needed a place to hide out till the speculation died down." Damian squinted into the late-afternoon sun, wondering when the inquisition would be over.

"I dunno what that craziness is about, but she looks like a nice enough girl. Mary said she reminds her of Ronnie," he said, referring to Damian's baby sister.

Normally that kind of statement would kill any building desire. When it didn't, Damian realized that Micki had a more powerful hold than he liked.

He glanced at Pops. "That ought to convince you I'm just doing a favor for a friend." For added luck, Damian crossed his fingers behind his back.

"Yeah well, Mary also said she looks like a keeper." As if Pops knew the conversation was over, he pushed the cart toward the Jeep.

Damian looked over at their topic of discussion. Oblivious, Micki had begun licking the liquid dripping from the bottom of the cone.

Drawing a deep breath, Damian strode over and cleared his throat.

She glanced up, red juice on her chin.

"Ready to hit the road?" he asked.

She'd been sitting cross-legged and, on hearing his voice, her feet hit the floor. "Ready." She glanced around. "Is there a garbage pail near here?"

He took the paper wrapper from her hand, walked to the curb and tossed it in the trash. Pops, he'd noticed, was still loading the groceries into the back of the Jeep.

Micki, in the meantime, had begun licking her fingers and he couldn't resist the temptation to stare as she sucked the juice off her fingertips one by one.

When she met his gaze, her eyes widened and her cheeks flushed. "Sticky," she explained.

He swallowed a reply that would surely have involved him offering to take over the job for her. "Let's go," he said gruffly.

He needed a cold drink and his big-screen TV where he could watch a game and distract himself from this woman. As if such a thing were even possible, he thought, wondering exactly what he'd gotten himself into.

CHAPTER SIX

UPON THEIR RETURN FROM TOWN, Damian sequestered himself in the den and flipped on the television to watch the Boston Red Sox play the New York Yankees. Since he hadn't invited her to join him and she was exhausted anyway, Micki retreated upstairs for a nap.

She woke an hour later and headed for the kitchen, intending to cook them dinner. She wasn't a gourmet chef, but she could whip up a passable meal for two. She didn't have to. An older couple was already at work.

She cleared her throat and walked into the room.

A gray-haired woman greeted her with a smile. "You must be Mr. Fuller's guest. I'm Rosa and this is my husband Tino." She gestured to a man who resembled Dom DeLuise. Robust and cheery, he waved, his hands full with a carving knife and breast of chicken.

"Micki Jordan," she said by way of introduction. "Can I help?" But even as she asked, she realized they were extremely at home in the kitchen. They worked in tandem, helping each other and knowing exactly where to find things in the drawers and cabinets.

"No thanks," Tino said, just as Micki had expected. "Go relax and we'll let you know when dinner's on the table."

"Okay." She lifted her arms in a halfhearted gesture, thinking she'd prefer to socialize than go off alone. "So have you worked here long?"

"For the last five years, every time Mr. Fuller comes to town," Rosa said.

"What do you do between visits?" Micki asked.

"If his family's here, we cook and clean for them. If not, we come in weekly to freshen the place up and keep it from getting musty while nobody's living here."

Micki nodded, though she wondered how they made a living on Damian's sporadic visits alone.

"When Damian was young, we were his neighbors in New Jersey," Rosa explained as she chopped tomatoes. "I'd do babysitting for his mother while she worked. She helped his father out at his car dealerships. Damian made it big, bought this place about the same time Tino had a heart attack."

She spared a loving glance at her husband. "He needed warmer weather and Damian needed caretakers. It's a win-win situation, though a much bigger win for us," Rosa said, clearly embarrassed.

"Don't sell yourself short," Damian said, joining them.

He stepped closer, his big body overwhelming

Micki from behind, his heady masculine scent sending warning signals to her brain. If she thought she'd slept off the effects of last night, she'd been sadly mistaken. Her reaction to the man was as potent as ever, which meant her plan to seduce him was still in full force.

"I see you met the best people around," Damian commented, affection in his tone.

"We met," Micki said warmly.

"We're almost finished," Tino said. "Do you want us to come back and clean up?"

Micki shook her head. "No thank you. I can take care of—"

"I'd appreciate it." Damian interrupted her.

He eased closer and leaned his head near hers. "They'll be insulted if they think they aren't needed," he whispered quietly into her ear. His breath was warm and his lips brushed against her hair. He might not have intended anything except imparting information but the result was erotic all the same and she shivered.

"Well, I need my rest anyway," Micki said.

Rosa nodded, pleased. "Dinner will be ready in a few minutes, so why don't you go sit and have a drink?" She gestured in the direction of the dining room.

Micki had expected a casual dinner, but as she headed to the other room, she found the rectangular table set with a delicate tablecloth, good china and two glasses of sparkling water poured and waiting for them. Surprised, she turned to question Damian.

He stopped short, nearly walking into her. "What's wrong?"

"Nothing, except...why the formality?"

He shrugged. "Rosa thinks company's a reason to use the good dishes."

"I would have thought this room was for show," she said, laughing.

"If it were up to me, that's what it would be for. My sisters decided if I was going to have a big house and help, I shouldn't be serving on paper plates in the den."

"They have a point."

He strode around her, pulled out a chair and waited for her to be seated.

Suddenly nerves took over as she found herself next to Damian at the end of the table. In the silence that followed, the atmosphere around them grew more intense. She became aware of the ticking of the clock on the wall behind her, a synchronized accompaniment to her heart as it beat heavily inside her chest.

She searched for an easy topic of conversation. He had his prearranged doctor's appointment the next day and Micki knew he put a lot of stock in the doctor helping him get back to work soon.

"So how 'bout them Renegades?" she asked to break the tension.

It worked. He grinned and raised his glass. "To the

division championship, then the NLCS and finally the World Series."

She lifted her water and clicked her glass with his. He seemed pleased at the topic of conversation and she didn't want to mess up by getting too serious. "I spoke to Sophie and she said the camp ran smoothly."

He nodded. "It always does. You Jordan girls have a knack for PR."

"Thank you. It's something we all enjoy, which I'm sure helps a lot. Nobody wants to get up and go to work every day and be miserable."

"Amen."

She smiled. "You love what you do, too."

"There's nothing more fulfilling than baseball."

She raised an eyebrow. "Nothing more fulfilling, huh? Are you absolutely sure? Because I can think of a few things that at least come close." And in case her insinuation wasn't clear, she reached out and ran her foot up and down his leg.

He blinked, obviously startled. Well, so was she. She hadn't thought she'd have the nerve to pull off Sophie's first suggestion.

"Micki Jordan, are you flirting with me?" he asked, stunned.

She tried for a relaxed smile. "I believe I am." Because she might never get another chance like this again. A rush of excitement flooded her veins.

Damian, meanwhile, still looked stunned.

"What's the matter? I can't imagine I'm the first woman who's propositioned you."

He placed the glass back onto the table and leaned closer. "Is that what you're doing? Propositioning me?"

She nodded slowly. "The question is are you up for the challenge?" Because Micki wanted him at peak levels.

Damian stared at the woman next to him. How had she gone from embarrassed ingenue to seductive vixen? And how did he get the shyer Micki back? No way did he want to be alone with the bold Micki, who seriously threatened his tenuous restraint.

"Oh, Rosa," he called. "Is dinner almost ready? I'm starving."

Micki met his gaze and chuckled. "I'll be sure to keep that in mind."

"Is everything a sexual innuendo where you're concerned?"

She propped her chin on one hand. "Only since I met you." She paused in thought. "Actually only since Carter got me drunk, then you kidnapped me to a remote island off the coast of Florida."

"I tried to talk you out of the strip joint," he reminded her.

"That brings me to another point. I thought you were a fun guy."

"I am a fun guy."

"You're going to have to prove it," she teased and his groin tightened with immediate need.

"Dinner," Rosa said, arriving with two plates, heaping with delicious food.

He'd hoped Rosa and dinner would break the tension, but as they began to eat, Damian realized they were just inching closer to the end of the meal and time alone—when he'd have to decide whether or not he wanted to meet Micki's challenge.

"Rosa, this is delicious," Micki said.

The older woman blushed. "Thank you. Steak, potatoes and green beans. All Mr. Fuller's favorites."

"So he ate his vegetables as a boy, did he?" Micki asked.

Rosa shook her head and laughed. "No but we've been piling them on his plate anyway. If we call them his favorites, we figure one day he'll forget and believe it."

"His mother's idea," Tino said, striding into the room with a wine bottle in his hand. "Wine anyone?"

Damian placed his hand over his glass. "No, thank you."

"Me neither."

Without warning, Micki ran her foot up and down his leg once more, blatantly teasing him. His gut twisted and he broke into a sweat. No way could he withstand a serious post-dinner assault.

"While you were having your wine, our daughter Sara called," Rosa said.

"The one who's getting married in a few months." Though he'd never been close with their children, Damian knew all their life stories and the depth of Rosa and Tino's love and pride in their brood.

"Well, not according to her. She had an argument with her fiancé and just like that, she called off the engagement." Rosa snapped her fingers.

"As if a promise means nothing," Tino said, his disappointment and concern clear in his tone.

"I'm sure she didn't break the engagement lightly," Damian said.

"That's what we need to find out." Rosa glared at her husband. She obviously wanted him to withhold judgment. "So we need to leave early, but I promise to come back and clean in the morning."

"That's not necessary." Micki waved a hand, calling attention her way. "You help your daughter. I'm happy to clean up."

"Are you sure?" Rosa asked.

Damian had every intention of letting them go to their daughter. "We can handle it," he assured her.

"Thank you," Tino said.

"Both of you," Rosa added. She untied her apron as she quickly walked back to the kitchen. A few minutes later, the door slammed shut behind the couple, leaving Micki and Damian alone.

Using caution, Damian turned to Micki. "I thought you wanted to get out of here as soon as possible." He hoped his reminder would get her to think about leaving again before he did something stupid. Like sleep with her.

"I changed my mind. I'm not so sure leaving is best for me after all. I like it here. It's relaxing, it's away from the press...and you're here."

Damian glanced toward the ceiling. How much could a normal guy take? She was sending out blatant signals and he couldn't deny his interest. Hell, he'd been interested for too long and now she was all but offering herself to him.

He'd never denied that he'd been spoiled, the baby brother of sisters who catered to his every whim and the athlete whose money assured him that any woman would do the same. Until now, he'd always known when to draw the line and respected the need to do so.

Micki deserved that same respect, but she so obviously didn't want it, and damned if he could stop himself from acting on what they both desired.

"You're serious?" he asked because he had to be sure.

"About you?"

He nodded.

"I can spell it out for you if you'd like," she said, leaning closer, her fresh scent enticing him. "I'm deadly serious about wanting you. About understanding your rules and not expecting anything beyond this. In fact, I'm so busy at home, I wouldn't have time even if you came crawling on your hands and knees."

He raised an eyebrow, wondering if he'd read her wrong in the past and she really was into short flings, or if she was telling him what he wanted to hear.

Either way, she'd given him a green light. He pushed his chair back and stood. Towering over her, he slid her chair back, too, then braced his hands on the armrests and leaned close, his lips inches from hers.

She swallowed hard and he sensed her nervousness, reminding him that despite the show of bravado, she wasn't the experienced, easy kind of woman he was used to. Somehow it made him desire her more.

He clenched his fingers around the hard wood. "I want you, too."

Her eyes grew wide, the blue pools deepening with pleasure. "So what's holding you back?"

"Not a damn thing." Without hesitating, he sealed his lips over hers and gave into the temptation he'd been fighting.

She sighed, the sound soft and full of complete relief as her lips parted and she took him inside. She tasted of pure woman. He slanted his mouth for better access and thrust his tongue deep and hard.

A part of him realized he was testing her, seeing if his unleashed need would scare her off, because he knew if he took this woman to bed there would be no holding back. He even wondered if a part of him hoped she'd retreat before it was too late.

But she wasn't running away. Instead she pulled him closer, wrapping her arms around his neck so he could continue his assault. And as he circled the warm, moist recesses of her mouth, their tongues tangling, their teeth grazing, he realized they shared an equally overwhelming desire. One that had to be sated immediately.

He reached back, untangled her hands and brought them down to her sides, while breaking the kiss slowly. Gently. In a way that let him savor every movement. The brush of his lips over hers, the soft licks of his tongue across the moisture they'd created, and the light nip of his teeth on her flesh.

She moaned and tried to entice him back into a soul-searching kiss, but he couldn't take another minute of kissing and teasing like they were horny teenagers who couldn't complete the act. Because they most certainly could.

"Let's go upstairs," he said, his voice hoarse with desire.

She nodded. "I think the dining room would be awkward."

"Not to mention hard on my back."

Micki grinned. "Not as young as you used to be, are you, Fuller?"

He laughed despite how true that statement was.

With Micki, he didn't feel the need to hide the painful truth. "Just keep that little secret to yourself."

She met his gaze, the moment suddenly too serious.

"I'm not too old for this." He bent down, lifted her into his arms, favoring his good hand, and carried her straight to his bed.

BE CAREFUL WHAT YOU ASK FOR, Micki thought as Damian swept her off to his bedroom in true fairy-tale form. But if he was her prince, he wasn't the permanent, happily-ever-after kind. Just the fantasy she'd dreamed about for most of her life, and one she had every intention of enjoying.

His bedroom was large with oversize shuttered windows, dark wood furniture, and a navy-and-cream color scheme, all dominated by a California king-size bed. When he laid her back against the pillows, butterflies filled her stomach, but no second thoughts raced through her mind. Apparently he had none either. He straddled her lower body with his thighs and his gaze never left hers as he pulled his shirt up and over his head.

Micki swallowed hard. For a woman who'd spent a lifetime in male locker rooms, she would have thought she was immune to a muscled body. No such luck. The man was sculpted and gorgeous, from his stubbled beard, sexy chest, down to the sprinkle of hair disappearing into the waistband of his jeans.

She'd examine what lay beneath that denim in a little while. For now she wanted to focus on his exposed upper body. "You have a golfer's tan," she mused. With one finger, she traced the tan lines that cut his forearms where his uniform sleeves ended.

He visibly shivered, reacting to her touch. "I'd prefer to call it a ballplayer's tan."

"Semantics." Emboldened, she drew an imaginary line beginning on his arms and traveling straight across his chest where his tanned neck abruptly changed to the paler hue.

She shut her eyes and continued to run her palm over his flesh, letting her senses take over. The texture of his hair-roughened skin, so different from her own, caused tremors of awareness to shoot through her body. As for Damian, when her fingertips touched his nipples, he sucked in a sharp breath. The sound echoed in her ears and gave her yet another taste of feminine power.

In the past, Micki had had her share of lovers. The relationships hadn't worked, not for her and not for the guy with whom she was involved. Most of the men had been sports guys she'd met through her job. Some had wanted an in with her powerful uncle; others had been interested in a short fling. The sex had been fine but had never been fulfilling. There hadn't been much give and take, and the relationships had left her empty in ways she hadn't understood.

As a result of those brief and ultimately unsatisfactory affairs, Micki could never have imagined affecting any man deeply on a physical level. Especially a man as sexual as Damian.

Once again, she smoothed her fingertips over Damian's hardened nipples, lingering this time, teasing him with her touch and lightly scraping her nails across his skin. He let out a groan of satisfaction that sent ripples of arousal straight to her core. *She* affected him. And the arousal in his voice caused dampness to pool between her thighs.

He touched her chin.

She opened her eyes and found herself looking into his chocolate-colored gaze. Warm and sexy, his stare was focused solely on her. "That's better," he said in a husky voice.

"Why?"

"I want to see your expression when I reciprocate." With a wicked grin, he eased her shirt upward.

She leaned forward to help and quickly her shirt ended up on the floor, leaving her in a bra that was quite different than what she was used to. Where she chose lacy fabric that left a lot to the imagination, the garment she'd found in the drawer showed everything to anyone who cared to look.

Damian did, his eyes growing wide. When Micki glanced down to see what had him so fascinated, she received a glimpse of her own breasts, plump and full inside the sheer material, her clearly visible nipples fully puckered and erect. Self-consciousness had her lifting her hands to cover herself, but he stopped her. He trapped her arms at her sides, holding them in place with his strong thighs.

"Do you want to know exactly what you do to me?" he asked. "Why I'm breaking a self-imposed promise to keep my hands to myself? Why I'm here when I should be with the team, injury be damned?"

Mouth dry, she merely nodded.

She expected him to cup her breasts in his hands and braced herself for the onslaught of sensation. He leaned forward and captured her nipple in his mouth instead.

Micki sucked in a startled breath. She glanced down to see his dark hair against her chest, tickling her skin. She felt a rush of warm breath and accompanying moisture, and a moan escaped her throat.

"I get it," she choked out. *This* was worth breaking the rules for.

He lifted his head and cool air brushed her damp skin. "No, you don't. Not yet." He placed his thumb over one distended nipple and pressed hard and deep until her hips bucked beneath him and she cried out with need. "But you will," he promised.

He obviously wasn't finished and she didn't know whether to beg for mercy or let him continue until she couldn't take any more. He grazed with his teeth, laved with his tongue, and finally suckled her nipple for a long, leisurely time until she writhed beneath him. The sensations tackled her body with unprecedented force, and with shaking hands, she reached for the button of his jeans.

Stripping off their clothes was a blur—who pulled off whose pants, who unhooked Micki's bra, she had no idea. All she was aware of was haste born of desire and building need. A need they both shared to get closer, to let skin touch skin with nothing in between.

She hadn't realized the implications of being so close to Damian. His heated flesh branded her and as he came over her, the silken strength of his erection pressed hard and hot against her thigh. This wasn't sex, this was intimacy and she'd have to live with that knowledge for the rest of her life, when Damian was long gone.

But while he was here, he was hers and she intended to savor the moments. Hooking her leg around his, she adjusted their positions, shifting him so that not only was he on top of her, but his member was poised at the place she needed him most.

"I was right," he said, his gruff voice rumbling in her ear.

"About what?"

He paused for a deep, wet kiss, his mouth melding with hers. God, she thought, the man was good.

"No matter how hard you tried to hide it, you are one hot woman."

Pleasure raced through her, chiseling away at the insecurities she'd harbored for as long as she could remember. His words also freed her to act on her desires and she slid her arms around his back, placing her palms against his buttocks.

"How long are you going to make me wait?" she whispered in his ear, letting her tongue glide along the outer shell.

He shivered and reciprocated with a nibble on her neck along with a teasing thrust of his hips. Their lower bodies met at exactly the right place. His erection ground into her feminine mound, setting off orgasmic-like tremors that were a mere prelude to the real thing.

In case he needed incentive, Micki reached down and wrapped her hand around his member. He was smooth with subtle ridges, and oh so hard and long.

"That's it." Damian had had enough. Enough teasing, enough foreplay, enough restraint. There was just so much a naked man could take.

Pausing only to grab protection, he then rose above her and spread her thighs with his hands. She met his gaze, eyes wide and imploring, with a trust that was humbling. But he wanted this woman as he hadn't wanted any other and as long as she wanted him, too, he wasn't about to stop.

Unable to wait another second, he nudged the head of his aching erection into her moist, warm sheath. She let out a sigh of longing at the same time he gritted his teeth and drove deep inside her. Her wet heat molded around him, cushioning him in a tight, suctioning hold. He thought he'd died and gone to heaven. He didn't know he could feel so good so fast, or so connected to another person.

Before he could dwell on that thought, Micki distracted him by wrapping her legs around him and hooking her ankles at the small of his back. Her hips jutted upward, their bodies met at exactly the right spot and after that there was no going slow.

He pulled out, then plunged fast and deep. Micki cried out but had no trouble keeping pace. Their rhythm was perfect, their bodies in unison. He pumped inside her and she met him thrust for thrust, her legs still wrapped around his waist. He couldn't resist kissing her again as they climbed higher and higher toward climax. She breathed harder in his ear, becoming more vocal with each successive bump and grind of their hips and bodies.

He wouldn't have believed she was so loud and expressive. Damn, but he liked it. Seconds later, everything inside and outside of him exploded as he came. And came and came.

He thrust in and out, drawing out every last incredible sensation and triggering Micki's release. She locked her ankles tighter around him, dug her nails into his back and lifted her hips high and hard.

She called out his name and touched a place he hadn't known existed. For the first time, a woman touched his heart.

CHAPTER SEVEN

MICKI AWOKE ALONE in Damian's bed and remembered that Dr. Maddux was arriving this morning to evaluate Damian's wrist. She hoped he'd have good news because Damian loved the game too much to be forced out before he was ready.

Since last night, Micki cared more about what Damian wanted than she probably should. Because of how he made her feel. Because of how she felt about him.

The man was a fantastic lover and knew how to make her feel like she was the only woman in the world who mattered to him, in bed and out. For the time being, she didn't mind living in her own deluded world. So much so that she got out of bed smiling and singing out of tune while she headed for the shower.

Half an hour later, she walked downstairs to the kitchen. Once there, she saw a note from Rosa telling them that she had left premade meals in the freezer.

One sniff informed Micki that Damian hadn't made coffee yet, so she set up a pot and waited for him to emerge from the basement gym where he was meeting with the doctor. She made herself a quick egg-white omelet and after she'd eaten and cleaned up, she decided she could no longer avoid calling her sisters.

She started with Annie since she wanted to check on her and the baby. She pulled out her cell phone, dialed and soon had her oldest sibling on the line.

"Good morning, big sister. How are you?" Micki's heart pounded in her chest as she waited for the reply.

"Baby and I are doing fine."

From the upbeat tone of Annabelle's voice, Micki believed her and she forced air back into her lungs. "You'd better follow doctor's orders and rest, no matter how hard it is for you to do nothing." While she spoke, Micki rummaged around for cleaning supplies and then wiped the countertops with Windex until they shone.

"I wouldn't put my anal personality before my baby's health. Besides, Vaughn's around 24/7 to make sure I'm a good girl."

"You're never good," Micki heard Vaughn joke in the background. "Say hi to your sister and reassure her I'm taking good care of you, babe," he said.

Micki smiled. In the time since Annie had married Brandon Vaughn, he'd grown on all the sisters. He was the brother Micki had never had. After all the years Annie had spent being the caretaker for Micki and Sophie, Micki was grateful her sister had found someone to cater to her for a change. Though she envied Annie and Vaughn, she didn't begrudge her sister her happiness.

Annabelle chatted about sonograms and bed rest, and Micki realized that while Annie had always been the caretaker, Micki had been taken care of. She wanted to be a caregiver, a mother one day. She hoped she'd eventually find a man, a partner who wanted to share her life and give her the traditional family unit she'd never had.

Suddenly Micki glanced around Damian's kitchen where she'd made herself at home. And she forced herself to remember that Damian would not be that man.

"So how's your forced trip to paradise?" Annie asked, her voice filled with concern.

Micki felt a smile work its way onto her face. "Actually not as bad as I thought. Turns out that after partying too hard and the PR fiasco, I needed some R & R after all. And…" Micki prepared herself to admit more to her sister when the sound of male voices and footsteps reminded her that she wasn't alone.

"Micki?" her sister asked.

"And I decided to see what paradise has to offer." Paradise meaning Damian, she thought, just as he entered the room with the orthopedist by his side.

Micki rushed her sister off the phone, promising to call back later. Heart pounding hard in her chest, she turned to meet Damian's gaze, not knowing what she'd find there.

He caught her questioning stare with a smoldering one of his own, the heat in his dark eyes telling her he hadn't forgotten last night. And the sudden smile that lit up his face indicated he didn't regret it either. Her heart melted at the sight of him and the honesty she saw there.

"Dr. Maddux, I'd like you to meet Micki Jordan, publicist extraordinaire. Micki, meet Dr. Maddux, bearer of bad news." Damian swept his hand through the air in a meaningless gesture yet the words he uttered were anything but.

"Thanks for coming, Doc." Damian spared a glance at Micki. "I'm going to walk him to the car that's taking him back to the airport."

She bit down on her lip and nodded. "I'll be here when you get back."

Damian's words had been vague, but decidedly negative. The next few minutes felt like a lifetime, leaving her on edge, flexing and unflexing her fingertips and pacing the floors. Finally the front door slammed hard and Damian rejoined her in the kitchen.

"What did he say?" she asked.

"Who's asking? Micki the team publicist or—"

"Micki your friend and I think you know that." She reminded herself that it was his pain causing him to question her loyalty.

He lowered his gaze. "I have tendinitis. Nothing some time off and immobility won't cure," he said with a hint of sarcasm in his voice. He raised his injured hand, pointing out the brace he'd been wearing.

Since that seemed like positive news, Micki knew there had to be more. "And?"

"And the numbness is probably a result of carpal tunnel syndrome. You know, repetitive motions such as throwing exacerbates it. After reviewing the X-rays, the bone density and the MRI results, and after a physical examination, the good doc said he also sees strong evidence of arthritis, which weakens the bones and will begin to give me aggravation down the line. Not too far down the line because the wrist is pretty fragile. So are the rest of the bones." He grimaced. "Welcome to old age."

She raised an eyebrow. Thirty-five wasn't ancient, but she'd heard it many times. Athletes counted age like dog years. "You aren't finished for the season are you?"

He shook his head.

"That's good. Though when you are, I know Uncle Yank has plenty of post-game work lined up for you. Or at least he's got some good ideas percolating."

Damian stared in wonder at her. He'd had crappy news and this woman wasn't pitying him. She was looking on the bright side.

"A good-looking guy like you, with all your sports knowledge, is pretty marketable, you know," she said in a deliberately smart-ass tone and patted his cheek with her hand.

He grabbed her wrist and pulled her close. She'd just showered and her hair smelled fresh and clean and her body was warm and willing, just as she'd been last night. He wrapped his arms around her waist and buried his face in the curve of her neck, wishing he could bury his problems as easily and as pleasurably.

He slid his fingers into the back pockets of her pants, cupping her rear and nestling his groin into the sweet V of her legs. "These jeans fit you like a glove."

"Your sisters are all different sizes but luckily I have an average body type that fits most anything."

He heard the self-deprecation in her tone and knew it was tied in with her tomboy image and her impression that somehow she was less feminine than her sisters. He knew differently. It was time she did, too. He might not be able to help himself but he could help Micki.

"You are anything but average," he said in a gruff voice and, in case she wasn't sure or didn't believe him, he rolled his hips, letting her feel the bulging erection that she'd caused.

She moaned in pleasure, a pleasure he understood. He'd walked into the kitchen, Dr. Maddux's words weighing heavily on his mind while his future and his career crashed down around him. And then he'd taken one look at Micki wearing a tight pair of faded jeans and a sunny yellow shirt and his mood had lifted. Just like that.

"You're just saying that to make me feel good," she said.

He shook his head, determined to win this argument. "I've been with many women—"

"Thanks for reminding me," she said wryly.

"And none has inspired me to do this." He stepped back, unsnapped his pants, then dropped and kicked them to one side of the room.

"Damian!"

"You know what they say, honey?"

"I'm afraid to ask," she said, her cheeks flushed red.

"If you can't take the heat, get out of the kitchen." He grinned and waited for her reaction.

She raised her hands to the bottom of her snug T-shirt and yanked it over her head. Same see-through bra as yesterday, pushing up her full breasts enticingly. His throat tightened as need pummeled him hard.

Nodding his approval, he added his shirt to their growing pile. Her jeans came next, his underwear, her bra and finally her panties.

She faced him without reaching for cover. He knew how difficult it must be to pretend she had no insecurities and he respected her all the more for making the attempt.

He couldn't tear his gaze from her full breasts and

the blond triangle of hair that beckoned to him. "You take my breath away."

"I know," she said, her stare focused on his member, which was thicker and harder than ever before.

"I'm glad I made my point."

She merely nodded and in the silence that followed, the air around them was dense with desire.

He picked her up and placed her on the kitchen table. Her eyes grew wide as her body came in contact with the wooden surface and she shivered.

"Cold?" he asked though he already knew. Her nipples had puckered and he reached out to roll one between his thumb and forefinger until she shut her eyes tight and moaned aloud.

"Which is it? Are you hot? Or are you cold?" he asked in a teasing voice.

She met his gaze. "You are so bad. I may be hot for you but the tabletop's freezing."

"Then let me warm you."

Her gaze never leaving his, she lowered herself back until she rested on her elbows. Her breasts thrust upward, tempting him to lick and taste. But Damian wanted her hotter than he'd had her before.

He pulled her closer to the end of the table and spread her legs wide, stepping in between her thighs.

"Damian," she said, her voice uncertain.

He was anything but. "Relax," he told her. He sat in the nearest chair and eyed her as if he were taking in a feast. Her thighs quivered and he sensed her tension. He didn't want her uptight, he just plain wanted her and knew just how to make her forget her insecurities.

He positioned himself directly in front of where she sat, legs open wide, waiting for him to take her. And he did. He leaned forward and slicked his tongue deep inside.

Micki sucked in a startled gasp. She couldn't believe she was spread out on Damian's table but her mortification gave way to complete and utter pleasure when his mouth made contact with her *there*. It felt so good, so right, she let out a loud sigh and gave up control, trusting Damian completely.

His tongue was wet, warm and giving as it slid over her folds. She experienced the glide of his tongue, mouth and, if she wasn't mistaken, his teeth. In and out, back and forth. She breathed in deeply and nearly passed out from the drugging sensations overtaking her body. It was one thing when they'd made love, another for him to want to pleasure her this way.

Without warning, he added his hand to his repertoire. His flat palm was hard against her mound as he began working her in a circular motion. The friction of his hand brought her instantly to the brink. Her hips rose and she jerked against him, pressing herself into his hand and his mouth. His tongue dipped deep inside her and his fingertip pressed the exact pressure point where she needed his touch the most.

When she needed more—stronger, deeper contact—he understood. He suckled her harder with his mouth, pulling on her sensitive flesh as her arousal built higher and higher.

She was so close and so out of control. Her hips rolled and her limbs trembled. "I can't—" The words ripped from her throat as her body bucked and sought a pinnacle it couldn't quite find.

"Yes, baby, you can. Get up." He pulled her upright and while she came forward, she heard the crinkling of foil as he took care of protection.

She didn't care where the condom had come from, she was just grateful he'd been prepared. Then she was off the table and in his arms, sitting astride him. Her legs bracketed his. Skin against skin, his thick arousal pressed hard into her thigh.

"Work with me, okay?" he asked.

She nodded. At this point she'd agree to anything.

He placed his hands on her hips and lifted her up so the tip of his erection was poised at her entry. "You're killing me," she told him.

"But you'll die happy," he said in a husky voice.

She laughed, then leaning forward, kissed him, sucking his lips into her mouth and teasing him mercilessly.

Seconds later, he reached out, his fingers finding her and spreading her slick moisture over her flesh. When he pushed one finger inside her, she sucked in a breath. Another finger joined the first and she gasped.

Then he removed his fingers and replaced it with his penis, thrusting upward at the same moment she pressed her hips down hard. He filled her completely. Thick and hard, she felt every silken ridge and each delectable inch. She closed her eyes and rocked against him, slowly at first, back and forth and then in a circular direction, each motion rubbing her pubic bone against him and making the spiraling sensations mount and build as she picked up a frenzied pace.

Somehow he managed to pump his hips upward and each thrust was in perfect synchronization with her need. She threaded her fingers through his hair and held on, kissing him when she could and just plain hanging on for the ride.

As he took her higher and higher, her world was reduced to nothing more or less than the point where their bodies joined. Her breath caught in her throat and she clenched her muscles tight around him. And finally he took her over the edge. Her entire body shook as she came, feelings and emotions colliding with physical sensations that she thought would never end.

Aftershocks shook her body but eventually the world around Micki came into focus. Her head was buried in Damian's neck and he held on to her waist, still deep inside her.

She tipped her head back and met his gaze.

Heavy-lidded and breathing raggedly, he managed to treat her to a sexy smile. "Very nice."

She felt a hot flush rise to her cheeks and tried to stand but he held on tight. "In a rush?" he asked.

"No. It's just—"

"You're not used to anything like this." One arm swept around the kitchen, encompassing the table and their chair.

She laughed. "You could say that."

"It's not a habit of mine, either." His voice was gruff, his gaze deep and serious as he smoothed his hands over her unruly curls. "You just make me crazy."

She swallowed hard. So he'd said, but she couldn't wrap her mind around this man wanting her so badly. "It was definitely good sex," she said, deliberately belittling what had just occurred.

Damian shook his head. "There's sex and then there's sex."

Which meant what? she wondered. What did he want from her? Right now she was off balance, shaken by the intensity of the encounter and the feelings she was developing for him. She wanted to put her clothes back on and gain some sort of leverage at least in her own mind.

He'd have to step up first, Micki decided. If there was more to this for him than a quick lay, he'd have to admit as much to her. "And which kind of sex did we just have?" she asked casually. She hoped.

The phone rang, cutting off any answer he might have had. She jumped off him, grabbed her clothes and scrambled for the bathroom, leaving Damian to answer the call naked.

Damian figured he'd never again look at the kitchen table or any meal he ate there the same way. He hung up the phone and pulled on his jeans, then picked up the rest of his clothes and headed for the shower. Anything to avoid telling Micki that it had been Coach Donovan on the phone. The doctor had filled management in on his condition and he had to regain control, convince them he was fine. He'd promised to return in twenty-four hours.

Which meant one more day with Micki.

He waited for her to shower and met her in the hallway. "Want to go for a drive?"

She met his gaze. "Sure. Care to tell me where we're going?"

He grabbed her hand, but not before taking the time to ogle her legs and amazing body in the ruffled black miniskirt and tie-dyed tank top she wore. "You really ought to dress up more often. It brings out the real you."

She tipped her head to one side, the damp curls hitting her shoulders. "How so?"

"This skirt is lively and fun. Like you. The top is flirty and sexy. Also like you."

He braced his hand on the wall over her head and

leaned close, inhaling the fresh, fragrant scent of her shampoo and savoring the excitement pulsing through his veins at the thought of spending another day alone with her. They might only have twenty-four hours but he intended to enjoy each one with no thought or pressure of his real life intruding.

"Did anyone ever tell you that you see what you want to see?" she asked through glossy lips.

He studied her for a moment. "I see what the problem is."

She narrowed her gaze. "I didn't know there was one."

"Just because you've outwardly made a transformation in how you dress, and just because my sisters' choice in clothing helps you along, doesn't mean you're used to it in here." He tapped the left side of her chest, above her heart.

She swallowed hard. "Am I that easy to read?"

"Only because I'm looking. I want to know all about you and I'm glad you're making it simple."

She squared her shoulders.

Obviously that notion bugged her.

"So you didn't tell me where we're going," she said, changing the subject.

"I'm going to show you around my part of the island."

A sudden smile took hold and he caught sight of two dimples in both of her cheeks.

"What's got you grinning all of a sudden?" he asked.

"Finally you'll be the one doing the sharing and I'll get to know more about you." She tugged on his hand like a kid anxious to get going.

"And this pleases you?" he asked, following her down the stairs and out the front door.

"Tremendously." She swung herself into the passenger seat of the Jeep and honked the horn. "Let's go, slowpoke!"

He laughed. The woman confounded him, astounded him. She aroused him and made him want to share. He'd never shown some parts of this retreat to anyone, male or female, not even his parents or sisters, but he wanted to share them with Micki.

He slid into the car, started the engine and they were on their way, only stopping at Pops' to pick up soda and sandwiches for lunch. Twenty minutes later, they arrived at a secluded part of the island where he'd bought undeveloped land and put his own stamp on it.

No matter how many times he made this trip, he still marveled at the beauty of this island, the lush palm trees, the blue sky dotted with perfect white clouds and the warm sticky air blowing on his skin.

Beside him, he could practically feel Micki quiver with anticipation and excitement. He enjoyed how much pleasure she took in exploring his island and appreciated that she didn't talk and pepper him with questions during the ride. Instead she remained silent beside him, as if she understood he desired quiet time and respected him enough to give him what he needed.

Most of all he was grateful for their ability to enjoy a comfortable sense of peace together, something he knew from overhearing his sisters was a rare gift between two people. He'd just never found that sense of rightness with any woman before.

He glanced over. Micki had shut her eyes and tipped her head back to let the sun bake her face as they drove. He admired her profile, the pert nose and the full lips he'd already learned by kissing, tasting and completely devouring. And he had to admit life felt pretty good right now.

Even if it was only temporary. His stomach plunged at the necessary reminder and the field came into view just in time, so he wouldn't have to think.

"We're here." Damian pulled up behind a metal backstop.

He'd wanted to share this with Micki yet he couldn't shake the fact that by bringing her here, he felt stripped bare and vulnerable in a way he couldn't understand.

Well, too late to back out now since they'd already arrived. Before she could ask questions, he hopped out of the car and strode to her side, helping her out. Together they walked toward his personal baseball field, complete with a pitcher's mound and all the requisite bases.

She turned to face him, curiosity etched all over

her expressive face. "If you build it, they will come?" Her blue eyes flashed with questions he didn't have specific answers to.

He merely chuckled in reply. "I guess, except that in my case, there is no *they.*"

"You built this for…?" She gestured toward the professional-size field.

"Me." His reply sounded ridiculous to his own ears, except it was the truth. "Growing up, I couldn't think of anything better than having my own place to hit a ball."

"Your own personal ball field."

He nodded. "So when I made the money, I built the field."

"At which point you could say you had everything you ever dreamed of?" she asked, too perceptively for his peace of mind.

"Not nearly." Looking into her gorgeous eyes, the reply had slipped out without permission. He sucked in a deep breath, but he couldn't take the words back, nor could he deny their meaning.

Not when he realized that now, at this moment, in his sacred spot with Micki, he had everything he'd never let himself dream of wanting.

He reached out and caressed her cheek with his hand. "You make it hard for me to concentrate on anything but you," he said, letting her into his innermost thoughts.

"That's what happens in paradise."

"You're doing it again."

"Doing what?" she asked.

"Denying your own power. When I complimented you earlier, you squirmed and changed the subject and when I say you distract me, you deny you're the cause." He let his thumb brush back and forth over her jaw. "I think that's why you draw me so much. You don't know nearly how much you can affect a man."

Her skin flushed pink beneath the summer sun. "You're a charmer, Damian."

"Can I take that as a compliment?" he asked, grinning.

"You can take it any way you want." Micki laughed despite how off center he had her feeling. He was right, of course. She wasn't used to compliments and intense stares from a man like Damian. A weekend like this was the stuff of dreams and she was happy to be here with him now.

"What are you thinking about?" he asked her.

She blinked and refocused on his handsome face. "This field. I'm wondering about your motives in having it built."

"You doubt I'd indulge my own childhood dreams?"

She shook her head. She didn't doubt his obvious motives. It was his subconscious ones that had her curious. "Are you sure you didn't build this for your own team?"

He let loose with a laugh. "Hell, I never want to be an owner. Too many damn hassles."

"I wasn't talking about you buying a professional team. I was talking about a different kind of legacy. I thought maybe you'd built this with your own kids in mind."

In the silence that followed, Micki wondered if she'd gone too far.

"I never gave it a thought," he said at last.

"You never thought about having kids that followed in your footsteps? Having kids at all?"

"I never left room in my mind for a family. Hell, I never left room for it in my life." He tipped his head to one side. "How about you?"

"Oh I definitely want a family," she said honestly. "When you lose your parents as I did, you know how much you missed growing up. I want that security for myself one day. You know, mother and father and kids. It's like setting all things right in the universe," she murmured, then realized how childish she sounded. "It's not everyone's dream," she admitted.

"But it's yours and I respect that."

She nodded. "What about after baseball? Have you thought about what you want after your ball-playing years are over?"

He shook his head. "In the beginning, I was too young and cocky, too full of myself to think about things like my career ending one day."

"You? Cocky?" Micki couldn't contain a wry laugh.

"Hard to believe, isn't it?" He laughed. "Anyway, for a long time I just concentrated on the here and now. On maintaining the status quo which was pretty damn good. And now when I should be at least planning for the future, I've got all I can do to keep myself healthy and in the game."

She knew how much the admission cost him and she appreciated being let in. She grabbed his hand and squeezed tight, letting him know she understood.

The aura around them had grown too serious, too intense, and Micki sought to break the tension. "Any chance you have a bat and ball in the back of the Jeep?"

"I sure do." His expression of pure relief told her he needed the break as much as she did.

He returned with a bat, ball and mitt in hand. "You sure you can handle me?"

Micki grinned. "Bring it on, bad boy." Because if there was any place Micki was in her element, it was on the field. Any field. She loved sports and had always excelled, thanks to Uncle Yank's expert tutelage.

And for half an hour she held up her end fairly well. He might be a professional ballplayer and a big, strong man, but he was injured and, between her swing and her ability to catch and throw a good distance, she managed to impress him anyway. Enough to have him running around the field and out of breath.

Finally, she realized he wasn't going to quit first,

so she dropped the ball she'd been about to pitch to him and wiped her sweaty palms together. "I'm starving," she called over to where he was taking some practice swings at home plate.

He leaned against the bat and eyed her with concern. "Are you okay?"

She nodded. "I'm fine. Just hungry."

He gathered the equipment together and they loaded it back in the Jeep. After washing their hands with bottled water, they sat down and ate in a shady spot beneath a large tree. The sun beat down overhead but the large leaves kept them from the worst of the heat and they enjoyed the turkey sandwiches Pops had made along with the chocolate-chip cookies Micki had added to their bag.

Full from food and exhausted from their workout, she raised her hands overhead and yawned.

"Lie down." He folded his legs beneath him and patted his thighs.

"You're a tough man to say no to." She did as he suggested, stretching out so her head lay in his lap and her body stretched out on their large blanket.

He massaged her temples with his fingertips and she relaxed, shutting her eyes and allowing herself to breathe easily.

They spent an entire day in each other's company doing nothing but just being together. She couldn't recall a time when she'd felt more at ease. She couldn't remember a time when she'd felt more like herself. She couldn't remember a time when she'd been happier. Or one that had ended so quickly.

They returned to the house long after the sun had set. Damian dropped his keys in the kitchen and, yawning, Micki waited as he hit Play on the answering machine.

First there was the usual litany of messages from his sisters and nieces, all of which she knew he'd return before they turned in for the night.

Then she heard a vaguely familiar masculine voice break the peacefulness of their day. "Fuller, it's Coach. Since you're flying in tomorrow morning, I expect you in my office at four and suited up with the rest of the team tomorrow night."

Damian's guilt-ridden eyes met hers. She didn't have to ask why he hadn't mentioned leaving before. Because if he had, they probably wouldn't have shared the same kind of carefree day. She wouldn't have seen his field of dreams and she definitely wouldn't have let herself pretend their time together didn't have to end.

"You can stay as long as you want," he said.

She shook her head. "No thanks. It's way past time I head home, too." She put up a brave front, a pretense that this particular ending didn't bother her at all.

Ironic that she'd been coerced into coming to the island in the first place and now she didn't want to leave.

DAMIAN AWOKE WITH MICKI in his arms. On the night-stand were two crinkled foil packets, evidence that they'd made love not once but twice last night. And not quickly or frantically either. Instead their joinings had been slow and leisurely, so neither one of them would be likely to forget this time on the island.

Now, Damian watched Micki sleep. Her blond curls were tousled around her face, much as they'd been after she collapsed on top of him. He liked when she was on top because he knew she was con-trolling the pace, sometimes squeezing her thighs together and milking him for all she was worth and other times releasing so her mound ground into him at just the right spot, all so she could make her cli-max and his that much stronger. In a few short days, he knew her that well.

She'd come to know him, too. Enough that when she'd heard the coach's voice, she hadn't condemned him for not leveling with her sooner. She hadn't com-plained about him having to leave. Not a single pout or whine, he thought. Micki didn't do any of the things that bothered him in other women and yet a part of him wished she would.

So he could find an excuse to walk away with no guilt? No regrets? No second thoughts? He'd have plenty of those, Damian knew because leaving her was the last thing he wanted to do.

And leaving her was exactly what he had to do in

order to preserve what remained of his career. If this time had taught him anything, it was that he'd been right about his inability to split his focus. When he was with Micki, he didn't give the game a second thought. Not even with Carter belting home runs and breathing down his neck.

He had to return to New York and deal with his life. Beyond the recent injury, he had the ongoing issue of arthritis to deal with and a talk with Yank was overdue.

It was time he faced the painful fact that this season, or next if he wanted to push it, should be his last. He'd buried the truth as well as himself inside Micki's willing body last night, but the sun shining through the bedroom blinds was a wake-up call he couldn't miss. A wake-up regarding many things. His career was just one of them.

CHAPTER EIGHT

ON THE PLANE RIDE HOME, Micki feigned sleep because it was easier than making small talk while looking at Damian's handsome face. They'd had their fling and it had been more than she'd ever dreamed of.

Yet it was time she faced a few harsh realities. Yes, she and Damian had shared some amazing, special, magic moments. Intimate moments, and not all of them sexual, she thought recalling their time on his baseball field. Yet obviously nothing he'd experienced with Micki had distinguished her from any of the other women in his life. Otherwise they wouldn't be on the verge of saying goodbye, she thought as Damian walked her to the limo she'd arranged to pick her up from the airport. She didn't want him to feel responsible for her for a second longer than necessary.

The truth hurt because despite knowing the score going in, she'd hoped for more from Damian. She wasn't going to get it. Time to move on with some great memories and enough of a confidence boost to send her into the dating world with a new look, new image and new attitude. And maybe she had some swampland she could sell herself and call it paradise.

Standing by her car, Micki turned to Damian. The least she could do was hold her head high while she proved to him she'd meant it when she'd said all she wanted was a short affair and she was enough of a grown-up to walk away with her pride intact.

Damian met her gaze, a serious expression on his face. "Micki—"

She shook her head. She didn't want to hear him belittle their time together. It was a turning point in her life and she'd never regret it.

"Thanks for kidnapping me." She didn't have to force a smile. Around Damian, it came easily.

"My pleasure." His voice held a sincerity that took her off guard.

"Don't be too hard on Carter," Micki said, covering a subject she knew was important. "He's young and stupid. He'll defeat himself. People like him always do."

Admiration filled his gaze. "You're smart."

"Yeah, well it doesn't mean I won't kick his ass first chance I get," she said, laughing. "I just don't need you to do it for me."

"And you're a tough lady, too."

She swallowed hard. "Sometimes I have to be." She placed a hand on top of the open car door, ready to escape inside.

He held her gaze as if willing her not to go.

"When can you play?" she asked although they'd discussed it already.

His expression tightened, his jaw clenched. "Another nine or ten days."

"Don't push it and try to be a hero," she warned him. "Ten days isn't so bad."

He leaned closer. "Between us?"

She nodded.

"It's that bad."

Micki understood he wasn't just talking about the ten more days on the DL. His career was near the end and he was trusting her with that information. She'd never felt more connected to another human being but there was little she could offer that he'd accept.

"If you ever need me—you know, to help you spin a situation or just to vent—you know where to find me." It was the best she could do.

A sad smile took hold of his lips. "You're special, Micki."

"Oh please."

"Stop doing that." He'd reached out and placed a finger over her lips. "Stop questioning yourself and how people look at you."

She shook her head. "That's not what I'm doing."

"That's exactly what you're doing."

"I am," she agreed, laughing. Why was it this man, who wanted to give and receive nothing, was the one who understood her so well?

"Well, next time you get the urge to fight a compliment, remember our weekend together, will you?"

She had a hunch she'd be remembering him a lot sooner and more often than that.

He reached out and hooked his hand around the back of her neck, pulled her close and sealed their lips in a kiss. One that was too fast and too brief—all too reminiscent of their time together.

"I'll do that." Micki forced a nod. She turned away before he could read the emotion on her face and slipped into the back of the car.

He shut the door for her and waved. "Take care." She was able to read his parting words on his lips.

Once again, she couldn't help but smile.

AN HOUR AFTER LEAVING Damian, Micki reached her apartment. She showered, changed and, since Sophie wasn't in her place across the hall, Micki took a cab over to Uncle Yank's. The doorman let her in and the elevator carried her to his penthouse apartment.

She rang the bell and a set of chimes went off that were so loud they scared her to death and had her heart racing like mad. His dog, Noodle, a Labradoodle he'd purchased because of the breed's intelligence and training in helping the blind, began a high-pitched bark that would wake the dead. A normal person would have bought a trained Lab, but not her uncle.

Without warning, the door from the apartment

across the hall swung open wide and an old woman in a brightly colored, decades-old sweatsuit strode outside, hands on her frail hips. "You tell that old man to muzzle the mutt and put a normal doorbell back on or I'm reporting him to the condo board, and don't think I won't." She patted her set hair and slammed the door shut behind her.

"And a good evening to you, Mrs. Murdoch," Micki called to her uncle's neighbor who'd lived there for years and was as likely to report her uncle as Micki was.

The same door swung open wide again. "He was much more reasonable when Lola came around," Mrs. Murdoch said.

"We all agree with you." Micki smiled at the older woman and eyed her uncle's closed door. He knew she was coming, so where was he?

"Well either he gets laid or he moves out. I'm not sure I can take much more of his obnoxious behavior. You tell him I said so, you hear?"

Micki wondered if the older woman was actually offering her services and bit the inside of her cheek to keep from laughing. "Oh, I'll tell him all right."

"Got to go. *Jeopardy!*'s on." Mrs. Murdoch slammed the door shut again.

Micki raised her hand to knock this time, when her uncle opened the door. "Sorry. I was in the john."

She rolled her eyes. "Too much information," she said, greeting him with a kiss.

"I can't believe you're back already. Is Damian that much of a dud?"

She raised an eyebrow, staring at her uncle. "You sent me off with him hoping we'd hook up?"

"Damn straight. So did you?"

Micki stepped around Yank and into his large apartment. They'd always been close and she didn't see any point in hiding the truth from him now. "Whatever we had was temporary and now it's over. So how did your doctor's appointment go?"

"Nothing's changed, nothing will. Are you telling me Fuller screwed you and took off?" Her uncle squared his shoulders, ready to fight on her behalf.

She shook her head. "Damian's a lot better than that and you know it or you wouldn't have sent me off to be alone with him."

"I—"

"You're caught red-handed. Now I'm going to forgive you for disregarding my feelings because I love you. And I'll tell you what you need to know about Damian. He's not capable of putting anyone or anything above the game, at least not at this point in his life, and he was honest about that. Okay? And now that I've bared my soul, I need you to do the same." She hugged him tight. "Are you saying the specialist couldn't help you?"

"It's a degenerative disease. My stage isn't early enough to change things and don't go yelling at me that I should've gone to him sooner because your sister already yelled enough for all three of you."

Micki swallowed hard. Twice in two days. Twice she had to face men she cared about and not show any pity no matter how much she wanted to. Damn men and their pride, she thought, taking a minute to compose herself before stepping back and facing her uncle.

"Well, you'll just have to carry on as you taught us to once we realized Mom and Dad weren't coming back, won't you?"

As if she understood, Noodle barked in agreement.

"You see? With Noodle by your side, you won't have any problems." Micki would see to it.

Her uncle grabbed her in a bear hug that expressed everything he couldn't say.

When they finally broke apart, she smiled at him. "So what can I make you for dinner?"

ALL THREE JORDAN SISTERS and Lola met at Annabelle's home in Greenlawn. They all sat surrounding Annie, who remained with her feet up on the couch, surrounded by her pets and plants. Some things never changed, Micki thought and a warm feeling filled her chest.

They'd chosen the location because it gave them privacy from Yank's prying and allowed Annabelle to remain off her feet as per doctor's orders. It had been a while since they'd all been together this way and they talked to each other, over each other and across one another. A true girls' meeting. Getting together with them reminded Micki of how much she'd missed their bonding time.

Annie clapped her hands, demanding their attention. "As much as we need to catch up, we're here for a reason."

They all nodded.

"I've tried to keep everyone up to date on Uncle Yank's condition. Does everyone understand the details?" Sophie, the sister who'd taken charge of the doctors and of the gruff man himself, asked.

"I'm confused," Micki admitted. "He lies and fudges the truth. One day he says he's fine and the next day he's wearing that talking clock like he can't read the dial on his wristwatch. I'd like an explanation I can understand."

"As you know, Uncle Yank has the wet form of macular degeneration," Sophie said. "Statistically, wet is less common than the dry form and accounts for ninety percent of all cases of legal blindness in people with the disease. It isn't curable and since Uncle Yank ignored symptoms for quite a while, the disease has progressed too much for any of the newer treatments."

"What exactly can he see or not see?" Annabelle asked.

Obviously Micki wasn't the only one who didn't understand their uncle's condition.

"It's hard to say. Maybe the explanation of what the disease involves will help."

This was Sophie in her element, Micki thought fondly.

"In clinical terms, macular degeneration is a physical disturbance in the center of the retina, which is called the macula." Sophie gestured as she spoke, pointing to her own eyes as an example. "The macula makes us capable of our most detailed vision—reading, driving, recognizing faces, watching TV, etc."

"Wow," Micki said aloud. Her throat grew tight at the thought of her independent uncle being deprived of the most basic tasks most people took for granted.

Since Uncle Yank had ignored his problems over the past year, Micki had as well. It was easier to push the truth away when not faced with it directly, but the time had come to cope head-on with all the repercussions.

Over the past few days, she and her sisters had spoken and agreed on a course of action. They just needed to bring Lola on board. The other woman was key as she had the ability to sway the important parties to their plan.

"I thought or rather I hoped that the specialist would tell him that surgery to remove scarring was an option to improve vision, but the disease progressed too far." Sophie's voice dropped low. "It's not going to get any better. It's going to get worse."

They all understood the implications.

Annabelle rubbed the slight bulge in her belly and sighed. "Can we suggest he move to some place with assisted living before it progresses to the point where he can't see at all?"

Micki shook her head, shuddering at the thought of their uncle's reaction. "Not if we want to live to tell the tale. That's a point he'll have to reach on his own."

"But the business affects us all, which is why I suggested we meet here to talk." Sophie's gaze swept over the group. "We need to think about the future today."

All three sisters turned to Lola.

"I am not coming back to work for him." Lola folded her arms across her silk blouse.

Though her outfit and overall look was still on the conservative side, she'd made many changes since leaving Uncle Yank's employ. Some of the alterations had been done in the hopes of enticing Yank to notice her before she left and those Lola had ditched fast, like too-youthful clothes. Other parts of her transformation remained, like her hair. She'd always kept the color a natural brown and the style pulled back into a bun. These days she had golden highlights and a chic shoulder-length bob that accentuated her graceful features. These days she not only worked for Spencer Atkins, she dated him as well. Together they attended industry events and were seen at the chicest restaurants.

Her uncle was a stubborn old coot, Micki thought

in frustration. He needed this woman now more than ever before.

All three sisters understood how hard it had been for Lola to leave Yank and none of them would be angry at her for refusing to come back. After thirty or more years with their stubborn uncle, nobody considered Lola selfish. In fact there was nobody more loving. The time had come when she'd needed some of that emotion returned.

"Nobody wants you to compromise the stand you've taken," Annabelle assured Lola. "But when he was first diagnosed, you mentioned a potential merger with Atkins Associates, remember?"

Lola winced.

Micki figured she'd probably recalled Uncle Yank's reaction to that suggestion.

"Why do you ask?" Lola's gaze narrowed.

Shifting positions on the couch, Annabelle sat up straighter as she explained. "Because the three of us have talked and we think that over time, a merger is the only way to save the sports agency part of the Hot Zone."

"And Uncle Yank's illness isn't the only reason," Micki said. "Let's face it. The newer agencies with their hotshot agents are snatching up the young athletes interested in money more than in loyalty. Uncle Yank needs backup and over time so will Spencer. A merger can benefit both agencies."

Sophie nodded in agreement. "Think about it. Uncle Yank brings young, raw talent with him in his other agents, but he's the big name. Same with Spencer. They're both too stubborn to realize they need successors. We could convince them that together they could be a powerhouse."

"A lasting powerhouse with a legacy after they're gone. Umm...I mean retire." Micki swallowed hard.

"So what do you think?" Sophie asked.

Lola rubbed her eyes and sighed. "I love you girls. I would do anything for you. Same for the business."

"And for Uncle Yank?" Annabelle asked, too sweetly, her intentions obvious.

Lola strode over and squeezed Annabelle's cheeks. "Sorry, honey, but you won't get me to pour my heart out. I'm over him."

"You taught us not to fib," Sophie chided.

"So who's ready for lunch? I brought us all Squagels from Cozy's," she said of the coffee shop located downstairs from the Hot Zone, specializing in salads and square bagels.

Annabelle sighed. "Mmmm. You are the best," she told Lola.

"But we still noticed that you changed the subject," Micki said.

Micki's stomach growled loudly and Lola teased. "Your stomach's on my side."

Micki laughed.

"I'll talk to Spencer. If he's still interested in a merger, we'll figure out a way to approach Yank," Lola promised, her voice somber. "He's away on business, so it might be a while though."

Micki paused. Now that she'd loved and lost Damian—in a manner of speaking—she felt an empathy with Lola she'd never had before. She couldn't imagine spending a lifetime side by side with a man who didn't return her feelings. Micki and her sisters were now asking Lola to come back into a situation from which she'd finally garnered the guts to escape.

She placed a hand on Lola's shoulder. "I understand all the reasons you don't want this merger to happen. We were selfish even to ask you to make such a sacrifice." She looked around at her sisters. "Maybe we should find another option."

Lola gave Micki a look of gratitude and for the first time Micki felt on more equal footing with the woman she'd always admired.

Silence followed and then Annabelle spoke. "Micki's right. We were so wrapped up with what to do about the agency we forgot to consider your feelings."

Sophie nodded. "We've been thoughtless. And you raised us so much better than that."

Lola paced back and forth across the room, stopping directly in front of where Annabelle lay on the couch. "Come here. All of you."

Micki and Sophie stepped closer.

"You've grown into such beautiful, smart, caring women. I'm so lucky to have had you in my life. You're the children I never had and I love you." She paused and Micki sensed she was holding back tears. "It's because I love you that I'm going to talk to Spencer."

"But—"

"I'm a big girl, Sophie," Lola said, cutting her off.

"If the merger happens I can still work for Spencer and not your uncle. I can retire if I want to. Don't worry about me, okay? Okay." She clapped her hands in front of her, a sure indication her decision wasn't open to argument.

Micki nodded slowly, accepting Lola's choice. "Just know we appreciate you backing us," she said and gave the woman a huge hug. "Now we need a deadline or we'll put off approaching those two men forever."

Lola nodded. "I can't say you're wrong about that."

"How about by Uncle Yank's annual birthday bash?" Sophie suggested. "By then we need to have spoken with them and coerced them into going along. Agreed?"

"Agreed," each of them murmured, leaving them with the knowledge that Uncle Yank's illness would forever alter all their lives.

Micki wondered how many more changes were in store.

YANK SAT AT HIS BIG OAK DESK and glanced at the photos on the corner. He couldn't see them well but he'd memorized their feel and order. He picked up the one with the rounded edges and ran his hand over the glass behind which lay a photo of Micki as a child.

Though he'd deny it aloud, he had a special place in his heart for the little one, as he liked to call Micki. How could he not? From the day the girls had come to live under his roof, she'd latched on to him like Noodle, who now lay under his desk. And Micki had never let go.

Unlike Annie who'd been older and aware enough to be scared and wary of her single uncle, Micki had immediately decided to love him and copy everything he did. From his weekly poker games, to visiting his clients on the road and in their locker rooms, Micki had insisted on trailing along.

At first he hadn't known what to do with her but he'd soon realized she was a joy to have around, even if he did have to learn to watch his mouth. Otherwise the school teachers called with complaints about her new vocabulary. The memory made him laugh.

So he blamed himself now that Damian hadn't come around as he'd hoped. Misplaced faith was a bitch, Yank thought. He'd mistakenly believed that if Damian spent time with Micki, he'd realize all that was absent in his life.

Just like you realize all you're missing? Lola's voice rose in his head once more.

Yank scowled. "Difference is even if I know what I'm missing, there's not a damn thing I can do to make you happy. You think you waited on me hand and foot before? What do you have to look forward to if I try to win you back now?"

Yank was a proud man and these truths hurt, but they had to be said, at least to himself. Talking back to himself was the only way he'd keep himself from picking up the phone, calling Lola and begging her to come home.

DAMIAN SLUNG A TOWEL LOW on his hips and made for the steam room attached to the team's workout area. He stepped into the moist heat, sat on a bench, leaned back and groaned.

His muscles ached from a good workout and his head hurt thinking about the meeting he had planned for this afternoon. Carole had called. She was in New York and had said she needed to talk to him. Not a good sign.

"God, I'm beat."

"Join the club," Roper said.

Damian shut his eyes and breathed in deeply, taking in the familiar smells that had always relaxed him in the past.

"How're the workouts going?" Roper asked.

Damian appreciated the small talk that would take him out of his own head. "Pretty good." He'd begun a slow routine of getting into shape with his trainer and the wrist was feeling surprisingly limber.

He'd be back on the field in a couple of days. Not a minute too soon considering that ass Carter had been playing with all the heart and soul Damian had possessed in his younger years. If he'd just lose the prick-like attitude, he had potential.

And it galled Damian to admit it.

"I'm sure the time off on the island helped," Roper said.

"It didn't hurt."

Roper's stare bored into him, making him uneasy. Micki's name had never passed the other man's lips but it hung between them anyway. Everyone knew Roper and Micki were close and it came as no shock that Roper would make his way around to discussing the island. They both knew Micki had everything to do with Damian's last trip down there.

"You did a decent thing, taking care of Micki," Roper said.

Bingo. Damian rolled his head to one side, his shoulders suddenly tense. "Just how tight are you two?"

Roper chuckled. "If I was Carter, I'd torture the hell out of you making you think there's more between us than there is, but you're my captain so I'll let you down fast and easy. She's like a sister to me."

"Okay then." Damian exhaled hard. He'd been

home from the island ten days and not an hour went by that he didn't think of her. "How's she doing?"

"Why don't you ask her yourself?" Roper asked, making Damian feel completely juvenile.

He let out a laugh. "I've regressed."

"Nah. You're just scared shitless because she's more than capable of handling you."

"She's probably the only woman who can." The words were out before he could censor them.

"And to think Micki was convinced she couldn't possibly interest a real jock because she's too much like one. Too much of a challenge, in other words."

"One of the guys." Damian repeated Micki's expression as if he and Roper shared equal insight into Micki's psyche. In reality, the other guy had much more knowledge and information than Damian had.

"Exactly." Roper nodded. "I'm guessing you showed her she was wrong?" His voice held typical innuendo but Damian knew Roper cared too much for Micki to indulge in locker room trashing. He wasn't prying, rather he was testing Damian's intentions.

"For a while." And then he'd given her the kiss-off at the airport, probably reinforcing her insecurities. No matter how unintentional, Damian had screwed Micki big-time.

"So why don't you call her and make it for a while longer?" Roper asked.

"Can't." Damian eased his legs out in front of him.

He'd begun to sweat and though normally at this point in the routine he'd be feeling mellow and relaxed, with Micki front and center in his mind, he was still wound tight. "I need to focus on rehab and playing."

"And that and Micki are mutually exclusive?" Roper asked, but before Damian could reply, the other man continued. "I'd guess so considering you have your hands full keeping Carter off your back."

A subject Damian could discuss with Roper without holding back. He and the other man had come up through the ranks together. They didn't have much in common except the game and mutual respect but it was enough to forge a bond between teammates.

"The kid has balls," Damian said of Ricky Carter. Damian understood the other man's drive and determination. He'd had it himself at that age. He'd also had respect for those who had come before him, and that was where he and Carter differed.

"If you need help stuffing him dick first into his locker, I'm your man," Roper offered.

"Thanks, John."

"My pleasure." Roper folded his arms behind his head and lay down on the long bench.

Silence descended but instead of releasing tension, their conversation had reminded Damian of all he'd left behind on the island in favor of the shit he'd returned to in his everyday life.

He wiped the sweat off his forehead with a towel

and copied Roper, lying back and closing his eyes. Better than facing what lay ahead.

CAROLE PACED THE FLOOR of her New York City hotel room, which was twice the size of her condo, a one-floor apartment that she paid for with her job as a legal secretary. Through her position at a law firm specializing in sports contracts, she'd met a variety of athletes at a variety of stages in their lives. Some, like Damian, were close to retirement and others, like Carter, had youth on their side.

She was attracted to them all and when they reciprocated, she indulged in what she thought was every woman's fantasy. Sleeping with ballplayers, *star* ballplayers, made her feel special and one step up from the other struggling working women of the world.

She'd never thought twice about her lifestyle nor had she had a problem moving on when a relationship had bored her—until Damian had come along. She'd enjoyed his company and looked forward to his return trips to Florida. She thought he'd felt the same way despite his reputation and so she hadn't seen it coming when his interest had faded. Not wanting to lose him, she thought that if she'd played it cool, he'd come to his senses and realize he didn't want to lose her. For a short time, her plan had worked because he had called, wanting to see her on his last trip to Florida. Then he'd unceremoniously dumped her that same night, passing her off to Ricky Carter like she was a piece of meat to be shared.

Not that she didn't like Carter. She did. A lot. Enough to have slept with him starting back in April, while she was still trying to hang on to Damian. She and Carter had had a good laugh over the fact that Damian had thought they didn't know one another. He'd even paid for their night out.

Still, in her heart, Damian's actions had stung. And now she had a major problem. A life-changing problem that would make living in her small apartment awfully cramped.

Her hand came to rest on her belly, as it often had since the stick had turned pink a few weeks ago. A baby. Jeez, how the frig had she been so careless?

She shook her head. Careless wasn't the right word. She might like men, but she was smart enough to use protection each and every time. With each and every man, though in the past six months, there had only been two of them.

Damian and Carter.

She couldn't know for sure whose baby she was carrying, but she knew who was better capable of supporting her and this child.

She knew what she had to do, which was why she was in New York now. She was so nauseous she thought she'd die and she knew it had nothing to do with morning sickness.

She was petrified of telling Damian and yet she knew that he was the only one capable of sparing her from the same fate as her mother—pregnant and alone, raising a kid on welfare, a revolving door of men passing through. In fact it had been this pregnancy that had forced her to face reality.

Her life had been too damn close to her mother's. One man after another, nobody ever staying long, nobody loving her. Carole wiped the tear that dripped down her cheek. Pathetic, that's what she was and she never even saw it happening.

The sound of someone knocking on the door startled her and she ran to the mirror to quickly check her makeup before letting Damian inside. He was her one chance to fix her life and she couldn't afford to mess up now.

CHAPTER NINE

SINCE RETURNING from the island, Damian's game was running smoothly. On the field, he was the Damian Fuller his coaches and fans expected. His first game off the disabled list, he'd played all nine innings, singled, doubled, walked twice and homered once. In the field, his work had been his best in years. Most importantly, as a team the Renegades had won this past series at home and they were still solidly in first place. Carter was pissed at being put back on the bench, but that was the kid's problem. Damian was at the top of his game again and that's all that mattered to him.

His coaches, his manager and most of his teammates were happy with his performance. The only one not taking his calls was his agent, and it didn't take a genius to figure out why Yank Morgan was upset. But the old man had sent his niece off to the island knowing full well that, to Damian, nothing came before his career. Yank couldn't possibly think Micki would change his mind—although Damian had to admit she was the only woman who'd ever tempted him to say to hell with his single-minded philosophy.

He found himself thinking of her at the worst moments. When he was in the field during a game, he'd remember her determined face as she pitched to him, how well she caught a ball and how her hair fluttered in the island breeze. He'd always catch his wayward thoughts before he screwed up on the field. Each time he'd push her out of his mind and promise himself *no more.* Then he'd imagine how much worse it'd be if he had to deal with her on a daily basis, and he'd assure himself that his decision to keep his distance was the right one.

Damian didn't think his agent would want him to screw up the end of his career over a woman. Not even the older man's beloved niece. And since he planned to stay away, Damian figured the old man would thank him for sparing Micki even more pain. Hell, Yank Morgan would come around in the end because, like Damian, he understood the game came first.

As a professional athlete Damian couldn't afford to let his emotions get the better of him. But as he walked into Carole's New York hotel where she'd asked him to meet her, his gut churned and even his chest hairs prickled with unease. Something about her coming to New York and calling him out of the blue just didn't feel right.

She greeted him warmly but her half smile did nothing to put his mind at rest, either.

"Thanks for coming, Damian." She led him into the oversize hotel room, lavishly decorated and probably a lot more expensive than Carole could afford.

Still he wasn't about to pry. "You're looking well," he told her. Not good, well. He chose his words carefully.

Though she looked beautiful as always, he had to be careful to keep his distance, both physically and emotionally. He didn't want her getting any wrong ideas about their relationship. Or lack of one. For him, things between them had ended the night they'd gone to Lacie's joint.

"So why make the trip north?" he asked.

"Sit." She gestured to the fabric-covered chair.

The flowers jumped out at him, big and ugly and as frightening to him as her somber tone of voice.

"What's wrong?" he asked.

"Did I ever tell you that my mother never married my father?" She let out a high-pitched laugh. "In fact she never knew who my daddy was."

They were over. Why in God's name were they talking about personal things like her past and scary notions like unmarried, pregnant women? "What's the point?"

She bent down and reached for his hand. "I don't know how to tell you this—"

"Just say it." His heart pounded a mile a minute and icy tentacles of fear crept up his spine.

"I know we used protection but…I'm pregnant." As if on cue, large teardrops fell from her already watery eyes. "And before you ask, yes it's yours."

"I wasn't going to ask," he lied.

She gave him a forced smile. "You're a good and decent man," she said softly and for a split second, guilt for distrusting her crept into his gut.

Then he reminded himself that this was a woman who'd slept with more ballplayers than just him. He'd never asked what she did when he was out of town, which had been most of the time, and she'd never offered details. He should have questioned, he realized now when it was too damned late. She was placing the responsibility squarely in his lap.

Damian was soaking in sweat, worse than when he played in Florida's sweltering heat, but somehow he maintained his composure and didn't let her see how badly his nerves had kicked in.

He ran a shaking hand through his hair. "Look Carole, you must realize this is a shock."

She nodded. "Of course I do. I've had some time to take in the news and you haven't."

"So you know I can't make any decisions right now." Hell, at the moment he couldn't even think clearly.

Only the irony of the situation swirled in his head. He'd always been so careful. He'd always looked out for himself and the women he was with. Wasn't that the point of protection in the first place?

"Dammit!" He slammed his fisted hand against the cocktail table, rattling the drinking glasses.

Carole wrapped her arms around him and laid her head on his shoulder. To her credit, she didn't try anything sexual. She merely touched him, emphasizing that they were in this together.

He patted her back uselessly. He didn't know how to help her, let alone how to help himself. "I need to go."

She rose to her feet. "I understand."

He drew himself upright. "I'll be in touch," he managed to promise.

"I know you will. You're a good man, Damian."

Her calm behavior was baffling him and he narrowed his gaze. The Carole he knew was all about how she looked and what she could get out of life. She epitomized the idea of *me*.

So why didn't the idea of having an unwanted baby have her ranting and raving? And why did she keep extolling his virtues? The answer was obvious. Because she wanted something from him. Whether it was marriage or money or something else, he wasn't going to sit here and try to figure out what right now. He needed to be alone to decide what *he* wanted.

Damian headed for the door and only began breathing again when he was solo in the hallway. Out of the blue, his entire life was in upheaval and nothing made sense.

One thing he did know with unqualified certainty— he didn't want to spend the rest of his life saddled with Carole as his wife.

MICKI NEEDED A SOCIAL LIFE. She needed something to think about other than her time on an island off the Florida coast with Damian. Not even waiting for Lola to talk to Spencer Atkins about a merger was enough to distract Micki's thoughts. Resigned to getting no agency work done while she was in this kind of mood, she turned to personal business instead.

First she e-mailed Sophie to see if she wanted to have dinner tonight, then she picked up the phone and scheduled a few appointments she had on her to-do list. Just when she couldn't think of anything else to occupy her mind, her office intercom rang.

She pushed the reply button. "Yes?"

"You have an unscheduled visitor," her secretary announced.

She shrugged. Whoever it was, it was better than sitting alone. "Send them in."

Micki stood at the same time the door opened and Damian walked in. Her heart leaped inside her chest and an amazing feeling of happiness surrounded her, lifting the cloud that had settled on her shoulders since they'd parted at the airport.

She'd been deprived and now she wasn't, and she shamelessly took in his appearance. He wore a pair of faded Levi's that did little to disguise the muscles beneath the jeans, along with a solid white T-shirt that accented his tan. He still had the scruffy beard she loved but his eyes were dim and he looked troubled. More troubled than the man she'd last seen worrying about his career, and she wondered what was bothering him.

She couldn't suppress the fleeting hope that maybe he'd missed her and that was why he'd come by. Heaven knew she'd missed him.

She strode around her desk, trying for a casually unaffected tone as she greeted him. "Hi there."

"Hey." He shut the door behind him. As he smiled, his gaze scanned her body for as long as she'd studied his. "You look great," he said at last.

She glanced down at her short pleated skirt and low-cut top. After leaving the island, she'd taken his advice and purchased more clothes that accentuated her feminine side. "Sophie and I went on a shopping spree."

He nodded approvingly. "Works for me," he said, his tone deeper than before.

He stepped closer and captured her in his arms, pulling her close and before she could blink, his lips came down hard on hers. His tongue plunged into her waiting mouth and she opened wide, accepting him because he had come for her. If she could have scripted the scenario, she couldn't have planned it any better.

She blinked and reality set in. Damian still stood before her.

She shivered and shook her head hard. "So what brings you by?"

He drew a deep breath and lowered himself into the nearest chair. "I have an appointment with your uncle."

"Oh."

"And I also need to talk to you."

She narrowed her gaze. "Okay."

He ran a hand through his hair. She'd never seen him so flustered before. "I need a friend."

She wanted to be more but knew she had to settle for whatever he offered. "You know I'm that."

He bowed his head. Almost as if he couldn't face her, Micki thought and her throat filled with fear. "What is it?"

A knock sounded on her door and Micki's secretary entered. "Today's papers are here," Amy said, interrupting them.

"Thanks." Micki didn't look over her shoulder at the other woman.

"I'll just leave them on your desk." Amy walked in and placed the papers down before taking off again.

"Sorry. Papers are a publicist's lifeblood," Micki explained.

He nodded. "That's sort of why I'm here."

She raised an eyebrow. "How so?"

"There's no easy way to say this so… Just take a look." He gestured toward the stack of dailies. "Start with the *News*. They're the most creative with the headlines."

Micki picked up the top paper, *The Daily News,* and flipped it to the back page. The headline read Miami Love Machine. Beneath it, the caption elaborated, "Miami legal secretary claims New York Renegades center fielder Damian Fuller is the father of her unborn child. Full story p. 72." The photo, which took up much of the back page, showed the woman Micki recognized as Damian's date from Tampa, leaving the Marriott Marquis on Broadway.

Micki's head swam with so many emotions she couldn't sort through them all. Shock, disbelief, pain and a completely unreasonable sense of betrayal all ricocheted around her mind and buffeted her body.

And to think she'd hoped he'd come to claim her as his own. Because even though he'd never promised her anything, Micki had held on to the hope that somehow she'd meant something to him.

This paper, whether or not it portrayed the truth, was proof of Damian's playboy ways and his inability to care for one woman long-term. Micki had been a fool to think otherwise.

She slowly laid the paper down on the desk. Swallowing her own pain, she turned to face him. He'd said he needed a friend. Somehow she'd be his friend. "What are you going to do?"

He shook his head and shrugged. "That's sort of what I wanted to talk to you about."

"Okay…. Forgive me for asking the obvious but is it yours?"

"I wish to hell I knew." He rose and paced the floor, ending up at the window overlooking the city.

She wondered if he found the same comfort in the sameness of the skyline that she often did, then realized that nothing would soothe her now.

"So you need to ask for a paternity test."

He turned and nodded in agreement.

Micki swallowed hard. "And if the baby is yours?"

When he didn't reply right away, she offered up an alternative that nearly broke her heart. "Marriage?"

"Hell no." He answered immediately. "Child support, yes. Support for Carole, maybe. But marriage?" Damian shook his head, then held it in his hands as if the pain were overwhelming.

"Are you asking my opinion?" she asked in disbelief. Nobody could tell him what to do.

He shook his head. "Back at the airport you said if I ever needed you for anything…to spin a situation or just to vent, I should come to you. So here I am." His smile didn't reach his eyes. "To tell you the truth, I didn't even think this would hit the papers. I had no idea till I woke up this morning but I guess it needs to be handled, right?"

"Right," she managed to say, stunned. "You want me to help you spin the story?"

He leaned against the plate-glass window, his dark eyes imploring as he merely inclined his head.

Her mouth grew dry at the thought of being his publicist for this very public, very painful ordeal. She definitely didn't think she could work by his side and deal with her very real feelings for him while at the same time he worked through a relationship with another woman that would last a lifetime.

Apparently he had no such trouble working alongside *her* in that capacity. The truth stung.

"You're the best at what you do." For the first time, a teasing grin curled his lips.

"Under any other circumstances I'd be flattered." She let out a bitter laugh.

"Micki—" He reached for her hand but she pulled back, not wanting to touch him and set off the sparks she knew would follow.

"I need to step outside for a minute." She needed time alone. Without meeting his gaze, she turned and walked out.

Once in the hall, she leaned back and forced air into her lungs. They'd been home from Florida for two weeks and he hadn't as much as picked up the phone. Now when he was in the ultimate kind of trouble, he showed up on her doorstep. Here she was again, Micki Jordan, every guy's pal, she thought in frustration.

But she didn't question what she'd do. Micki could never turn down anyone in need. She knew better than to think she could ignore Damian's plea. If he needed her professional help, she'd provide it.

But no way would she give of herself emotionally again.

"YOU'RE AN ASS, Fuller," Damian said, swinging his hand uselessly in the air.

He couldn't believe he'd been so damn stupid. Selfish. Unfeeling. He'd woken up hungover and needing someone. Micki had been the only person who'd come to mind. The only one he'd wanted to share his pain with and the only person he trusted enough to ask for help. Unfortunately in all his thinking about himself, not once had he taken her feelings into account.

The news had hurt her, that much was obvious. If there was one person on this earth he'd want to protect from pain, it was Micki. Too late now, he thought, disgusted with himself.

He knew she'd walked out so she could be alone and retreat behind every emotional wall she could find. He didn't blame her. If he had a brick wall he could hide behind, he'd be there in an instant. Problem was, he didn't have that luxury. Nothing would make Carole and her pregnancy go away. He couldn't change the fact that he was back-page headlines again, this time with a scandal that would do far more damage than good.

He couldn't deny he needed Micki's unique ability to spin a story his way nor could he ignore that it might be the only way for him to keep her in his life. At least until he sorted through this personal mess and came out the other side. Right now Micki was his lifeline and he needed her. Apparently knowing he was selfish and doing something about it were two different things.

Without warning the door swung open wide and Micki walked back inside, her sister Sophie and her uncle Yank right behind her.

He stiffened, ignoring the embarrassment he felt at being caught with his pants down by people he admired and cared for. "Why do I have the feeling I'd rather face a firing squad than the three of you?" he asked.

"Well, I don't know," Yank said, his voice laced with sarcasm. "Maybe because you can't keep your pecker in your pants and now we've got ourselves a situation?" The older man picked up the paper and flung it Damian's way.

Damian winced. It was bad enough he'd still have to explain this mess to his family but now he was faced with Micki's. "I really don't see how that's relevant to my career."

"He really doesn't see how this is relevant to his career," Yank mimicked him. "I'll tell you how. I can book you on comedy shows and channels for idiots if this kid turns out to be yours. Want to know what was waiting in the wings for you?" Yank asked.

Probably not, Damian thought. "What?" he asked instead.

"*GMA* special sports correspondent, that's what. You see, you might not have wanted to talk about your career beyond playing ball but I had your back. Always."

"And I appreciate that. I admit this isn't the responsible image I want to project and I'm not proud of any of this. But plenty of famous people have survived worse scandal. I don't see what you're so worked up about," he said, his voice trailing off as his gaze shifted from Yank to Micki.

Damian knew exactly what had the old man so riled up and there wasn't a damn thing he could do to make things better. The man was already pissed at how Damian had handled his relationship with Micki. Now this. Who could blame Yank if his anger was more personal than professional?

Then there was Micki who hadn't met Damian's gaze since bringing her partners into the room.

"Look," Micki said, stepping in front of her uncle. "I spend my days spinning scandal for a living, but I thought we needed reinforcements on this one. You had an appointment with Uncle Yank anyway and I figured Sophie would be of help since I'm not exactly an unbiased third party."

In other words, she was hurt, and afraid her emotions would get in the way of doing her job. "You aren't about to pass me off to your sister, are you?" he asked Micki, ignoring the other two people in the room.

Silence followed and his gut churned at the thought of losing the only person he trusted.

"It would serve you right if I did, but no I'll help you handle this," she finally said.

Well that was something, at least. "Okay then, what's the plan?"

Sophie picked up a pen and began making notes on a pad in her hand. "In cases like these, having the right person standing by a man in times of scandal can save a reputation. In your case it's going to be Micki who holds your hand through this mess." Her frown told him how much Sophie hated the idea of her sister being subjected to being in the role of his savior.

But obviously they'd discussed it briefly before coming in here because neither Yank nor Micki argued the point.

Still Damian was confused. "I'm not sure I understand what you're suggesting."

"I'll explain. First you're going to issue a statement with your publicist by your side. That would be me," Micki said in case he missed the obvious. "You are going to admit you made a mistake and state that once the facts are verified, you plan to do the right thing. You're going to be a stand-up guy, just like your fans and the kids who look up to you expect."

He nodded. So far so good. Relief filled him as he realized that he'd been right in coming to Micki for help. Not just professionally but personally as well. He couldn't wrap his mind around how to handle any of this and he could already see that she'd help him get his head on straight. He'd owe her big time for this, Damian thought.

"Next up is handling the actual…umm…situation," Micki said, her cheeks turning red in embarrassment.

"What she's referring to is whether you've dealt with the issues surrounding this pregnancy," Sophie said, rescuing her sister. "Did you talk to the woman about a paternity test?"

He shook his head. "Not yet."

"Did you think about meeting with a lawyer?" Yank asked.

Again, Damian said, "No. I just found out. I can't even imagine how the damn story got leaked so quickly."

"Probably the doctors or nurses the woman saw. Somebody saw a chance to make a buck," Yank muttered.

"You need to set up those appointments," Micki instructed him, back to her professional mode. "What's your schedule look like?"

Damian groaned. "A series of home games and then a week on the road."

She nodded. "Okay, lawyer and doctor appointments first."

"You need to find out how far along this woman is and then talk to someone about when it's safe for paternity tests to be done."

"My sisters have an ob-gyn. I can set up an appointment with him. He's a family friend and I'm sure he'll fit me in around game times."

His sisters. Shit. The thought of facing them and their questions made him squirm.

Sophie nodded. "Good. At least we have a plan of action. Right now Micki will go with you and help deal with the press. In case you didn't realize, they're already outside the building and clamoring for information."

"Yeah, they were camped outside my building this morning." He winced at the memory. "There's no media quite like New York's."

"You got that right. Screw up and they're all over you," Yank said. "I got one question."

"Shoot." Damian wasn't about to hold anything back now.

"If the kid's yours, do you plan on marrying this broad?"

"Hell no. I don't believe in screwing up Carole's life or the kid's life just because protection didn't work," he snapped.

Yank cleared his throat. "You're saying you used protection?"

Micki looked away.

Damian ran a hand over his warm face. "Yeah, Yank. I did."

"Well that's something." The older man met his gaze with a sympathetic look of his own.

For a brief second, Damian didn't feel like the pariah in the room or the man who'd let this entire family down.

What a freaking mess he'd made. He and Micki hadn't had a commitment; they'd had what should have been a brief fling. Yet he couldn't shake the self-disgust flowing through him at the thought of disappointing her family and hurting her.

"I say we deal with the press immediately," Micki said, interrupting his thoughts. "The more time you let go by, the more speculation they'll shovel and the more dirt they'll dig up on both you and Carole. You ready?" she asked Damian in her most professional, distant voice.

"Ready as I'll ever be."

She nodded. "Then let's do it. I'll brief you on what to say on the way downstairs." Micki strode out of the room, pad in hand, all but ignoring him.

At this point the only thing he had going for him was the fact that she and her family agreed she'd stick by his side. He intended to hold her to her promise.

RICKY CARTER SAT in his small apartment and watched Eyewitness News at Noon. Thanks to his discreet contacts, Damian Fuller's paternity scandal had headlined the back of every newspaper in the city. Now Carter watched his captain and the man whose position he coveted step in front of microphones and speak from the heart.

No prepared statement for Fuller, Carter thought, taking a swig from a bottle of beer. Instead the man had the fans eating from the palm of his hand as he extolled the virtues of always using protection, explaining how mistakes happen anyway and promising to do the right thing. Then he asked for time to figure things out and requested the media focus on what was important at this time of year—the Renegades making it to the off season.

He shook his head in disgust. Everything the man touched turned to gold. Nothing Carter did made a difference or brought Fuller down, and he ought to know since he'd tried his best.

Carter had made sure to let the reporters who covered the team know at which strip club they could find Fuller. Carter had hoped they'd bash Fuller for partying at Lacie's the night before a charity event. In-

stead he'd been branded a hero for rescuing his
agent's niece. Nice piece of spinning by the Hot
Zone, Carter thought, frustrated.

Even now Fuller had the sexy little publicist standing by his side despite his fall from grace. The same
woman who'd eyed Carter with disdain looked at
Fuller with adoring eyes.

"The story of my life," he muttered.

But it wasn't just Damian's dumb luck eating
away at Rick now, it was his own actions that bothered him. When he'd hooked up with Carole, he'd
eyed Fuller with envy. Silently sabotaging the Renegades captain had been too easy to resist, and for a
while nobody had been hurt in the process.

Until Carole had gotten pregnant.

He and Carole had come together in fun but somewhere along the way, he'd begun to develop feelings
for her. Hell, he'd even thought she felt the same
way. But then she'd ended up pregnant, insisting the
baby was Damian's. To add insult to injury, she'd
been refusing to return Carter's phone calls.

Carter had been so pissed about the pregnancy, so
angry at Fuller, he'd wanted to get back at his captain. Carter had revealed Carole's pregnancy to the
press. But soon after making the call, the anger had
subsided and he realized he'd set Carole up for pain
and humiliation—something he'd never intended to
do. He'd called the press first and realized he'd be

hurting Carole later, after it was too late to take back the story.

He picked up the phone and dialed her hotel room. He knew she wasn't leaving the city until tomorrow and wanted to make sure she was okay while she was here.

The phone rang and rang on the other end until he was about ready to hang up.

"Hello?" Carole said, out of breath.

"Hey, babe, I've been trying to reach you."

"Carter?"

"Who were you expecting? Never mind," he said, before she could answer. He was certain he didn't want to know. "How are you feeling?"

"A little queasy. I've been spending more time than I'd like in the bathroom."

Maybe that's why he hadn't been able to reach her. He glanced toward his fridge. "You should try drinking Coke. It'll help. At least that's what my sister said when she was expecting."

"Thanks for the advice, Rick."

He swallowed hard. "No problem. So how are you handling…the rest of it?" he asked, referring to the media attention and hoping she wouldn't make him spell it out. He felt bad enough already.

She inhaled and he heard the long pause at the other end. "It's horrible. The reporters are all over the lobby. I had to ask security to sneak me down the service elevator tomorrow morning just so I can make my flight. I can't believe someone at the doctor's office would leak the news about my pregnancy. I feel so violated."

Carter's gut cramped. "What makes you think it was them?"

She sniffed and he imagined her wiping her eyes as she spoke. "Nobody else knows Damian's the father except you and me and I know you wouldn't hurt me."

She trusted him, Ricky thought, fighting the wave of nausea that overtook him as he faced the reality of what he'd done. In his zeal to take everything Damian Fuller had, he'd hurt this woman in the process. He hadn't meant to. He cared about her too much.

Way too much.

If she knew he'd been sabotaging Fuller, she'd dump his ass even as a friend. And he didn't want that. As much as he and Carole had often joked about Damian's arrogance and downfall, she was now carrying Fuller's kid.

Or was she? he wondered, as Damian's words from the press conference played back in his head.

Rick always wore a condom—it was ingrained in his head by his father—and he'd used one with Carole. She'd said she always made a guy use protection, too, but when she'd told him about the pregnancy, she'd said there was one time she and Fuller hadn't used birth control. He'd believed her.

"Hey, babe?"

"Yes?"

"Did you and Fuller use protection?"

He listened closely, waiting for an answer.

"I already told you about me and Damian. Why are you asking me again?"

He shrugged. "Something Fuller said to the press about using protection and accidents happening anyway."

She let out a too shrill laugh. "What else is he going to say? That he's not the hero the world thinks he is?"

"I understand, babe. And I'm here for you no matter what."

"That's so sweet." She paused. "But we can't see each other anymore. And Damian can't know we've ever been together, you know that right? Because if Damian will, ummm, marry me and give the baby a name, you know I have to do it. Promise me, okay?"

Rick shut his eyes tight. His position on the field, his number at bat and now his woman. What the hell else did Fuller need to hang on to that ought to be his? Carter wondered.

He couldn't live with making Carole such a promise.

"Oh I'm going to be sick again. I've got to go," she said and slammed the phone in his ear.

Apparently he wasn't going to have to promise her he'd keep his silence, after all. Which was a good thing since long after she'd hung up the phone, and long after the Renegades had won their 4:00 p.m. game, Rick tossed and turned in his bed, something eating away at him.

Something Carole hadn't said.

She hadn't answered his question about whether she and Fuller had used protection. After telling him about her pregnancy that first time, after explaining she and Damian had made that mistake just once, she'd evaded reassuring him directly ever since. Which left Rick with lingering doubts about Carole's initial claim.

Never mind the fact that she might have been with more guys than him and Fuller. Rick didn't want to deal with that thought at the moment. But if she and Fuller *had* used protection, just like she and Rick had used protection, then there was a fifty-fifty chance the baby she was carrying was his.

CHAPTER TEN

MICKI'S HEAD POUNDED as she somehow made it through the day. Although she, Sophie and Uncle Yank had all agreed they needed to stand by Damian, only she had a personal stake in the news he'd delivered. Only she was hurt by the fact that he'd possibly fathered a child. And only she disagreed with his decision not to marry Carole.

Nothing ate away at her more than a child deprived of a parent, perhaps because she'd lived the nightmare herself. She couldn't understand how Damian could willingly opt out of his child's life. She figured it was because the baby wasn't a reality to him yet. Once it was, if it was, then she hoped he'd do the right thing and be a full-time parent by marrying Carole. No matter how much Micki was hurt by the thought.

In the meantime, she'd guide him through the PR aspects of his situation and make sure he played well to his public. All of his publics, which in a star athlete's case included his coaches, the people who paid his salary, and his fans, including the parents of the kids who idolized him.

At least he was a quick study. She'd briefed him on the elevator ride down and he'd aced the brief statement to the reporters and the few questions she'd allowed him to take. He'd come across as a concerned man, a fallible human, and a star who was acknowledging his place in the public eye and using his mistake to educate America's youth.

He'd returned to the office and used the conference room to schedule the meetings Sophie had suggested. First up was the doctor who'd explain the ins and outs of safe paternity testing. He had an appointment for a consultation tomorrow. Once he had an understanding of the facts, he'd have to confront Carole and request a test. Those were the more personal aspects of this situation and he didn't need Micki around for that, she thought gratefully.

A knock sounded on her door and she glanced up. "Come in."

Sophie stuck her head inside. "Want to grab a bite to eat?"

Micki shook her head.

"Okay then good thing I figured you'd want to be holed up in your office. We'll just eat here." Sophie pulled a paper bag from behind her back and proceeded to unload the goodies she'd bought from the café downstairs. "I've got two iced coffees and two

Squagels with cream cheese. Comfort food including a brownie for dessert."

"I appreciate it, Soph, but I'm not hungry."

Her sister shrugged. "So you can keep me company while I eat."

A couple of minutes later, Sophie had spread everything out across Micki's desk, leaving her no choice but to stare or pick at the food she'd brought. Micki decided to pick.

"I'm sorry you have to go through this." Sophie met her gaze. "Damian's a jerk."

"He's not." Micki shook her head, surprised to find herself defending him. "I mean in reality, he's no different than thousands of other people who end up with unplanned pregnancies. He's just famous, that's all."

Sophie took a bite of her bagel and Micki waited while she chewed and swallowed. "You don't hold it against him?" her sister asked.

"I don't like that it happened. I don't like the feeling that I'm having his past affairs thrown in my face as a direct reminder that the man doesn't commit to anyone." Micki's throat filled as the enormity of another woman having Damian's baby overwhelmed her. She swallowed hard and continued, "But when all is said and done, this isn't about me. He was honest and up front from the beginning. He said no strings. I agreed." She ripped a piece of the bagel and popped it in her mouth.

Sophie reached across the desk and covered Micki's hand with hers. "That doesn't mean you aren't hurt."

"I never said I wasn't." She followed the bagel with a long sip of iced coffee.

Sophie sighed. "Is there a chance the kid isn't his?"

Micki shrugged. "I guess so. There's also a chance the woman isn't really pregnant. I mean her breasts are fake so there's every chance this baby is, too." Then, catching herself, Micki slapped a hand over her mouth. "That was uncalled for."

"But I bet it felt good." Sophie grinned.

Micki laughed and finally relaxed, grateful she had her sister to share this rough time with. "Any word from Lola?" she asked, changing the subject to their next problem.

Sophie shook her head. "Apparently Spence has been away on vacation and she hasn't been able to talk to him. Either that or she's avoiding it. Who can blame her?"

"Well I have my hands full with Damian's mess, so it's just as well I don't have to deal with any more upheaval at the moment."

"Amen." With that, Sophie collected the garbage and rose from her seat. "But you know Uncle Yank's birthday is in a few days. Spencer will be back by then. We're all going to have to deal with this soon."

Just then, Amy knocked and entered. "I'm leaving for the night."

Micki waved her hand in the air. "Enjoy your evening."

The other woman smiled. "You, too. Oh, since you asked me to hold your messages all afternoon, here they are. The only one that can't wait is on top." The secretary handed Micki the pink stack of papers before taking off.

"Anything interesting?" Sophie asked.

Micki glanced down and groaned. "Just a message from Damian that he's sending a car to pick me up around eight. He says I should plan on swinging by the stadium for him and then he has some things we need to do."

Sophie frowned. "If he's asking for evening work, tell him you expect overtime pay."

Micki had spent the day at her desk. She glanced down at the flirty miniskirt she'd chosen this morning, when the sun was still shining bright and the newspapers hadn't yet hit her desk. Now it looked tired and wrinkled. "I can't go out like this. I look like hell."

"Then it's a good thing you have a chance to go home and change."

She closed her eyes and let out an exhausted groan. "I can't imagine what he could possibly need from me tonight."

Her sister grew suddenly quiet, causing Micki's nerve endings to prickle uncomfortably. "What is it?"

Sophie leaned closer, her soft gaze settling on

Micki. "I was just thinking… What if Damian just needs *you?*"

Sophie's question haunted Micki for the next few hours. It haunted her as she changed into jeans, sneakers and a T-shirt. It haunted her as she returned to the office and then climbed into the back seat of the limo he'd sent to pick her up.

And it haunted her now as she waited in the car outside the stadium for Damian to emerge after the press conference following tonight's game. Huge floodlights lit up the night sky as people swarmed out of the various exits, animated and flushed with excitement, thanks to the latest Renegades win.

Micki watched from her back seat in the limo, protected by the complete anonymity afforded by the tinted glass windows. She sat in her private world and contemplated her sister's words.

What if Damian just needs you?

Damian had never hinted that he wanted anything more than professional help but there'd been moments when she'd caught his gaze and the connection between them had returned as strong as it had been on the island. As much as she didn't think he'd contemplate resuming their relationship when his life was such a mess, neither one of them could deny the chemistry. A powerful attraction she needed to control.

Nothing could happen between them again. Not

if this baby was his. Micki would never allow herself to end up in the middle of Damian and Carole's relationship, nor that of Damian and his child. She respected the sanctity and traditions of marriage and family too much.

She doubted she had much to worry about anyway. Damian hadn't been in touch with her—not until he'd gotten into trouble and needed her help.

As much as she wanted to hate him for getting himself in this situation, she couldn't. And as much as she wanted to pound him in the head until he said Carole was lying, she couldn't do that, either. What she intended to do was quite ironic, actually. She was going to become the one thing she'd made a special effort *not* to be—Damian's buddy, pal and friend. And if she hated him for anything, she hated him for reducing them to that.

THE POST-GAME PRESS CONFERENCE ran long. Instead of discussing the game, reporters wanted to talk about Damian's personal life, which he and Coach Donovan had already declared off-limits. Still, they were reporters, which meant they didn't take no for an answer. They asked, he declined to reply. It took him longer than he'd have liked to finally make his way down to the limo and meet up with Micki.

The chauffeur opened the car door and Damian slid in beside her. Her eyes were shut and he had a chance to study her. Her hair fell in gentle waves around her softly made-up face. Just her presence gave him the sense of peace and comfort he lacked.

The driver slammed the door closed and she bolted upright in her seat.

"Hey." He smiled at her startled expression.

"Hi." She ran her hands up and down her bare arms and shivered. "I fell asleep."

He nodded. "Sorry I ran late." He tapped the Plexiglas partition, indicating the driver should go, and the car started up for the trip to Jersey.

"Congratulations. I was listening to WFAN. You have another win under your belts."

"Thanks."

She eyed him warily, obviously still uncertain how to act around him now.

He had no answers for her or for himself. All he knew was that she provided an anchor in his turbulent life and he'd missed her desperately in the time they'd been apart. He was grateful to be with her again and though he hated the circumstances that had brought them together, he had no choice but to accept them and begin to cope.

"So when do I get to hear why you needed me tonight?" she asked. "What's the PR problem?"

He knew he couldn't play innocent or dumb so he opted for the truth. "My family." He leaned back in the seat and shut his eyes, exhaustion overtaking him.

"Are you for real?" She blew out a puff of air in frustration. "I don't hear from you for two weeks and then when I do, you've got a paternity scandal hanging over your head. I agreed to help you out, but since when did that include explaining your actions to your family?" she asked, obviously appalled he'd brought her along for this trip.

Well, hell. "They're going to grill me mercilessly."

She arched an eyebrow. Her expression lacked any sympathy at all. "So? You deserve it. But personal issues don't fall under my job description."

He reached out and grabbed her hand. Her skin felt soft and smooth, like the skin on her belly and the flesh on her thighs, he recalled, his body growing hot and hard with the memory. So aroused that focusing on explanations was difficult.

He understood her anger but couldn't find the words to explain that in the mayhem since Carole dropped the bomb, Micki was the only person he felt comfortable with. He didn't understand the connection that drew him to her either, but the fact remained that he needed her, more than just on a professional level. For the first time in his life, he was looking to a woman for emotional support.

He ran a hand over his face. "I'm a freaking mess," he admitted, meeting her gaze. "My wrist hurts every time I pick up or hit the ball. It doesn't matter how well I'm playing, I've got to live with the fact that it's taking everything out of me just to get through every game. Then I've got Carole who I can't even begin to believe, but I can't afford not to."

"Go on," she said, softly.

He swallowed but his mouth tasted like pitcher's mound dirt. "If the kid is mine, what the hell kind of father will I make?" he asked, voicing his fears aloud for the first time.

To Micki. Which proved to him that keeping her by his side was necessary to his sanity.

She covered his hand with hers. "If it comes to that, you'll make the best kind of dad."

"When you say it, I can almost believe it," he said, forcing a laugh.

"You should." Light danced in her eyes for the first time all evening. "Didn't you say your father was amazing? We learn by example, so what makes you think you'll be any different?"

He turned her hand over and looked at the fragile skin on her wrist. "*You're* amazing," he said, gratitude and something warm he didn't want to examine too closely filling his chest.

Without warning, she jerked her hand back. "I'm just stating the facts," she said, putting distance between them once more.

He didn't have to guess why. He was a man with baggage and risks, and as much as he wanted to bury himself inside her and forget his problems, that would only add one more complication to an already screwed-up mess.

"There's something I want you to consider," Micki said.

"What's that?"

She twisted her hands together, a sure sign he wouldn't like her request. "I grew up orphaned."

He nodded. "I know."

"And I believe that in the best of all possible worlds, a baby should have both parents around. If the baby is yours, you need to consider marrying Carole and giving the child a real family."

Her voice broke on the word *family*. So did his heart. In all his thinking, he'd forgotten that Micki had been raised by her bachelor uncle. She'd missed out on parents in her life and obviously she still felt that loss.

Damian breathed deeply and leaned forward in his seat. "I understand where you're coming from but you need to understand that this isn't all about me not wanting to marry Carole. It's about the baby, too. Sometimes you can do a child a bigger favor by not raising it in a home where there is no love or caring."

She spread her hands wide. "I don't know."

"Growing up, didn't you have everything you needed in your untraditional home with your uncle, Lola and your sisters?"

She nodded.

"So I guess you need to consider that by not marrying Carole, I may still be doing right by this baby."

"If it's yours."

"If it's mine," he agreed and hoped with everything in him that Carole had been as unfaithful as he suspected.

He glanced out the window and realized they were close to his sister's house where his entire family waited. "There's just one more thing." Something that had been weighing on his mind.

"What's that?"

He placed an arm behind her head and leaned close enough to smell the scent of her skin. His groin ached with the need to bury himself deep inside her and thrust hard and fast until the outside world disappeared and all that remained was *them*.

Instead he cleared his throat and forced himself to remain focused. "I appreciate you agreeing to stay by my side." He owed her his thanks and probably much more.

He turned his head and his lips touched the side of her neck. When she didn't push him away, he let his mouth skim her soft flesh. Just for a moment, he promised himself. No more.

He grasped her arm and raised it to press a gentle kiss on her exposed flesh there, letting his tongue linger. He didn't know if it was his words or his touch that got to her but she trembled and a soft sigh escaped from the back of her throat. She wore a soft T-shirt that gathered in the middle, accentuating her breasts, and her nipples puckered beneath his gaze. She pivoted toward him and just as he thought her lips would touch his, the car jerked to a sudden stop.

"We're here." She jumped back, obviously shaken by what had almost transpired between them.

He clamped down on his disappointment, telling himself the interruption was for the best.

She straightened her top and fussed with her hair. "So how do you feel about explaining yourself to your sisters?" she asked in an obvious scramble for conversation.

"I don't relish the idea of discussing my stupidity or my sex life with my sisters and my parents any more than I enjoyed revealing it to you." He reached for the handle at the same time the driver opened and held the door for them. "But I got myself into this mess and my family deserves to know what's going on, so…I'll let them skewer me."

She glanced down. "You know, I do admire how you're facing up to all this."

"Thanks," he said, surprised. He reached out and tipped her chin upward.

He took in her flushed cheeks and pouty glossed lips and curled his hands into fists to keep from kissing her. Really kissing her this time.

He knew he had to focus on less pleasant tasks right now. Like facing the firing squad he called his family.

MICKI WOULD FEEL A LOT BETTER about herself if the kiss hadn't happened because she hadn't let it, not because of the fortuitous timing of their arrival. Thank God they'd reached their destination or else she'd probably be kicking herself for letting him kiss her. For kissing him back. And for allowing him to do whatever else to her in the back seat of the limo despite her promise to herself to keep her distance.

Now, introductions behind them, Damian sat next to Micki in the family room of his sister Brenda's house and took his punishment like a man. Apparently in his family, punishment meant a grilling by all interested parties.

Beside her, Damian clenched his fists, and sucking up the embarrassment, he let the questions fly.

His father paced the floor in front of Damian's seat on the couch. "Sum it up in a nutshell," Mike Fuller said in the same tone Micki could imagine him using with his kids when they'd screwed up during their youth.

"A woman I used to see claims she's pregnant and I'm the father."

"Claims?" His mother jumped on the uncertainty.

Damian nodded. "I'll be checking out both parts of her statement."

"So the baby might not be yours?" Ronnie asked.

"Or she might not even be pregnant," Brenda said confidently.

"All possibilities, I suppose. As much as I don't want this baby to be mine, I'd hate to think she'd outright lie about something like this."

"With your finances, that's the first thing you need to consider." His father stopped and shoved his hands in his front pants pockets. "Didn't I teach you to use protection *each and every time?*"

Micki felt her cheeks heat up and flush at the older man's frank talk.

"I used protection," he said, looking his father in the eye. "Each and every time."

As he had with her, Micki recalled. Each and every time.

His father nodded, relieved. "Well that's something."

Her uncle had said the same thing.

"Maybe the condom broke," Rhonda offered.

"Three kids, only thirteen months apart. You ought to know," Marissa said.

"Leave your sister alone," Marissa's husband Dan said, jumping in only to call his wife off. "Ours are eighteen months apart so I don't know why you're giving Rhonda a hard time," he said with a wry smile.

Ronnie snickered.

Marissa nudged her husband in the side. "Spoil-sport." But she spoke in a teasing tone.

Micki couldn't suppress a smile at the byplay among the family members. She, Annabelle and Sophie could always go at one another given the slightest provocation but at the heart of all the needling in her family was a basic love and respect. Micki sensed the same thing here.

"Girls," Adrienne said, clapping her hands. "Dan's right. Now's not the time to tease each other. We've got important issues to deal with."

"Your mother's right. Now's the time to rally around your brother." Mike walked over and placed an arm around Damian's shoulder in a sign of unwavering support.

Obviously it didn't matter how bad his children's sins, Damian's father would always forgive them. Just like Uncle Yank who'd flown to Florida in a heartbeat to be with Micki. Who'd have thought her untraditional family and Damian's had so much in common?

"When will you have answers?" Brenda asked.

"I have an appointment with Gary Kernan tomorrow to get the rundown on testing. I promise to fill you in as soon as I know something."

Ronnie reached for her brother's hand. "Gary and his partners delivered all our kids. He's the best."

"And you can trust him to be honest and discreet." Brenda's husband Steve chose his moment to add to the conversation.

Micki also picked up on the love and respect between Damian's parents as well as between his sisters and their husbands. He truly did have the best role models for happy relationships, she thought. Yet he'd backed away from forming any of his own in favor of focusing solely on his career.

It was something she'd analyze further later, but for now, since Damian had chosen to bring her here, she was going to do her best to help the family deal with the crisis.

"Excuse me," Micki said.

"Yes?" Damian's mother asked. "You've been so quiet until now. What's on your mind?"

Micki smiled. "I was hoping I could give you all a quick PR course before we leave tonight," Micki offered. "Because Damian won't be the only one who's going to get cornered or pestered for answers."

All of the Fuller family's eyes turned her way.

"We're happy to hear anything Damian's publicist and friend has to say." Adrienne seemed to welcome her with her warm gaze and soft voice.

"Okay then. Just a few helpful hints in case the press gets ahold of you."

"We've all been screening our calls with caller ID," Brenda said.

Micki stood and took center stage among Damian's family. She was used to public speaking but in this case she felt scrutinized in a more personal way. No doubt his sisters wondered about the true nature of her relationship with their brother, but there was nothing Micki could do about it. Damian's recent exploits would cause many people to wonder. It was something he'd have to live with. Something she'd have to ignore now.

"Screening calls won't stop a determined reporter from accosting you in the supermarket or while you're taking the kids into dance class. But you have a few strategies at your disposal."

"Such as?" Damian's mother asked.

Micki held up one finger. "There's the old 'no comment' and keep walking." She raised a second finger in the air. "There's the redirect in which you just tell them to call your brother's publicist and hand out my card that I'll leave with you all." She paused and lifted a third finger to join the other two. "Or you can just tell them to go away or you'll call the police and report them for harassment, especially if they're bothering you when the kids are around."

Damian watched Micki take charge of his boisterous family. Obviously in her element, her suggestions were to the point, succinct, and also well thought out. She impressed him on so many levels he couldn't begin to count them all.

He hadn't thought to ask her to coach his family but he was grateful she'd done so on her own. As for his sisters, to Damian's amazement, his talkative nosy siblings had shut up and were listening to Micki intently. His mother was scribbling notes on a small pad she always kept in her purse and his father was watching Micki with a huge grin on his face, no small feat considering his worry over Damian's messed-up life.

"Any questions?" Micki asked.

"I have one." Ronnie, his youngest and most outspoken sibling raised a hand in the air.

"She's not a teacher and you aren't in school," Marissa said, laughing.

"Well whatever. I just want to know if you're here because Damian's paying you to help him."

"Or if you're here because you care about Damian," Brenda chimed in, helping Ronnie out in embarrassing him.

Damian didn't meet Micki's gaze. Instead he jumped up from his seat. "Hey, that's uncalled for. I'm the only one who can put Micki on the spot and that's not going to happen right now. We have to get back to the city, so the inquisition is over."

The trio didn't argue, which meant they knew they were out of line. Damian used the next few minutes to hug, kiss, say goodbye and thank them all for being in his corner even through such an awkward mess. Even Micki was treated to warm hugs and kisses goodbye, making Damian happy he'd brought her along.

Ronnie promised to fill her husband in on the conversation since he'd gone home to relieve the babysitter. But it was Marissa's and Brenda's older teen-age girls who concerned Damian most. He knew the teens looked up to their famous uncle and so he promised to have a talk with his older nieces when this all blew over, including discussing the uncomfortable topic of safe sex.

It was the least he could do in exchange for the public scandal he'd caused.

MICKI SLEPT ON THE RIDE BACK to the city, waking up just as the car came to a stop in front of her building. She glanced at her watch. It was almost midnight. She was beyond exhausted from a very emotional day and night, and her body ached from the uncomfortable position she'd been in.

She rubbed her eyes and focused on the handsome, sexy man sitting before her. "I fell asleep again," she said, embarrassed.

"Don't worry about it. So did I." He stretched and her gaze fell to the muscles in his forearms and his tanned skin.

Her mouth grew dry and she wished she had a bottle of water to quench her thirst. Better that than wishing she could kiss him and find the moisture she was lacking.

"In the end it was a good idea to bring me tonight."

Damian smiled. "Left alone, who knows how my sisters would have handled the reporters." He grimaced at the thought of subjecting his family to scrutiny they hadn't signed up for. "You helped my family out a lot. I appreciate it."

"Well your family is special and I'm glad I got to meet them."

"They said the same thing about you." He paused before saying what was on his mind, then decided what the hell. "Actually the last thing my father said was that I should grab onto you and not let you go."

His genuine, warm smile stole what was left of Micki's breath. "That's sweet."

She stepped out of the car, Damian right behind her. When she turned, she found herself staring into his compelling eyes. The hot and humid summer air wafted around them, increasing the heat that rose between them.

She tried to hang onto her focus and keep her desire at bay. "I've been wondering about something."

"Shoot."

"Your parents are happily married, and so are your sisters. They all have kids and they obviously get through any problems together."

He tipped his head to one side. "What's your point?" he asked.

She struggled to find the words and decided just to state her thoughts no matter how personal they seemed. "I guess I'm wondering why, faced with all that, you fight so hard against settling down yourself?"

He shook his head and let out a soft, sexy, rumbling laugh. "I've asked myself the same question many times." He braced his hand on the top of the car and leaned his head against his shoulder. "Do you put a lot of stock in birth order?"

Interesting question, she thought. "A fair amount, I guess. I mean because I was the youngest, Annabelle felt she had to protect me most after our parents died. She took the brunt of the burden and shielded me from the possibility of foster care if Uncle Yank didn't want to raise us. She was an adult way before her time."

"And I was the baby who never had to grow up," he said. "My sisters catered to me and mothered me. And I've been lucky in that everything I've wanted has come pretty easily."

She immediately waved away his point. "You're known for your work ethic so I wouldn't say things came easily," she chided.

"I'm not saying I didn't work hard at my career but I had more lucky breaks than most." He shook his head and laughed, a self-deprecating sound that told Micki he'd given her original question way more previous thought than she'd given him credit for. "When everything goes your way, you get spoiled. *I* got spoiled. Hell, I *am* spoiled. I'm also petrified of losing everything I have," he admitted.

"So…"

"I work overtime to maintain the image, including the perception of the partying guy with no injuries and no weaknesses."

"And you think if you let yourself get involved with anyone who means something to you, you'll lose the one thing that means everything to you. Your career."

"I'm amazed you get it," he said, his tone filled with surprise and an almost reluctant admiration.

She glanced down at the sidewalk, scuffing the bottom of her shoes against the pavement. "I guess that's what comes from my spending a lifetime hanging around with professional jocks. I understand the world you deal in."

"We do have that world in common," he said gruffly.

Emotion emanated from him and shook her up inside because, although tonight had been about business, she somehow felt closer to him than she had before. Given the circumstances, closer unnerved her.

"But as much as I stand by my choices to keep my career going, I was a damn idiot to get involved with a woman like Carole. She was a meaningless fling and now I may be tied to her for the rest of my life."

"Payback's a bitch," Micki said, forcing a chuckle. But the pain in her heart wasn't at all amusing. Because, as he'd spoken, she'd realized that their time on the island was probably also a meaningless fling.

Suddenly he reached up and stroked her cheek

with the back of his hand. "You and I weren't the same as me and Carole," he said, reading her mind.

"I didn't think I was."

He shook his head. "Yeah, you did. And I can't say I gave you any reason to believe otherwise."

She forced a smile. "Not to worry, I know where we stand."

"No, I don't think you do." He stared at her, his gaze compelling and enigmatic all at the same time. "Let me walk you inside?"

She shook her head. "I'm fine."

She watched the struggle inside him until finally he stepped back. "Okay then. I'll meet you outside the doctor's office tomorrow?"

She blinked, surprised. "The paternity test consultation? You don't need PR help for that."

"You're right. I don't. But I do need you by my side for moral support."

Micki groaned. "Damian…"

"Please." He met her gaze, his eyes imploring and his tone holding a desperate quality she couldn't resist.

"Sure." She heard herself agreeing, her stomach in knots over involving herself in something so personal.

He exhaled hard, obviously relieved. "Thank you. Again."

She forced a smile. She certainly couldn't say it was her pleasure.

"Sleep tight," he said in a husky voice.

She forced a smile. "You, too."

Later that night, alone in her bed, she didn't have to wonder why she felt so empty and alone.

CHAPTER ELEVEN

MICKI HAD A LONG DAY AHEAD of her and no time to come home in between meetings, work and the dinner party for Uncle Yank's birthday. With no alternative, she took the dress she'd bought for the occasion, zipped it into a garment bag and took it with her to work so she could change there. She arrived at the office by 7:00 a.m. to reschedule some appointments and leave a few notes for Amy before heading over to the doctor's office on Park Avenue to meet Damian.

She had knots in her stomach over the idea of discussing paternity tests and Damian's sexual relationship with another woman. She understood his need to have someone there for support, but after thinking things over and over last night, she'd decided she wasn't the right person for the job.

She turned the corner and found Damian already standing outside the door, leaning against a black iron handrail. In his jeans and light blue Polo collared shirt, he was the sexiest man on Park Avenue. In fact, he was one of the only men on this part of Park Avenue so early in the morning, which was a good thing because she didn't think she could handle this conversation in front of an audience.

"Thanks for coming," he said, walking toward her.

She gathered her courage as she launched right into the speech she'd prepared last night. "I completely understand you needing moral support and I want to be there for you. I really do. But this is just too much. I don't belong here and I'm really not comfortable sitting down with a doctor discussing how long ago you impregnated another woman." She forced the words out in a rush or she knew she'd never say them at all.

She was as much as admitting she had feelings for the man and that really wasn't something she'd ever wanted him to know. Not when he was incapable of reciprocating. "So now that you know how I feel, I can get back to the office."

Micki turned and started down the street, searching for the nearest taxi as she ran. She still hadn't made peace with her high heels and she wobbled more than once, turning her ankle painfully and destroying any hope she had for a dignified exit.

"Micki!" Damian called after her.

Thank goodness a yellow cab with its lights on rounded the corner. She waved. The car came to a screeching halt. At the same time she reached for the door, Damian caught up with her. She opened the door but he held it, preventing her from getting in.

"Micki, please. I just want to talk to you," he said, breathing heavily.

She swallowed but her throat was tight. "When I agreed to help you out I didn't know how hard it would be," she admitted, her heart pounding in her chest, proving her words with each heavy beat.

"I didn't realize either," he said softly, his breath warm against her neck.

"Hey lady, you getting in or not?" the cabdriver asked impatiently.

Micki turned to Damian whose gaze was soft and understanding. "Just sit in the waiting room and as soon as I'm finished, we'll talk."

Her head throbbed, her ankle hurt and her heart ached like mad. "I must be insane," she said more to herself than to Damian. She glanced at the cabbie through the open passenger's side window. "I'm sorry to have taken your time," she told him and slammed the door shut instead of getting inside.

"Thank you." Damian grabbed her hand and held on tight. "I already told you I can act like a spoiled son of a bitch sometimes." His lips turned upward in an embarrassed grin but his relief at having stopped her exit was palpable.

"Yeah, you did." But for some reason she was still standing by his side.

An hour later, he walked out of the doctor's office and insisted they grab a cup of coffee. She'd already

touched base with Amy at the office and knew her
11:00 a.m. appointment had canceled, freeing up her
time, so she agreed.

They settled into seats at Sara Beth's Kitchen and
quickly placed their orders. Micki was grateful for
the fresh, hot coffee but she wasn't much interested
in her Danish.

Damian guzzled his caffeine, needing the fortifi-
cation desperately. When he was finished, he placed
his mug aside and met her gaze from across the small
table. For several moments, he simply stared at her,
unsure of what to say or where to begin.

He only knew he owed her an apology. Silence
surrounded them and though it was morning-rush
time, the restaurant was atypically quiet for a week-
day. He'd brought her here because they had a lot to
discuss and he didn't want to do it over the phone.
Until she'd nearly bolted on him this morning, he
hadn't realized how much he counted on her comforting presence and solid support.

In the instant she'd taken off down the street, he'd
been forced to acknowledge that she was so much
more than a friend who was holding his hand through
a crisis. He didn't know how much more and at this
moment he couldn't see the point in delving too
deeply. He also didn't think she'd appreciate hearing
he was coming to care for her deeply—not when another woman and her baby stood between them, as

did his fucked-up life and the career he was still trying desperately to hang on to.

He dragged his chair closer, moving so he sat directly beside her. His thigh brushed her bare leg and he savored the warmth of her body heat. "I'm sorry this has been so hard for you."

"Professionally it's the right way to handle things."

"But like you said, this morning's appointment wasn't at all a professional request."

She shook her head. "Never mind that. Friends stand by friends."

His gut churned uncomfortably at her casual use of the word.

"So what exactly did the doctor say?" she asked.

Her question forced him to focus. "Are you sure you want to hear about it?"

She nodded slowly. "I didn't want to be there for the discussion. I can handle hearing the news from you."

"Basically he said there're three types of testing." He reached into his pocket for the brochure the doctor had given him and scanned the paper again so he could accurately explain. "Two are invasive and could be dangerous to the fetus. The last one is a simple blood test involving just the mother and potential father's blood samples. The lab extracts fetal blood cells from the mother's sample and compares the DNA to the potential father's. That would be me." He pressed his lips together, anger at himself welling up again.

"When can it be done safely?"

He glanced at Micki, whose normally flushed skin had grown pale during this awkward conversation. "Any time after twelve weeks." Damian had already done the math. Assuming Carole had gotten pregnant their last time together in April, they were just approaching twelve weeks. "Which means we're pretty close to being able to do the test," he said, sparing Micki the details.

"I see. And how is Carole handling all this?" she asked, her voice tight as she unsuccessfully tried to withhold any emotion.

"I don't know," he said, gripping his coffee cup tighter in his hand. "I haven't been in touch with her."

"That's awful!"

He winced. "It's not as cold and callous as it seems." He glanced down, embarrassed about what Micki must think of him. "At first I needed time to digest the news. I needed time to arrange things like this test. And I needed to deal with the idea of possibly being a father."

"And have you?" she asked.

He shrugged, uncertainty still rioting through him. "I don't know. I can accept it if the test is positive. It's hard to deal with it when it's not even a reality yet."

"I understand that."

"But thanks to you I'm taking steps in the right direction and beginning to wrap my brain around it. On the way over this morning I called my lawyer to set up an appointment to put a trust fund together if the baby is mine." He looked into her blue eyes. "I needed to do all these things before I could go to Carole and discuss things coherently."

Micki exhaled slowly. "I can't imagine what this has been like for you. I know that you're in limbo with Carole and that you're worried about your career, and I know that you're taking a beating in the press—"

"The hell with the press. This mess has taught me that the only opinions I care about are the ones held by the people I—" He'd been about to say *love*.

A word he never used or even thought about. Sitting across from Micki, knowing his feelings for her were growing beyond simple desire or gratitude, it unnerved him to do so now.

"Are you okay?" Micki placed her hand over his.

To Damian it was like touching a match to a wick. His candle was on fire, he thought, holding back a laugh. Who'd have thought his feelings for this woman could lighten his mood and make him happy at a time when he felt like his life was strangling him?

Looking at her, her soft skin and moist lips, listening to her reassure him and tell him she believed he could handle things, *he* started to believe.

"Actually, I'm fine." Suddenly, his beeper went off, interrupting them.

"Excuse me." He checked the number and muttered a curse. "I was supposed to be at the stadium for an early workout." He'd completely blanked on his priorities—not a good sign.

"Someone's screwed," Micki said helpfully.

"Gee, thanks." Despite himself, Damian laughed. He was on his feet and tossing money onto the table in seconds.

They headed for the street together but when he tried to give her the first cab, she waved him away.

"I'm not going to take this one now and have you hand my head to me on a platter later. You take the first one." She swept her hand in a gallant gesture that had him laughing once again.

Before he got in the car, he turned to Micki. "One question. What made you stick around this morning and not just walk away?" He needed to know what held them together on her side of things.

She shifted from foot to foot before meeting his gaze. "You need me," she said simply, then pivoted to walk away.

It wasn't a declaration of love or even lust. But it was an acknowledgment of a bond and the genuineness of those words meant more than he cared to think about.

Anyway, he had no time to linger, no time to waste. Acting on pure instinct, he pulled her close and kissed her hard on the lips before sliding into the cab and slamming the door shut behind him.

The taxi sped away, leaving him alone with thoughts he didn't want to have. Panic over being late. Panic over Carole. Panic over losing Micki when this was all over.

Instead of thinking, he pulled out his cell phone and searched for Carole's number in Florida. Surely she was home or at least on her way by now. Thanks to Micki's reaction, he'd had a revelation, a feeling of what it might be like to be the one in Carole's shoes, uncertain of what life had in store. He certainly couldn't live with himself if he left Carole thinking she was in this alone.

Her answering machine picked up on the second ring and after waiting through her recorded message, he said, "Hey, Carole, it's Damian. I know things can't be easy right now…umm…I'll be away on a seven-day road trip and then let's plan on getting together to talk when I get home. If you need anything in the meantime, you can reach me on my cell." He reiterated the number, though he was sure she knew it by heart, and hung up, feeling better for having checked on her.

He leaned back in the cab and shut his eyes. Just like at night, his thoughts overwhelmed him. In the deepest recesses of his soul, Damian couldn't imagine fathering a child with Carole. He couldn't imagine the careful planning of his career exploding in his face now, when it was almost over. He still had a chance to go out on top and he didn't want to blow it.

He knew he was possibly the baby's father. But when he tried to do as Micki suggested and face the reality, to view this kid as his, the only child he could envision had blue eyes not brown and naturally blond curly hair, not the kind that came from a bottle.

Unwilling to follow that train of thought, he glanced at his watch. Dammit, he was so late.

To his never-ending shock, he started to laugh. He'd never been late for a practice, let alone a game. He'd spent his entire career ensuring he remained focused on his goals. And now, when he was preoccupied and completely screwed up, when he ought to be pissed as hell at himself for every wrong move recently made, he felt lighter than he had in years.

MICKI LOCKED HER OFFICE DOOR and drew the shades on the glass windows that made her office visible from the hallway. She'd already freshened her makeup. She had about half an hour to change and make it to her uncle's annual birthday party at his favorite restaurant.

Annabelle was doing better and she'd gotten her doctor's permission to attend the party as long as she stayed off her feet while there and didn't overdo. They'd kept the invitations to a minimum this year, mostly family and a few friends…including Lola and Spencer Atkins.

Separately the two were Uncle Yank's closest

friends, even if he and Lola were estranged at the moment, but as an item they were an explosive combination destined to incite Uncle Yank to riot. Micki groaned, knowing it was going to be an eventful night.

She slipped on her new high-heeled shoes, straightened her skirt and opened her office door in time to find Damian on the other side. Since leaving him this morning, she hadn't let herself dwell on him or his situation or else she knew she'd get nothing done. But he was here now and, apparently, *eventful* was an understatement, she thought, surprised by his unexpected appearance.

He scanned her from her sandals up to the hem on her short skirt, lingered on her tight top and ended on her freshly made-up face.

"You look fantastic," he said, the heat in his gaze and his husky tone unmistakable.

Warmth spread and the old pulse-pounding desire rushed through her at his compliment. For a brief moment, they were back on the island, unencumbered by life and reality.

"Thank you," she murmured. She met his gaze and realized he was clean shaven. He was also well dressed in a pair of tan slacks and a black button-down collared shirt with a teasing sprinkle of chest hair peeking out from the opening.

A quick inhale told her he was wearing a sexy cologne and Micki knew she was in trouble. Since he'd played an afternoon game and his apartment was downtown in Gramercy Park, he'd gone out of his way to be here.

She moistened her lips. "So…what brings you by my neck of the woods?"

"You do. You and your uncle. I'm here to take you to his party."

She narrowed her gaze. "I don't mean to be rude but I don't remember seeing you on the guest list." And she'd kill whoever added him because tonight was to have been the only free time she had all day. Breathing time. Alone time without being tortured by wanting what she couldn't have.

"That's because when I called your secretary to find out your plans for the evening and she told me about the party, I called Sophie and invited myself." He treated her to his most endearing grin and her stomach flipped in anticipation.

Of what she didn't know. "I can't imagine Sophie just told you to come."

"Actually, she did. Are you ready to leave?"

Micki silently promised to murder her meddling sister. "I was going to drive my car so I could get home easier."

"I'll make sure you get home and you can take a cab to work and pick up your car tomorrow."

"Presumptuous."

"And bossy," he agreed with a laugh. "Stop fight-

ing me or you'll be late for the party. I'm leaving for
a series of away games tomorrow. I'm just asking you
to spend time with me tonight. Fun time. No thoughts
of problems or PR or anything stressful." He held out
his hand toward her. "Please."

She shut her eyes, tired of her constant internal
fight. She still held on to her notions about family and
she was adamant about not coming between Damian
and his. But he obviously wanted to spend time together and she desired the same thing. They didn't
have a future but why couldn't they have time *now?*

She opened her eyes and saw the opportunity to
forget her problems and just have a good time. "Yes.
Yes," she said, unable to resist.

He banged one side of his head with his hand.
"Say that again? I'm sure I heard you wrong."

She grinned. "You thought you'd have to work
harder, didn't you?"

"Maybe but I'm not complaining."

She placed her hand in his and pulled him close.

He met her gaze, desire flaring in his expression. "Micki…"

Her name was meant as a warning, she knew.

For the first time in what seemed like ages, she
heard Roper telling her to step up and take what
she wanted. One night of fun, she reminded herself and rose to her tiptoes to touch her mouth to
his. She lingered for a while, just savoring his

warm lips and his arousing masculine scent that had her stomach flipping in purely sensual anticipation. Micki's bones seemed to turn to liquid and she thought she'd melt right on the spot. When he lifted his hands and cupped her face, holding her head in place so he could take control, all the yearning and desire she'd been holding back rose to the surface.

He tipped her head and slid his mouth over hers, moving his lips deftly from side to side in a kiss that suddenly turned hot. Drugging. Her chest rose and fell and her breasts grew heavy, aching for his touch. She stepped closer, so her chest brushed against his, but the light friction did little to ease the building, burning need. She moaned and curled her hands around the fabric of his shirt. It was all she could do not to strip him right here and make up for lost time.

"Ahem. I know my eyes are blurry but I think I'm seeing clearly enough to know this ain't the place for hanky-panky," Uncle Yank said, interrupting them.

Damian jumped back first, while Micki closed her eyes so she could take a minute to compose herself. "Ever hear of knocking?" she asked her uncle.

"Ever hear of *behind closed doors?*" he retorted.

She let out a frustrated groan.

"I'm sorry," Damian said, stepping farther away. "That wasn't appropriate."

Micki blinked. "Oh this is great. You're apologizing to my uncle for kissing his twenty-six-year-old niece!"

"It's a matter of respect," both her uncle and Damian said at the same time.

"Well at least we agree on something." Uncle Yank nodded, obviously pleased.

Micki pushed her curls out of her face, completely mortified by the two men and their frank talk. Because she'd been such a tomboy, she'd never gone through a traditional dating phase that included Uncle Yank interrogating boyfriends. She didn't want to begin one now.

She stomped over to her desk and picked up her purse, which she'd forgotten the first time she'd tried to leave, and turned to the two men standing by the door. "Well, don't we have a party to get to?" she asked.

With any luck her uncle would have his driver waiting and she could get a minute alone with Damian before heading over to the large family gathering.

"We sure do. Let's get a move on so I can open my presents." Uncle Yank shoved Damian through the door first, then held it open for Micki.

"We'll meet you there," she promised.

"I thought we'd go together." Her uncle rubbed his palms in anticipation, not the least bit concerned that three was a crowd.

"I'll drive," Damian offered.

"Fine," Micki muttered. A short drive with her

uncle as chaperone wouldn't be so bad. They had all night to enjoy their time together.

And to see whether or not they planned to go any further than that kiss.

DAMIAN WANTED TO SURPRISE Micki and spend time with her before his road trip. Just the two of them hanging out, having fun, no talk of anything serious. Instead he'd ended up having to invite himself to Yank's party if he wanted to see Micki at all before he left for the week. He'd had to do some fancy talking to get Sophie to let him come.

Hell, he'd had to flat out beg. Damian knew he'd look out for his own sisters the same way. Considering Sophie had threatened to rip his hotshot balls off if he hurt Micki again, Damian considered himself fairly warned.

He'd been prepared for Micki to be wary and he hadn't been disappointed. He'd sensed the war going on inside her as she'd fought not to let herself get close to him, but somehow she'd ended up not only giving in, but treating him to a hot, sensual kiss.

He wasn't stupid enough to think they were picking up where they'd left off on the island and he knew damn well it wouldn't be a good idea. But he could admit to himself that the cold showers he'd been taking since she'd come back into his life just weren't cutting it. He was walking around with a permanent hard-on courtesy of Micki Jordan and that kiss had been an appetizer that had him hungry for more.

Now he and Micki, along with Yank and a curly-haired cream puff of a dog walked into the restaurant. "Morgan party," Yank said to the hostess, using his gruffest, meanest voice.

The young woman's gaze darted from Micki and Damian to Yank and then lower to his pet. "I'm sorry, Mr. Morgan, but there are no dogs allowed. The health code prohibits it," she explained.

"I may be going blind but I ain't deaf and I don't really think you just told me I can't bring my Seeing Eye dog into this establishment."

Micki stifled a groan.

The hostess peered down at the unkempt dog who resembled a mop more than a well-trained assistant. "Oh," she said, skeptically.

Seeing as how the thing kept pulling against his leash in a blatant attempt to take off at a run, Damian could understand the girl's confusion. "How about you talk to your manager and see if you could make an exception for the gentleman and his...er...guide dog," he suggested.

She nodded, and headed down a hallway, presumably to a back office.

Damian bit the inside of his cheek to keep from laughing. "So now the poodle's your guide dog?" he asked.

"It's not a poodle, it's a Labradoodle," Micki replied to Damian before turning to her uncle. "Why couldn't you leave Noodle home?"

"Noodle the Labradoodle?" Damian asked in disbelief.

"Don't you dare make fun of this girl. At least *she's* stood by me."

"Veiled reference to Lola," Micki whispered in Damian's ear.

"But why didn't you just leave her home?"

"Because she's my date." Yank's surly tone was obviously meant to warn Micki to back off and leave him alone. If Damian was a betting man, he'd wager she'd do neither.

Micki burst out laughing. "Do you really think Lola's going to be jealous of a dog? And do you really think a dog is going to keep you warm at night? Or are you counting on your stubborn streak to do it instead?"

"Missy, I'm still older than you and I know what's best."

"Then why are you still alone?"

"Okay, time out," Damian said, stepping between Yank and Micki. "Before one of you says something you'll regret."

At that moment, the hostess returned and told them, "The manager's willing to make an exception for you, Mr. Morgan, but you need to keep the dog in the private room."

"It's discrimination, that's what this is," Yank muttered.

"He'll keep the dog out of sight and thank you," Micki said to the other woman.

She nodded and led them the long way around the restaurant to the back room they'd rented for the event.

Yank went first and Damian followed behind, surprised when Micki reached back and grabbed his hand, pulling him alongside her.

"He's so tense about seeing Lola and Spencer Atkins together that he's close to insane." Micki gestured to her uncle and the dog.

"I can't imagine what he's going through, what with his eyesight deteriorating and the woman he loves having moved on."

"With his best friend."

Damian shook his head in sympathy. He glanced at Micki and realized that she'd been supporting him while her own situation wasn't exactly calm and quiet.

"I didn't realize about Yank's eyes or how much Lola's desertion has hurt him. You've been going through a lot of craziness yourself."

Micki paused outside the private party room. "Uncle Yank all but pushed Lola out. If he'd just given her an inkling about his real feelings instead of treating her like his slave and servant…"

"They have an odd history," Damian said.

"Amen."

"But between his health and the PR agency, you've been dealing with a lot." He lowered his head. "And then Carter spiked your drink, Yank pushed you off on me and sent you to the island—"

"We slept together, came home and went our separate ways and then you showed up at my office to tell me another woman might be carrying your child. Does that about sum it up?"

He waited for her voice to turn from matter-of-fact to bitingly sarcastic but it didn't happen. Instead she laid out the facts and started to laugh.

"Just what's so funny?" he asked.

"My soap opera of a life."

"I'm sorry for adding to the list."

Micki shook her head, an unbelievable smile on her lips. "Don't be. If you hadn't come around, I might be bored."

The sound of raised voices traveled from the room next door. "Something tells me being bored wouldn't be a remote possibility. Let's see what's going on."

Micki shot around him and he followed her into the room. Her uncle stood on a chair surrounded by decorations the family had strung around the room. Paper streamers were taped onto the ceiling, green and white helium balloons floated at will, and a store-bought Happy Birthday sign dangled precariously from the wall.

Damian wanted to ask Micki about the significance of such obviously childlike party symbols, but Yank was pontificating from on high. Loudly.

"...And since it's my birthday—and I thank you all very much for coming—I thought I got to decide who I wanted here. And I can tell you right now, I don't want to party with the lovebirds." Yank pointed first to Lola, then to Spencer Atkins, who were on separate sides of the room, whether out of deference to Yank's feelings or pure irony.

Yank's always wiry hair stood on end and his face flushed red with pure jealousy. Damian leveled a side-long glance at Micki. He couldn't be responsible for his actions either if she walked into a party with another man—a notion that rattled the hell out of him.

Suddenly Yank, who was still ranting from his perch in the center of the room, lost his balance. Without warning, he wobbled, pitched to one side and fell before anyone could help him.

"Uncle Yank!" All three of his nieces ran to the older man's side, but Lola got there first.

"You frustrating, crotchety, old coot!" she yelled, bending down at his side. "Where does it hurt?" She spread her hands all over him, her concern and love so real even Damian could feel it.

"My leg," he muttered and rubbed a place high on his hip.

Damian winced. "Somebody call for an ambulance," he yelled to the waiters nearby.

Yank was still yelling at Lola to get the hell away and let him be humiliated in peace.

Uncomfortable making them a spectacle, Damian stepped back.

Micki slipped her hand into his. "There's not much we can do. The hostess already called 911," she said.

"I ain't going in an ambulance," Yank blustered.

Noodle *woofed* in agreement and licked Yank's face, the dog's concern obvious.

Spencer Atkins stormed over to his best friend. The two men couldn't be more different in looks, Yank in his button-down Hawaiian shirt and Atkins in his double-breasted suit. "Shut the hell up, will you? Your mouth is what got you into trouble in the first place."

Yank scowled at his friend. "You stole my woman—"

"I was never yours to begin with. You didn't want me," Lola said, tears streaming down her cheeks and causing her makeup to run.

If she cared about that or her hair, which had fallen from its bun, or the fact that her blouse had pulled loose from the back of her skirt, she didn't show it. All her concern was lavished on the man lying on the floor.

"I wonder if he'll come around now," Micki whispered. "I mean it feels like his last chance. If he pushes Lola away this time, it's probably for good."

The overwhelming emotion of her family situation struck Damian hard. "Hopefully this'll smarten him up. It can happen to even the dumbest jock," he said, hoping to lighten the mood.

She laughed and hiccupped at the same time.

"Coming through." The paramedics came in and the next few minutes passed in a blur as they carefully loaded the older man onto the stretcher.

"Come on. I'll drive you and Sophie to the hospital." Damian tugged on her hand.

Annabelle and Vaughn were already halfway out the door. Micki relayed the offer to Sophie, who held a squirming Noodle in her arms, and they all headed for the exit.

At the door, Micki turned back to the dwindling crowd. "Happy birthday, Uncle Yank," she said to the almost empty room.

They reached the street as Yank was being placed in the ambulance. "I'll ride with you," Lola said.

"Why don't you ride with your boyfriend?" Yank asked.

"You old fool, he isn't my boyfriend," Lola said. "He's my friend."

"You dress like that for your friend?"

Apparently Yank's leg wasn't as badly bruised as his ego, Damian thought.

"I dressed like this for you. Spencer wouldn't care if I ran naked through Central Park! He's gay!" Lola said, then helped the ambulance men push the stretcher inside. She shot a look of regret at Spencer. "And for forcing me to reveal that secret, you can damn well ride alone. Spencer will take me to the hospital!"

The other woman stormed off, head held high.

Damian turned to Micki. "Is my mouth hanging open?" he asked.

"No more than mine is, I'm sure."

"Spencer Atkins is gay?" Damian ran a hand through his hair and laughed.

"What's so funny?"

He shook his head. "Your uncle just lost his last excuse. He's going to have to step up or step out of her life for good."

"Umm," she said in a low voice. "There's something you should know but you can't repeat it until it's official."

Damian raised an eyebrow. "You've got me curious."

"Well, the Hot Zone is going to be merging with Atkins Associates. It's mostly because of Uncle Yank's eyesight. It'll benefit him to have someone he trusts handling his clients."

"He trusts Atkins?"

Micki nodded. "Like a brother. Like you said about Lola, a strange relationship. Anyway, he agrees the merger's necessary but he's not taking it well. That probably explains his ranting back there. It's hard for him to give up his independence."

"Wow."

"Well, now you've been entrusted with privileged information. Repeat it and I may have to shoot you." She grinned and his heart twisted inside his chest.

His seven-day road trip was looking damn good about now.

CHAPTER TWELVE

TWO DAYS AFTER her uncle's accident, Micki was still annoyed with fate. Just when she'd decided to make use of the makeover changes she'd done inside and out and enjoy one more night with Damian, fate had held her to her original promise to keep her hands off.

Uncle Yank had broken his hip and needed immediate surgery to repair the damage done in the fall. Between recuperation and physical therapy, he was looking at a long haul. She spent the night of her uncle's party at the hospital. Since they'd sedated him for the pain, he hadn't been able to have a coherent conversation with Lola, so that relationship was still on hold.

Meanwhile Micki and Sophie were taking turns dog-sitting Noodle the Labradoodle who refused to eat, sleep or drink alone. Uncle Yank had spoiled the pooch rotten and if they didn't keep up his bad habits, the dog cried day and night. The neighbors had left notes of complaint on both Sophie's and Micki's doors, forcing them to take Noodle to work along with them. They'd also been alternating visiting hours at the hospital in order to take any burden off of Annabelle who'd been ordered by the doctor to take it easy on her feet and on her stress levels.

Though she wished her uncle hadn't hurt himself so badly, Micki didn't mind the added chaos in her own life. With Damian out of town, she was happy to have her mind occupied with other things. When she had time to think, she tortured herself with what might have happened had she not been stuck at the hospital their last night together.

Her body tingled at the thought of making love with Damian once more, of what his hot, hard body felt like pressed against hers as he drove into her again and again and again.

She sighed, then caught herself and realized she was moaning aloud while sitting in her office going over paperwork.

"Nice, Micki," she muttered.

"Woof!" Noodle answered her from her perch on the chair reserved for clients. Apparently Uncle Yank gave Noodle the run of the furniture as well as his life.

"You miss him, don't you, girl?"

The dog let out a whine, laid her head down on the expensive leather and covered her eyes with her paws.

"I'll take that as a yes," Micki said, laughing.

She checked her watch and realized it was almost time to relieve Sophie at Uncle Yank's bedside. It had been two days since the accident and the doctors wanted him up and out of bed to begin the difficult process of making him mobile in order to prevent pneumonia or infection from setting in. It wouldn't be fair to subject Sophie to that hell all by herself.

Micki grabbed her purse and walked out of her office. "Amy, if anyone needs me I'm at the hospital. I'll check in when I can, okay?"

"Don't worry about anything on this end. We've all got things covered. You just get your uncle back to his cranky old self."

"Put that way, it shouldn't be all that hard after all." Micki laughed. "Wish me luck," she said and headed for the hospital and the grouch of the century.

YANK LAY IN HIS HOSPITAL BED and pretended he was sleeping while Lola paced the floor, muttering to herself. Only a blind man couldn't see he had a choice to make, he thought wryly. He just wasn't ready to make it yet.

"Why the hell didn't you tell me Spencer was gay? Why didn't he tell me himself?"

Lola turned around, obviously startled he wasn't sleeping. "Why? Are you interested in him?" she asked.

"Ha-ha."

Lola walked toward the end of the bed. "How are you feeling?"

At the reminder, he winced and pushed the pain

medication button on his IV. "Like I broke my hip and had major surgery."

She nodded. "I figured."

"You're avoiding my questions."

She grabbed a chair and pulled it closer to his bedside, then smoothed her skirt and sat down.

Her new position gave him a direct view of the tank top beneath her blazer and her cleavage, which looked damn good for a woman her age.

"I didn't tell you because it wasn't my secret to tell and Spencer didn't tell you because…I don't know why. He kept it quiet because the industry's so male-oriented, he didn't want to make any of his clients uncomfortable."

"That's bullshit," Yank muttered. "Nobody cares about his personal life, only his ability to negotiate the best damn contract he can."

Lola's eyes sparkled with appreciation and he squirmed beneath her gaze. He wasn't used to her looking at him with anything other than frustration and disgust. He'd nearly forgotten what her approval felt like.

It felt good.

"I sent Sophie home for a shower and Micki's coming back in time for the physical therapist to help get you out of bed."

"I can't move."

"You have to move or else you'll end up with

twice as many problems. Here." She shoved a con-
traption the night nurse had brought by. "Breathe into
this and make sure you get that pressure thing up to
ten. You don't want to get pneumonia on top of everything else."

He scowled. "Damn bossy woman."

"And you love me, Yank Morgan—don't tell me
you don't."

"Even if I did, and I ain't admitting nothing yet,
don't you think you deserve a helluva lot better than
a man who's going blind and now has a busted hip?"

She glared at him, the frustration and annoyance
back full force. "Don't you think that's my decision
to make? That's been my point all along."

"Are you saying I could tell you I love you just so
you could turn around and make the 'decision' to say
I'm not what you bargained for anymore?" he asked,
outraged by the thought.

Lola treated him to a smile he couldn't figure out.
"I'm not saying yes or no. Life's full of risks and it's
time you took one." She rose from her seat. "One beyond standing up on a chair and ranting like a fool,"
she muttered and headed for the door.

"Where are you going?" It wasn't easy to admit
but he didn't want her to leave.

"I have a lunch date and then I have to get back
to work. I promised the girls I'd start going over the
files and figure out who can cover your clients while

you're laid up. The merger's got to be on the fast track now."

He'd had a hard enough time swallowing his pride and agreeing to join his firm with Atkins but he couldn't let the agency flounder and the girls' PR business suffer. What with the young agents nipping at his heels, it was a smart business move. That didn't mean he had to like it.

"Okay. Make sure Irwin draws up the paperwork. I want my lawyer doing the drafting," he said to Lola.

"Then I suggest you talk to one of the girls and have them arrange it. I don't work for you anymore, remember? And I didn't hear *I love you, Lola,* or *I'm sorry, Lola,* come out of your mouth, so I don't really feel compelled to help you out." She reached for her purse, which had been lying on the moveable tray. "Besides, I'm still working for Spence and until the merger's complete, that would be a conflict of interest."

Yank punched his covers with his hand. "Of all the—"

"Good morning," Micki said in a too-cheerful voice as she walked into the room.

The little peacemaker had probably heard the arguing from the hall and decided to come fix things.

"What's going on?" she asked.

Lola smiled and kissed her on the cheek. "Nothing you need to worry about. I was just leaving, so he's all yours."

"Oh joy," Micki said, laughing.

"When are you coming back?" Yank asked Lola.

She turned. Her eyes held a fierce determination he'd seen only once before, when she'd given him her ultimatum and then walked out.

His stomach churned in anticipation.

"I'll be back when you have something to say that I want to hear." She waved goodbye and walked out the door. Out of his room and out of his life.

"Pardon my French but I suggest you shit or get off the pot, Uncle Yank. The woman may have the patience of a saint but even saints have their limits and she's obviously reached hers," Micki said.

He leaned back in his bed, everything in his aging body aching. "I need a nap."

"You need to get out of that bed," the chipper physical therapist they'd met yesterday said as she strode into the room.

And with that, Yank entered a hell that was second only to watching Lola leave him again.

THE RENEGADES SPLIT the two-game series with Los Angeles. Tomorrow was a travel day, which gave the team some freedom tonight although Coach Donovan insisted they remain in the hotel and hit their rooms by midnight. Damian sat at the hotel bar, nursing a beer with his teammates, participating in jokes and wondering how Yank and Micki were holding up.

He didn't plan on calling Micki, thus proving to himself that while he was on the road, only his career mattered. But that hadn't stopped him from tossing and turning in his cold, lonely hotel bed, wondering what she was doing, what she was wearing to bed and most of all whether or not she was missing him.

He rose and walked over to the bar to order a fresh drink.

"Hey." A drunken Carter sauntered up beside him.

Although Damian had watched him down drink after drink tonight, Carter had been unusually quiet and subdued this road trip, making Damian wonder what trouble the rookie had up his sleeve.

"How's it going?" Damian asked.

The other man shrugged. "It's going."

Damian waited for Carter to leave, but he lingered, then grabbed a stool and sat down.

As team captain, Damian had listened to the guys when they'd had problems that might interfere with their game and he'd given advice based on his years in the league, but in the short time Carter had been with the Renegades, he'd never come to Damian for a damn thing. As far as Damian could tell, Carter needed no one except his ego.

As Micki had once said, he was young. He'd learn.

The way the kid lingered now, apparently he wanted something.

"Two Guinnesses," Damian said to the bartender,

ordering Carter's drink of choice tonight. Damian waited for them to be served and turned to the rookie. "Okay, what gives?"

The younger man tipped his head to one side, then raised his glass. "To peace."

His words took Damian off guard. "As I recall, you rejected the same offer a few weeks back."

"A lot's happened in a few weeks. Enough to make me respect my *elders*."

With Carter's irreverence, the tension eased from Damian's neck and shoulders. "That's the smart-ass rookie I know."

"Tell me something." Carter wasn't slurring his words but his tone definitely indicated he was drunk and Damian knew the other man wouldn't be talking to him now if he were cold sober.

"What's that?" Damian asked.

"How the hell do you do it?"

Damian raised an eyebrow. "Do what?"

"Always come out on top, smelling like a rose." Carter nudged his elbow against Damian's. "Come on, share your secrets."

Damian glanced at the other man's glassy eyes and rolled his own. "You really are trashed. How the hell can you think I come out smelling like a rose when my life's for shit right now?"

Carter glanced away. "Well yeah, but you'll come out of it. You always do."

Damian groaned. "If anything it comes down to how you live your life. I may be a selfish SOB at times but I never deliberately intend to screw with anyone else. Maybe it's good karma. Then again, good karma wouldn't have me with a pregnant ex-lover."

Carter shook his head. "I hear you, man. I haven't exactly been living my life in a way that has much to do with goodwill towards men, if you know what I mean." He took a long pull of his beer.

"You've been a prick," Damian agreed.

"Yeah. And it isn't working for me too well. I'm thinking I've got to figure out your angle, since you seem to be doing something right." He slung an arm over Damian's shoulder in a brotherly gesture Damian didn't trust for a minute.

Damian wrapped his hands around the beer glass. "So what's with the change in attitude? Coach giving you shit?"

Carter raised his head, meeting Damian's gaze. "I'm giving me shit. Actually, a woman's giving me shit. Do you know what it's like to fall for someone who won't give you the time of day?" He let out a sarcastic laugh. "No of course you don't. All woman fall at your feet."

"Tell me something, Carter, because this jealousy of yours is getting old. Would you really want to be in my shoes? Thirty-five, one year left on your contract and a pregnant woman claiming you're having a kid you never wanted or planned?"

The rookie burst out laughing, taking Damian by surprise.

"What the hell's so funny?"

Carter rested an arm on the bar and leaned toward Damian. "Well here's the thing. My woman is *your* woman and as long as you're in the picture, she won't have anything to do with me. Won't return my calls. So would I want to be in your shoes? Hell yeah." With that astonishing proclamation, he downed the rest of his beer and gestured for yet another.

"I think you've had enough. We're playing tomorrow," Damian reminded him. He sifted through Carter's words in his mind. "My woman's your woman? Micki Jordan?" Even as Damian said her name, he knew that the notion was an impossible one.

Carter's belly laugh caused more than one person at the bar to turn and glance their way. "Don't you see the irony? You don't even want Carole and she's slobbering for whatever you'll give her. I'm willing to take full responsibility for the kid and she's discounted me like I'm dirt."

Nothing the guy said made sense but if Damian had to guess, he figured Carole and Carter had slept together and Carter had fallen hard. Problem was, Damian had hooked them up just a few weeks ago so unfortunately there was no reason for Carter to "take responsibility." "Listen, buddy. You sober up and we'll talk more tomorrow."

"You're dismissing me the same way she did."

Damian rose to his feet. "Do I need to remind you about the facts of life? Even if you slept with Carole, she says she's almost three months pregnant. That makes you an impossible candidate."

"Not if I slept with her for the first time back in April, which I did. To get back at you. I just didn't expect to develop feelings for the woman."

Hot damn, Damian thought, he'd been right all along. Carole had been sleeping around while they were together. He hadn't figured Carter in her travels, but what the hell. Anyone she'd been with gave him that much more hope that he wouldn't be tied to her for eternity.

"So when I handed her over to you?" Damian asked.

"We had a good laugh," Carter admitted. "Oh and while we're spilling our guts?"

Carter was spilling, Damian was listening, but he wasn't about to remind him and ruin the momentum. He wondered what else the rookie was about to confess.

"Yeah?"

He shook his head and actually looked sheepish for a brief moment. "I'm the one who led the photographers to Lacie's. I hoped you'd get caught with your pants down and get some negative press for a change."

The confirmation of something Damian had suspected all along should have infuriated him but, coupled with Carter's admission about Carole, Damian found himself in a forgiving mood.

"And instead they decided I'd rescued Micki and I was a hero. Must've pissed you off."

Carter nodded. "Enough that when you didn't show up for practice and Sophie Jordan said you were doing rehab work at your island home, I called the airport and had them hijack your bags." Again, the other man glanced away, obviously unable to look his captain in the eye.

"What else?" Damian asked in a lethally low tone, his forgiveness now coming in short supply.

Carter rose to his feet and stumbled unsteadily. "Promise you won't hit me."

This had to be bad, Damian thought and winced before even hearing the news. "Just spit it out."

"I was the one who leaked the pregnancy news to the press and before you say I'm an ass, I'll do it for you. I'm sorry. I didn't mean to hurt Carole. I was just looking to get back at you." He rubbed the back of his neck. "Which doesn't make it any better, I know. But losing Carole taught me a lesson and I'm damn sorry." He hung his head.

Damian didn't know how much was drunken rambling, how much was truth, but at least Carter had developed a conscience. Enough to confess his sins, and those confessions had Damian wondering. And gave him legitimate reason to demand a paternity test from Carole without feeling guilty.

"Let's go get you sobered up," Damian said, not bothering to address anything Carter had admitted.

"You aren't going to kill me?"

Damian glanced at Carter's pale face. "Nah. I think I'll spare you. But if this repentant stuff is all an act and you pull a stunt like that again? I'll be using your balls for batting practice."

Carter grinned, a drunken grin. "Fair enough."

"Carole know about any of this?" Damian asked.

Carter shook his head. "But I'm going to tell her because, starting tomorrow, I'm turning over a new, responsible leaf. She's gonna see I want to be in her life even if the kid turns out to be yours."

Damian shook his head and prodded the drunken man toward the bank of elevators in the hall, all the while wondering if fate would be kind to Damian Fuller, the man who'd been given everything.

And hand him this one thing more.

MICKI OPENED A BAG of Tostitos she'd bought in the hospital cafeteria. She popped open a can of Diet Coke for herself and put Uncle Yank's can on his bedside tray for him to enjoy later. While he dozed, she curled up on the chair in his private room and settled in to watch TV. Despite her best intentions, the channel landed on WPIX and the Renegades came into view on the small screen.

The Renegades were in the field, down by two runs in the seventh, no outs, bases loaded. She watched a ball fly toward center field. She raised the volume.

"…And Fuller goes back, back to the far wall. He's there. He jumps. His hand hits the wall as the ball lands in his glove but he manages to hold on to it! Fuller prevents a grand slam but can he keep the number of runs down to a manageable level?"

Holding her breath, Micki leaned forward in her seat.

"Rodriguez scores on the sacrifice fly! Fuller throws to third and Baressi holds up at second base. Damian Fuller keeps the damage to one run."

Micki let out a long stream of air. "That was close."

"He's got some mileage left in him yet," Uncle Yank said from his bed.

She turned. "You're up!" she said, surprised.

"What do you expect when you blast the television like that?"

"How are you feeling?"

"It hurts."

She knew what the admission cost him. "Sophie's been making phone calls. We're getting you the best physical therapist there is. You'll be up and about in no time," she promised her uncle.

He nodded. "You're good girls. I don't tell you that often enough."

Micki smiled. "Yes you do." She rose, walked to the bed and leaned over to place a kiss on his cheek.

"Oh shit. Make it louder," her uncle said, suddenly agitated and pointing wildly toward the TV.

Micki turned and grabbed the remote, which was wired to his bed. She raised the sound but she'd already caught sight of Damian in the outfield, surrounded by his coach and trainers.

"…And Fuller is helped off the field. We don't know the full extent of the injury or if it's related to his last stint on the DL but as soon as anything comes our way, we'll report it back to you."

Micki hit the mute button once more. She met her uncle's worried gaze with one of her own. Her stomach plummeted because she knew, whether or not this injury kept him out of the game, Damian was going to take it as yet another sign that the career he loved was coming to an end.

"This can't be good," she said aloud.

Her uncle shook his head. "But you can't fight age forever," he said, thoughtfully.

Micki wondered if he was referring to Damian or to himself.

CHAPTER THIRTEEN

DAMIAN'S SEVEN-DAY ROAD TRIP was cut short by a plane ride home to see Dr. Maddux and undergo a full battery of tests on his wrist, including X-rays and an electromyogram that recorded the electrical activity of the nerve and muscle cells in his wrist. Maddux said he'd call him with the results, but it didn't take a damn machine to tell Damian that there was pressure on the nerve and swelling there, too.

Based on the tingling numbness and almost complete lack of feeling in his thumb, Damian figured it didn't matter much what the diagnosis was, his season just might be finished.

Not to mention what was left of his career.

He poured himself a second shot of whiskey and sat down in his favorite leather chair in his den. He left the plasma screen black, not wanting to flip channels and see what was happening in a world that for him was falling apart. How much more crap would be dumped on his head before it was all over?

Damian wondered, feeling sorry for himself and not giving a good goddamn.

The doorbell rang and he ignored it. He wasn't in the mood for company, especially his sisters, the only people besides his parents that Rafael, the doorman, would allow up without calling first.

The buzzer sounded a second time and then a third. Obviously Rafael had told them he was home. With a curse, Damian rose and headed for the door, intending to kiss whichever well-meaning sibling was behind it hello and then goodbye.

"Don't you realize when someone doesn't answer the door he doesn't want to be bothered?" he asked at the same time he pulled it open wide.

"Hello, Oscar," Micki said with a big smile.

He scratched his head, his slightly inebriated brain not comprehending her reference.

"Oscar the Grouch. Now let me in so we can talk." Without waiting for permission, she ducked under his arm and strode inside.

He slammed the door shut behind himself. Micki was the one person he wanted to see and the person he'd been avoiding. He figured he'd dumped enough of his problems on her without adding his injury to the list.

He followed behind her, taking in the sweet curve of her rear end encased in tight denim and the hint of skin at her waist peeking out below the cropped top. Her hips swayed as she walked and his groin grew thick and hard with wanting her. At least some part of his broken-down body still worked.

"So how'd you get Rafael to let you in?" He slammed the door shut behind him.

She shrugged. "I was just honest. I told him you'd been through a lot and you needed a friend. He looked me in the eye and buzzed me right in. I think if I'd said I'd come to seduce you he'd have tossed me out on my rear end."

Damian laughed despite himself. "He's definitely done that before for me. He's a bouncer in his spare time."

"You need security to keep the women away, huh?"

He could tell she was deliberately keeping the conversation light for his sake and decided the hell with it. He wasn't in a light mood and she might as well know it going in.

"Right now I want everyone to stay away." He caught himself immediately. "Except you." He hadn't wanted company but with Micki he didn't feel the need to entertain her or make small talk.

She'd never been to his apartment, yet she made herself at home, heading straight for the den and his oversize club chair. Since she'd taken his seat, Damian eased himself beside her on the arm of the chair.

"So how bad is it?" she asked, reaching for his good hand, the one not in a brace.

"Can't feel my thumb and the rest of the hand tingles like it's asleep."

"What do the doctors say?"

He shrugged. "They're being deliberately vague till the tests are read. They're still mentioning carpal tunnel and a pinched nerve but nobody's willing to commit to anything."

Micki swallowed hard. She'd come here because he'd ignored her calls on both his cell and his home number, and she'd realized he was probably holed up here throwing a pity party for himself. She glanced at the half-full glass of whiskey and frowned. She hated that she'd been right.

Damian was the least self-pitying man she knew but the potential for bad news was strong and he'd spent who knows how long denying the inevitable.

"Don't take this the wrong way and jump all over me, okay?" she asked.

He tipped his head towards her. "I promise not to take it the wrong way. As for jumping you—"

She laughed. "Those weren't my exact words."

"They work well enough for me," he said in a husky tone she couldn't mistake.

A tremor of awareness shot through her but she forced herself to keep her focus. He might not realize it, but he needed sound advice and she was here to give it to him. "Didn't you realize something like this would happen eventually?"

"Ever hear of denial?"

She thought of her Uncle Yank. "I'm vaguely familiar with the term. Look, you're thirty-five and have a multimillion-dollar contract. You've been selected for ten consecutive All-Star appearances, you've won an All-Star MVP award, five Silver Slugger Awards and ten consecutive Golden Gloves and that's not the half of your accomplishments. That's a lot to be proud of no matter when you have to step down." She glanced up and noticed the satisfied expression that curved his mouth into a sexy grin.

"Has someone been reading up on me?" he asked.

She nudged him in the side with her elbow. "Don't be so arrogant. I just happen to know these things."

He burst out laughing.

She ignored the burn in her cheeks. "My point is—"

"I get your point, Micki. I just can't accept it."

"Well maybe it's time you do." She let out an exasperated groan. "Maybe it's time that spoiled little boy who thinks everything comes so easily acknowledges that his time in the field and at the plate has passed. That doesn't mean the future doesn't hold great things."

She slid forward and rose from her seat, certain he needed time and space to absorb her words.

"Wait." His hand on her shoulder stopped her.

"I think I've given you enough to think about. I should go."

His hand curled tighter around her, his fingertips branding her with their heat. "What if I don't want you to leave?"

Micki's heart skipped a beat, maybe more, before it kicked in once more. "You aren't upset about what I said?"

He let out a harsh laugh. "Sure I am. That doesn't mean I'm upset with you."

She turned to face him. "Nice distinction. Another way of not dealing with your feelings?" she asked lightly, though how she could speak with both his large, warm hand and his chocolate gaze on her was beyond her.

Her mouth had grown dry and not because of the sexual tension, though it was strong. Something had changed between them.

For the first time since they'd returned from the island, for the first time since the paternity scandal, Micki truly felt as if they were back in their easy, comfortable state.

And because of that connection, the teasing took on more sensual, provocative undertones. Desire raced through her at the thought.

He raised his hand and cupped her cheek. "Know what I like about you?"

"What's that?" she asked, trembling as she spoke.

His thumb caressed her face. "You don't pull any punches. You tell it like it is. And you aren't afraid to go head-to-head with me."

"I learned from the best." Once again she thought of her uncle.

"Well you should know something. Your guts and your spirit? They turn me on."

His voice was gruff and, combined with his purely masculine heat, it turned *her* on. Still, before she'd consider sleeping with him, she had to make some things clear.

"Damian?"

"Hmm?" His gaze bored into hers.

She gathered her courage because what she was about to say was the last thing she wanted, but she had no choice. "This can't be more than a one-time thing."

One more time together before the paternity results came in. Micki knew that once they determined whether or not he was the father, she'd lose him one way or another. To his new life with a baby or to his old life that he couldn't seem to let go of.

He stared into her eyes, his hand caressing her face, remaining eerily silent as he pondered her words. She trembled with passion and desire, ready to jump him at a moment's notice. But Micki needed confirmation that they agreed on the ground rules.

She swallowed hard. "Do you understand?"

A muscle ticked in his cheek. "I ought to. They're my damn rules."

It had been a while since she had had the freedom to act on her feelings and she did so now. Slowly she reached out and smoothed her fingers over the lines of tension on his face, trying not to let her emotions show. "And? Do you want to go along?"

"I want," he said in a deep voice. "I want you badly."

His words freed her from worry or from thinking about anything except tonight. A seductive smile curved her lips.

He slid his hand from her cheek to her shoulders, his fingertips dipping below her neckline. His touch was hot on her skin, his intent to tease and arouse obvious—and effective.

She trembled, her nipples puckering into hard knots beneath her lightweight T-shirt as she reached for the opening on his collared polo shirt.

He stopped her, grabbing her wrist with his good hand. "I think I can maneuver things better in the bedroom."

"Tonight you don't have to worry about maneuvering or using that wrist at all," she promised him. "Tonight it's all about you."

Damian appreciated the sentiment but he wanted to make love to Micki hard and fast, to block out everything around him but her.

"Show me the bedroom," she said, her voice low and husky.

Apparently she was calling the shots tonight. Fine by him. He didn't want to think, not even about her words. She hadn't sugarcoated her feelings and because he trusted her judgment, he'd think about what she said—but he'd do it tomorrow. As she'd pointed out, they had another agenda for the rest of the night.

Her hand in his, he led her down the hallway ending at his large master suite. She stepped ahead of him toward the bed, a place he'd only slept alone. Despite all the women who'd passed through his life, he'd protected and held onto his privacy both on the island and here at his apartment. Though Micki had shown up uninvited, he had no second thoughts about sharing his personal space. She'd already become intimately involved in his life and having her here felt right.

The bedroom lights were on dimmers and he lowered them enough to set the mood. He joined her by the bed, where she'd already begun to strip off her clothes. He had every intention of following her lead.

He reached for the snap on his jeans just as Micki came beside him wearing a nude-colored bra that revealed soft mounds of flesh and delectable cleavage, along with her darkened nipples pressing enticingly into the see-through lace. His gaze fell lower, to her flat stomach and matching panties, also nude, that teased him with a glimpse of triangular shadow.

"You're fast," he said, approvingly.

"Aah, but I intend to go slow." A provocative smile lifted her lips.

She pulled his shirt from his waistband, then slipped the garment up and off easily. Instead of turning to his jeans next, she dipped her head and placed her lips against his abdomen. With excruciating patience, she teased him, running her mouth over his bare chest, leaving a moist trail in her wake. Cool air rushed over his dampened skin and he shivered.

"You like this?" Micki asked, at the same time she splayed her hands over his chest, her fingertips grazing his nipples, turning them into hardened peaks.

He let out a rough growl as desire shot through him, the ache traveling straight to his groin. If she wasn't going to move things along, then he intended to. He needed her too badly.

He unzipped his jeans and quickly shoved them aside.

"Commando," she murmured. "Now that I like." With both hands, she eased him onto the bed and once he was on his back in the center, she straddled his waist.

He slid his hand to the back of her neck, pulling her close for a hot kiss, holding nothing back. He thrust his tongue into her open mouth, delving into the deepest recesses and finding so much more than an answer to his sexual need. Kissing her soothed his pain and eased the ache in his soul.

She squirmed on top of him, her body grinding against his, as desperate as he was to get closer despite the silky barrier that still separated them. He hooked his one thumb into the thin band and slid her underwear down her soft thighs.

"Please tell me you have protection," she murmured.

He nodded. "Not because I bring women here, but yeah, I do." She exhaled a sigh of relief and he laughed. "It's good to know the wanting's mutual," he said, tucking her hair behind her ear.

She grinned. "Very mutual."

He retrieved the foil packet from his nightstand and handed it over to her. "The hand's not working well enough for me to do it myself." He eyed her warily as he pushed himself against the pillows and waited for her to take over.

She ripped the foil, an expression of concentration on her face. She held up the condom to the light, eyeing it this way and that. "Is there a trick to this?"

"You'll figure it out." He clenched his jaw, his throbbing arousal making it difficult to focus.

His groin jutted upward and she began to roll the thin sheath over him, her fingers brushing his penis. Her lack of skill and yet complete determination was endearing and arousing at the same time.

Once protected, she straddled him, poised directly over where he needed her most. Not about to be completely passive, he reached out and tested her wetness, slipping his finger between her damp folds.

"Oh wow." She shuddered and clenched her legs around his hand.

Damian grinned. "At least I haven't lost my touch."

"Nobody will ever accuse you of that," she said and began an easy slide down his shaft.

She was hot and tight, and fit like a glove. He let out a prolonged groan, his body shuddering from the need to thrust. But he wouldn't, not until she'd begun her ascent and he knew he could take her along with him.

Damian already felt the urge to come but he wasn't about to do it alone. He thrust upward, making sure she felt the full force of their connection. A connection he welcomed as much as he fought to control.

She grabbed his hand and began a steady rocking motion, grinding herself against him each time she encased him completely in her luscious body. He shifted, adjusting his weight and thrusting upward, over and over again.

They reached a mutual rhythm, one that came so naturally it would have been frightening if he'd had the time to think. He didn't. He could only focus on sensation. On feeling.

She was equally lost, her breath coming faster and faster and faster. Soft cries escaped from the back of her throat and her nails dug into his shoulders as she rode him harder, her body pulling him along for the ride.

HOT NUMBER

Finally her body squeezed even tighter around his. The closer he came to release, the thicker and harder he grew. His muscles tightened and he lost himself inside her.

In more ways than one.

MICKI SCOURED THE CABINETS in Damian's kitchen but there wasn't much to eat or even use to create a meal. Instead she pulled out the box of cocoa mix and used the microwave to make hot chocolate. Just as she finished the preparations, Damian strode into the room, wearing a pair of gray sweats and nothing more.

The man took her breath away. Her emotions were mixed, a bittersweet feeling washing over her because her one night had passed. No matter how spectacular it had been, it was over.

But not until she walked out of this apartment. Placing the two mugs on the table, she joined him. "You're quiet this morning," she said, wondering what he had on his mind.

He glanced into his cup. "Did I tell you that Carter and I had a man-to-man talk while I was on the road?"

She shook her head. "You didn't mention it."

"I guess I had other things on my mind."

"So what'd the swine have to say?" She leaned forward on her hand.

"He took a stab at being human."

She raised an eyebrow. "Are you kidding? What's he really want?"

"My thoughts exactly but I don't think you're going to believe the answer." A smile curved his mouth and she was tempted to taste the hot chocolate right off his lips. "He wants Carole."

Micki choked on her drink.

"There's more. Apparently their relationship began way before I ever handed Carole over to him. They hooked up back in April."

Micki opened and closed her mouth. "Are you saying the baby could be his?"

"Could be. He's had it in for me for a long time. He's been after my job, my woman—he told me himself." Damian shook his head. "He was the one who called the press that night at Lacie's and the one who sidetracked our luggage. And, he was also the guy who revealed the paternity scandal to the papers."

"Quite a stand-up guy," Micki muttered, never forgetting for a minute that he'd deliberately gotten her drunk that night, which had led to her public humiliation.

Damian rocked back in his chair. "I wanted to throttle him but then I realized thanks to his being a slimeball, he may have taken the load off my shoulders. And the kicker is? He wants to. Even if the baby's mine, he wants to marry Carole."

Micki gnawed on her lower lip. "This is so bizarre I don't know whether to cheer or hit him with his own bat."

Damian nodded. "Join the club."

"When do you plan on talking to Carole?" Micki asked.

His expression turned thoughtful. "The series of away games are over soon. As soon as Carter's home, I figured we'd do it together. Hard to believe the guy who sabotaged me might be my only chance at freedom."

More than anything, Micki wanted Damian free from Carole and this mess but at the same time, she knew what freedom meant to Damian. No personal responsibilities, no heavy-duty relationships, just a man and his career, she thought.

A man minus Micki.

DAMIAN GLANCED DOWN at his hand. He knew better than to attempt to flex. The pain wasn't worth the effort and immobilization was the best medicine for now. Doctor's orders, Damian thought. The doc had called with his test results soon after Micki had left.

Damian was glad she'd missed the call so he could wallow in his grief in private before sharing the news. Apparently he had nerve damage or at least slight nerve damage. Once this flare-up subsided, he could choose to finish out the season, but if he continued to play, he'd be guaranteeing himself an awful lot of time on the disabled list next year and risking nerve damage that would likely be both major and permanent.

Which meant he had to make a decision. If he were honest with himself, the time had been coming for a while now. He just hadn't wanted to face it. Denial at its best, as he'd told Micki.

Micki. Who else would have the guts to throw his inadequacies in his face and make it seem like she was doing him a favor? He bit back a grin at the feisty way she'd confronted him. At the time, he'd silently applauded her nerve.

Hell, the verbal slap she'd provided had awakened something dead inside him. And that spunk of hers turned him on. When he was with her, not just in her bed but by her side, the bad didn't feel nearly as awful as he knew it should.

Damian wasn't a man who wanted women in his life or interfering in his business. That rule didn't apply to Micki. Ever since that New Year's Eve kiss, something had been building between them. He'd denied it, a tactic he now realized was his specialty when he didn't want to face an issue. And when denial had no longer worked, he'd ignored the attraction as if it would disappear. But their chemistry had been stronger than he knew and by the time he'd taken her to bed, she'd already become a part of him.

The best part, he thought. Even then he must have

sensed how much he needed her because he'd blindly shown up on her doorstep after Carole's declaration and he'd wanted her by his side ever since. She—and her family—had given him direction and instructions on steps to take in order to cope with the scandal, and somehow she'd kept him focused when he could have spiraled out of control in a panicked frenzy. She'd refused to let him give in to self-pity over his hand and showed no mercy when it came to making him face the future.

What future? he wondered. With the exception of saving his money for a rainy day, he'd never planned for a day without baseball.

"Maybe it's time you should," he said, mimicking Micki's words.

But first he had to deal with Carole and figure out that part of his life. Between him and Carter, Damian was looking at a fifty-fifty shot the baby was his. Not good odds.

But he believed he could handle the possibility. As Micki had correctly pointed out, he had the best role model to make it happen. If the kid was his, Damian knew he'd be as good a father as his old man had been to him. He knew this thanks to Micki.

Damian rubbed his eyes and walked to the window overlooking the park below. Man, he was tired and not just from making love to Micki late into the night.

He was emotionally drained. For many reasons.

Not the least of which was Micki herself. What would her role be in his life once he no longer had the baby scandal as an excuse to keep her by his side.

CHAPTER FOURTEEN

DAMIAN AND CARTER STRODE UP to Carole's apartment door together. They'd agreed not to tell her they were coming to Florida, afraid she'd have time to regroup. They wanted her moment of realization to be genuine. They wanted to see her reaction to the fact that both men knew the truth. At the very least, their alliance ought to at least frighten her into being honest. There was a damn good chance even she didn't know whose baby it was, but they were going to find out.

"You ready?" Damian asked Carter.

"As I'll ever be." He rolled his shoulders beneath his sport jacket.

The kid had dressed up for the occasion. Damian glanced down at his ripped jeans and good-luck jersey and shrugged. It wasn't like he wanted to make a good impression at the moment. As for Carter, Damian had to admire the kid for going after what he wanted, this time in an honest way.

Poor Carole wouldn't know what hit her when Carter got down on one knee. Damian had no idea how she felt about the rookie and though he shouldn't care after what Carter had put him through, he couldn't help but hope Carole would see some good in Carter and give him a chance, for her sake as well as the baby's. No matter who the biological father turned out to be.

Damian drew a steadying breath and knocked on the door. He heard Carole's muffled voice and then the door swung open wide.

"Damian?" Her gaze shifted to the man beside him. "Carter?" The color drained from her cheeks. "What are you doing here?"

"I take it you mean what are we doing here together?" Damian asked.

She didn't reply, just stood and stared. Obviously she hadn't been expecting company because she wore no makeup, a pair of baggy sweats and an oversize T-shirt that accentuated her breasts, made even larger by the pregnancy.

He didn't think he'd ever seen her looking so... real. For the first time, Damian saw beyond the artificial persona she deliberately put on and caught a glimpse of the woman Carter had fallen in love with. For his sake, Damian hoped Carole's heart was equally real.

"I don't think you want to have this discussion in the hallway," Carter said, stepping forward. He grasped her elbow. "Come on, babe. Let us inside."

She squirmed and waved her hand, gesturing for them to enter.

Damian understood her discomfort. He felt it, too, and he stood by the window while Carter made himself comfortable on the couch.

Beside him, Carole clasped and unclasped her hands. "I can't imagine why you're here together," she said, letting out a nervous laugh.

"Oh I think you can," Damian muttered.

"You were with both of us around the same time," Carter said calmly. He grasped her hand. "Now I don't hold it against you, babe. We just want to know whose baby you're carrying."

She blinked, as if stunned by the statement. "I told you it's Damian's." Her voice rose to a high pitch.

"Yes, you did. Unfortunately those are just words. We need proof."

Damian remained by the window, separated from the couple and distanced emotionally, but his heart pounded a mile a minute and his throat was raw. "We used protection," he reminded her.

"So did we," Carter said.

Damian paced the length of the window, turned and walked back again. "So unless you have a magic way of determining whose kid this is, we need to run a paternity test."

"No!" She shouted the word and both men jerked their heads her way. "It's Damian's," she insisted.

Damian saw the other man's jaw clench and could practically read his mind. Once again Carter was coming in second to the almighty Damian Fuller.

"Why is it so damn important that he be the father?" Carter asked.

Carole wiped a tear from her face and then another.

Sensing she had reasons he didn't need to hear, Damian stepped toward her. "I'm going to leave you two alone to talk. And when we're finished, I would be grateful if you came back to New York with Carter so we can have the test done. If not, we can do it down here, but Carter would miss a game and that's really not fair to him—or to the team. They need him."

Shock registered on Carter's face. Unadulterated awe. "You mean it?"

"Hell, rookie, of course I mean it. In the last week, you've become more than a man I just might be able to admire one day. You're a damn good player." As much as Damian spoke a growing truth, he said the words for Carole's benefit. Because she seemed leery of the notion of having Carter's kid.

She was selling the man short, Damian thought. Not that Carter hadn't done everything to earn the reputation, but he was changing and he deserved the benefit of the doubt.

Carole hadn't met Damian's gaze. "Carole?" he said.

She lifted her damp eyes.

"I mean what I said. I want that test done even if I have to get a court order to do it."

She blinked. "Don't do this, Damian."

"It won't be an issue," Carter promised, his hand still covering hers, only now he squeezed it tight.

Damian nodded and headed for the door, trusting Carter to handle Carole. He hoped like hell his gut instinct was right and the kid not only had a good heart, but finally had grown up, too.

CARTER WAITED until Damian walked out before turning to Carole. With no makeup and everyday clothing on, she appeared frail and vulnerable. He'd never seen her look more beautiful. It made him all the more anxious. Because if he didn't get every word right, he'd lose her forever.

"We're alone. So how about you explain to me why it's so important that Fuller be the baby's father?" he asked.

Her hands shook as she reached for the box of tissues on the end table. "You have to understand that I didn't set him up. I didn't want to be pregnant."

Carter nodded. "I understand. So…"

"He's established. He has his career set and he's financially more than able to provide—"

Rick felt as if he'd been sucker punched. "So that's it? He's got money and I don't?"

"My mother never knew who my father was. We

never knew where our next meal was coming from. Each guy she met she hoped would be Mr. Right. Most of them couldn't put a meal on the table." She shook her head, the tears flowing down her cheeks.

Carter swallowed hard. "I'm not as wealthy as Fuller yet, but I more than get by."

She raised her moist gaze to his. "What if you get hurt before your first big contract? What if you have a bad season and nobody wants you or arbitration doesn't work out?"

"What if I get hit by a bus crossing the street? Babe, life is a risk. All you can do is live it the best way you know how and be happy doing it."

"When did you become so philosophical?" She sniffed and he pulled a tissue from the box and gently wiped her tears.

"About the time I realized I might lose you." Carter knew he'd come this far, not just in miles but in personal growth. He might as well risk it all. "I love you, babe. Even if the baby is Fuller's, it'll be okay."

Carole stared at Ricky Carter in shocked disbelief. "Love?"

One minute her childhood poverty was rising to suffocate her and the next minute this man was trying to make her fears disappear. But as much as he tried, he couldn't do the one thing she needed and that was guarantee her she wouldn't end up alone and on welfare, reliving her mother's unstable life.

"Yeah. Somehow during all this, I ended up falling in love with you. And let's face it, we are alike enough to make this work."

"Two peas in a pod?"

He nodded, his dimples showing as he smiled. "Listen, babe, we're both driven. We're both not above using other people to get what we want. You knew this baby could be mine and you would have passed it off as Fuller's."

She winced as he laid out her sins. "I never meant to hurt you."

"And I never meant to hurt you when I called the papers and told them Damian was going to be a daddy. I was just so angry he was getting something else I wanted again—"

"You told the papers? Something else you wanted? I don't know which statement makes me angrier. That you'd betray me or—"

"In the heat of the moment," he said, his eyes downcast, his remorse seemingly honest.

"Or that you think I'm a possession to be had by you or Damian!"

He shook his head and laughed, taking her off guard.

"What's so funny?"

"You're doing the same damn thing with that unborn baby. You're using it as a possession to give to Damian or whomever you think is the best daddy at this moment. Like I said, we're alike.

Similarly driven. So let's turn all that energy towards one another—and the baby—instead. What do you say?"

Inside, Carole was shaking, her stomach in knots, nausea rising up her throat. "Did you forget that there's a fifty percent chance the baby's Damian's?" she said, admitting a truth she could no longer deny.

"Not at all. But let me lay out a few facts for you."

She drew her tongue over her dry lips.

"First, even if Damian's the father, he has no intention of marrying you."

Her stomach cramped at his words. "You can't know that for sure."

"He told me and if you ask him outright, he'll tell you the same thing. Oh, he'll do right by you and pay you so you and the baby are comfortable, but you are never going to be a family."

She swallowed hard, unable to reply.

"Unlike Fuller, I plan on marrying you whether or not the kid is mine. I plan on supporting you and your baby regardless and I plan on giving you the family you're looking for. Want to know why?"

"Why?" she whispered.

He took her hand again, his touch warm and reassuring. "Because like I said, I love you." He squeezed her fingers. "But you're scared and I don't expect you to be able to deal with all this right now. So let's take it one step at a time."

Carole rose but the blood rushed from her head and she grew so dizzy she had to sit once more.

He pushed her head downward between her legs. "Relax and breathe," Carter instructed her.

She did as she was told and slowly she began to feel better. "I'm okay," she mumbled.

"Sit up nice and slowly."

She lifted her head and met his gaze. "I'm better. Thanks."

"I'll take care of you, babe. I promise. Now how about we take that test?" He reached behind him and pulled an airline ticket out of his pocket. "We can be on the 5:00 p.m. tonight."

She grasped his hand, suddenly seeing him as her only lifeline. It didn't matter that she loved him, too, and always had. Love had never been enough to make any of her mother's men stick around.

Why should she be any luckier?

THANKS TO A BAD HEAD COLD, Micki stayed home from work. When boredom set in and she couldn't stop thinking about Damian's trip to Florida, she began cleaning her apartment, tackling junk drawers, cabinets and closets. With the amount of garbage she'd collected, the dust bunnies did nothing to help her already stuffed nose and itchy throat. She was surrounded by junk and completely miserable when the doorbell rang.

She sniffed, grabbed a tissue and headed for the door. "Who's there?"

"It's Roper."

She let her friend inside. "What are you doing here?" she asked.

"And a welcome to you, too. I called the office to see if I could take you for lunch and they said you were out of the office today. I figured you could use some company what with Damian being in Florida and all."

Micki scowled. "You're subtle as ever, John. I'm not home wallowing. I'm sick."

He studied her intently. "Red nose, no makeup… Yep, you're sick." He headed for the kitchen and picked up the phone.

"What are you doing?"

"Ordering you the best chicken soup in Manhattan. Luckily they deliver." He called in the order and, since the thought of hot soup sliding down her raw throat was heavenly, she didn't argue.

They settled into her den. Micki grabbed an afghan blanket and wrapped it around herself to keep warm. "So why are you really here? Is it because you think with Damian off talking to Carole, I'd be a basket case?"

Roper chuckled. "You said it, I didn't. Have you heard from him?"

She shook her head. "And I don't plan to." She glanced down. "It's over," she told her best friend.

"Because?"

"Baby or no baby, Damian lives a lifestyle that has no room for commitment. And I want that." She blew her nose into a tissue. "I want someone who can balance a career and a family."

John leaned forward in his seat. "And you think Damian doesn't want that? With all the changes in his life at the moment, I'd think some stability would be nice right now."

She shook her head. "He's overwhelmed with the paternity thing. If it's his, he's going to have his hands full adding a baby to his list of responsibilities, which he admits he has trouble prioritizing."

"And if it isn't his kid?"

Micki let out a laugh. "Come on. You know him pretty well. He'll be so damn relieved he's off the hook, he's going to return to focusing on what's left of his career. He's certainly not going to do a one-eighty and want a serious commitment when he's just escaped one."

"Says you."

"Says logic, common sense, and I'd bet Damian if you asked him," Micki argued. She'd thought these issues through long and hard. Her conclusions hurt, but they made perfect sense.

"If I asked him he'd say he couldn't have gotten through any of this without your support. The man needed you."

Micki cringed at her friend's words.

"What? What'd I say?" Roper asked, obviously reading her expression.

She stretched her legs out in front of her. Her body ached and she wondered if maybe she had the flu. "You nailed the other thing I've been thinking about. My whole life, I've always been taken care of. First by my parents, then by Annabelle and Uncle Yank. I've always needed other people. For the first time, someone needed me. Once Damian has his answer, once he knows whose baby it is, he's not going to need me anymore."

"All your clients need your expert advice and spin on a situation. You must know it's true, otherwise you wouldn't be as successful as you are." He ran a hand through his neatly combed hair, a sure sign Micki was confusing him.

"It's not the same thing as with the people who hire me." Something special existed between Micki and Damian, something that transcended a client-publicist relationship.

Someone she cared about had relied on her for a change. Losing him saddened her because she'd grown used to the way he'd come to need her and she liked knowing he looked to her as someone important in his life, someone he could trust with his deepest secrets. She'd spent a lot of time lately trying to come to terms with the fact that that part of her life was over.

Roper let out an exasperated sound. "Well if it makes you feel any better, I still need you," he said, treating her to his endearing grin.

The man obviously still didn't get it, which was just as well. She didn't need him psychoanalyzing her at the moment. She sneezed.

"Bless you." Roper stood. "I really should get going before I catch whatever it is you've got. I don't want to miss the autism benefit at the Pierre tomorrow night. Are you going to be up to it?"

She nodded. "After all the work Sophie and I put into it to pull it off, you'd better believe I'll be there. The Renegades will get some extremely positive press from this."

"And we're playing so well, ticket sales are up anyway. It's all good," Roper said. "But you need to rest up."

"After my soup gets here, I could use a nap," she admitted.

"Feel better," he said as she walked him to the door.

"Thanks."

"And cut Damian some slack. The guy's been through hell but it doesn't mean things are over between the two of you."

Micki ignored him. She'd already said goodbye to Damian in the place it counted most. Her heart.

THE BALLROOM in the Pierre hotel sparkled as much as the celebrities who were attending the benefit in their designer gowns and jewels. Considering the money laid out per plate for this event, everybody had pulled out their finest formal wear. Even Micki had purchased a new gown.

The light pink chiffon complimented her skin tone, or so the lady at Saks Fifth Avenue had told her. Unfortunately, she had no place in the strapless gown to hide tissues and so she'd loaded up on Benadryl in an effort to dry herself out. She couldn't speak without sounding like a frog and her head felt like it was about to explode.

A trip to the doctor this afternoon had resulted in the diagnosis of a sinus infection and so she was on antibiotics as well, but she still wasn't about to miss this big event.

After checking on a few things, Micki headed for the bar and asked for a glass of ice water.

"You'd better make sure no one spikes your drink," a familiar voice said.

Micki drew her shoulders back and turned to face Rick Carter. "Long time no see. I'm sorry I can't say I missed you," she said to the man who'd started her roller-coaster affair with Damian Fuller.

Carter inclined his head. "I'm sorry for changing your drink order that night. I'm sorry for a lot of things," he said.

She narrowed her gaze. "You look like the Carter I know but you don't sound like him." She knew his situation with Carole had to have changed how he viewed life, but considering how he'd treated Micki in the past, she wasn't about to give him the benefit of the doubt so easily.

"I don't blame you for hating me. I just wanted to say I was sorry and maybe one day we can get past it and be friends?"

She nodded warily. "Apology accepted." She'd been taught manners, after all. "As for the future, you'll understand if I reserve judgment."

"Fair enough." He started to walk away and paused. "I really am trying to turn over a new leaf. Even if that paternity test doesn't name me—"

"You took the test already?" Micki asked, stunned.

"We sure did, though it takes two weeks to get the results."

"I see."

She knew Damian had gone to Florida with Carter but she hadn't known the result of their discussion. She certainly had no idea they'd all taken tests. Because she hadn't returned his calls, Micki thought. Instead she'd had her secretary keep her up to date on anything Damian needed professionally, and there'd been nothing. So how could she have known?

"Well good luck. I hope things turn out the way you want them to."

He inclined his head. "Thanks for that."

He walked away, leaving Micki alone with her ice

water and stuffy nose. Her head hurt badly. As long as things here were under control, she might as well tell Sophie she was heading home.

Micki looked around for her sister and finally spotted her red dress across the room. She started toward Sophie when a firm hand on her shoulder stopped her.

"Going somewhere?" Damian asked.

Micki stepped back and looked into his dark gaze. "I didn't realize you'd be here."

"Why not? All the Renegades were on the invitation list."

She shrugged. "I know. I just thought…you wouldn't be in the mood for a party."

"I'm not. But (a) it's for a good cause, (b) you put the event together and (c) I knew you'd be here. Any one of those reasons works for me."

His grin turned her insides into a mushy mess. "Well thanks for coming but I was just leaving."

His smile quickly faded. "Why the rush? I was hoping to talk to you."

As much as she'd love to spend more time with him, Micki had already decided to protect her heart. "I'm not feeling well. Why don't you call me?"

"Because you don't answer my messages. Come on, one dance. We'll talk and then you can go home and take care of that cold," he said, his voice gruff and just short of pleading.

Before she could reply, he grabbed her hand and

led her out to the dance floor. He wrapped an arm around her waist and pulled her toward him, his body flush with hers.

Her back tingled where his palm rested. "You don't want to get too close. You'll catch my cold."

"I'm not worried. So how's your uncle doing?" he asked, his breath warm against her ear. His body moved in a graceful glide around the dance floor, sweeping her along with him.

"He's fine. Driving people in the rehab place nuts but he shouldn't be out of commission too long."

Damian nodded. "That's good. I'll get by to see him this week."

"He'd like that."

"And the merger?" he whispered the private words so no one else could overhear.

She shook her head. "Slow as you'd expect with Spence and Uncle Yank pulling from opposite ends. They'll run up hefty lawyer bills but it'll get done."

He chuckled, the low rumble of laughter in his chest reverberating against her. "And his eyesight?"

"He doesn't complain. He never did. I think he's too busy hiding how he really feels."

Damian raised his hand, still in a brace. "I can definitely relate to his situation," he muttered.

"Any improvement?" she asked, gently touching his hand.

"Not considering how long it's been immobilized.

I've had some physical therapy, too. It's August and the play-offs are in sight for September. I just don't know if I'll be playing in them."

He sounded resigned but more accepting than she'd heard him before. She wondered what, if anything, had changed in his mind but decided not to ask. She couldn't keep her distance if she let herself get wrapped up in his emotions.

They continued to move together in rhythm. He intertwined his fingers with hers and pulled her hand tighter against his chest. The gesture felt intimate somehow and, despite herself, Micki trembled.

"We took the paternity tests," Damian said, breaking the silence.

She nodded. "Carter told me."

"I'd have told you myself if you'd returned my calls. Carole is not happy. For some reason I can't fathom, she wants this kid to be mine."

"Good genes?" She strove for a lighthearted laugh.

"All I care about is whether you like what's in my jeans." He treated her to the sexy wink she adored.

"Maybe that's the problem," she murmured. "I like it too much."

His heartbeat slow and steady, both soothing and arousing, reminded her of all she couldn't have. Suddenly she jerked away from his warm body and solid hold, not caring if she drew attention, just needing to escape from all that she could never really have.

"We had our one last time," she said. Then Micki ran for the door before she changed her mind and indulged in another.

CHAPTER FIFTEEN

THE MINUTES OF THE CLOCK on the doctor's office wall ticked slowly by. Damian had met Carter and Carole at the office for the paternity results and they all sat in the cramped Manhattan space, none saying a word.

Damian hadn't seen Carole since their last discussion in Florida. Since Carter had taken it on himself to make her travel plans and pick her up at the airport, Damian had stepped aside. The other man deserved a shot at proving himself to the woman he obviously loved. Carole shot him daggers with her not-so-subtle glares and Damian figured she was royally pissed because he'd allowed Carter to take over.

Well, hell. The two of them had a strange relationship but damned if he'd stand in the way. Once Carole got over her obsession with Damian, she'd see Carter had potential. Damian glanced at the clock and wondered if the results would let him walk away and leave these two to figure out their relationship or if he'd forever be the obstacle between them.

He rubbed his hands together—the brace was now for bedtime only—and realized his palms were sweating. A sure sign of nerves. How could he not be stressed when his mind was juggling thoughts of his career and possible fatherhood. And then there was Micki…

All of which added up to Damian's mental and physical exhaustion. He hadn't been sleeping well at night. Nighttime was the worst because then not only was he concerned about his injured hand and the daily workout routines—which hadn't been as productive as he'd have liked—but thoughts of Micki surfaced and wouldn't leave him alone.

She haunted his nights in ways no woman ever had. With two major problems in his life, he found himself wanting to discuss his options with Micki. He wanted to hear her tell him that he would make a good father because when *she* said it, he believed. When he gave himself a pep talk, it was Micki's voice he heard, reassuring him and convincing him he could be a better man.

No woman had ever made him want to be a better man before.

"Are you all ready?" Dr. Kernan joined them, walking into his private office and interrupting Damian's thoughts.

Carole rose to her feet. In her high heels and skirt, she was the woman he remembered, dressed to impress. But he noticed that her suit jacket was buttoned over her skirt, leading him to believe she no longer had the flat abdomen he remembered.

At the thought, his stomach cramped badly.

"Frankly, Doctor, I think we wasted your time. I already know that Damian is the father and I'm so sorry time was taken away from your other patients to inform us of something we already knew." She shot the other man a pleading glance.

For a brief second, Damian almost felt sorry for her but then he remembered the hell he'd been living with ever since her announcement and her deliberate omission of Carter's part in her life.

Rick placed an arm around her shoulder and, though she stiffened, she didn't pull away. "Babe, you need to face the truth. It's a crapshoot. Fifty-fifty. Doc?" he asked, turning to the older man.

Dr. Kernan glanced at the folder in his hand. "As I explained the day we did the test, I extracted the fetal cells from the mother's blood sample and compared blood types to both possible fathers."

"As I said—" Carole began, but Carter cut her off.

"What do the results show?" he asked.

Damian held his breath.

The doctor met Damian's gaze. "I can guarantee you one hundred percent, you are *not* nor can you possibly be the baby's father."

Damian blinked, certain he'd heard incorrectly.

"That's not possible," Carole said, her voice trembling with pure fear.

Her reaction assured Damian he hadn't misunderstood. "Not mine?" he asked.

The doctor who'd delivered all of his sisters' children walked over and put a hand on Damian's shoulder. "Not yours," he said, loud and clear.

Damian forced air into his lungs. It wasn't easy and he realized he was dizzy. He rubbed his forehead.

"What are you saying?" Carole asked.

Damian glanced at Carter whose face was flushed red. The other man hadn't asked if he was the father. Carole might claim that she'd only been with both men, but Damian couldn't help questioning that. Carter wanted this baby and a life with Carole, for better or for worse, Damian thought wryly. Would the rookie be disappointed in life yet again? At least he couldn't blame Damian this time.

He drew a deep breath and rose before the doctor could announce the next set of results. "I think this is where I take my leave." Damian turned to his teammate. "Good luck," he said and, avoiding Carole's gaze, he headed for the door.

He didn't want to be around to witness either Carter's triumph or his humiliation.

It wasn't his business. Not anymore.

CAROLE'S HANDS SHOOK as Damian walked out the door without sparing her a glance. He disappeared along with her hopes and dreams for a solid future for herself and her baby. It wasn't that she couldn't support herself. She could. She always had. And it wasn't that she was in love with the man. If love were the sole criterion for security, she'd lasso Carter and marry him today.

The doctor stood before them, that damning folder in his hand.

"So it's a done deal?" Carter asked. "It's mine?"

A wave of dizziness swept over her and she lowered herself into the nearest chair. The doctor came up behind her and eased her head down slowly until it rested between her legs.

"Easy," Dr. Kernan said. "Just stay in this position for a bit."

"Are you okay?" Rick leaned down beside her. "I already told you we'll get through this together and that was before Damian was out of the picture. We're gonna be fine, babe," he said in a reassuring voice.

A lump rose in her throat. Carter's words only made her feel that much worse. The poor man had too much faith in her, Carole thought. She didn't deserve for him to love her. She didn't deserve for him to care.

It didn't matter that she'd learned her lesson about chasing fantasy instead of reality. It didn't matter that she'd learned the hard way she should have valued herself and her body enough to hold out for a man who truly cared instead of settling for scraps from the big stars.

She'd sacrificed her self-respect long ago. After watching Damian walk out of the room, she now promised herself to start fresh. She'd make a life for herself and her baby and it'd be a better one than her mother had been able to give her. There'd be no men wandering through at all hours and there'd be nourishing meals on the table. She'd see to it.

Though her heart pounded in her chest, she was starting to regain her composure. Carole slowly lifted her head. "Let's do this," she said, wanting the official announcement over with.

Dr. Kernan flipped his folder closed. "Congratulations," he said, his gaze meeting Carter's. "You're the proud father-to-be."

"Woo hoo!" Carter pumped his fist in the air and the doctor laughed. "So is it a boy or girl?" Carter asked.

Dr. Kernan slapped Carter on the back. "I know you're excited but why don't we ask the mother whether she wants to know the sex?"

Carole was still focusing on taking deep breaths and trying mentally to get herself and her life in order. She was going to be the mother of Carter's child, and she was going to be a mother who set a fine example for her…

"What is it?" she asked the doctor.

"You're having a girl. Congratulations."

A broad grin spread across Carter's face as Dr. Kernan shook first his hand, then Carole's.

"You folks have been through a lot. I'd urge you to get some old-fashioned family counseling for the baby's sake if not your own. I can recommend some names if you'd like. Think about it and get back to me." He placed his pen into the pocket of his white coat. "In the meantime, good luck. I suggest you contact an OB of your choice and begin regular appointments if you haven't already," he said, his gaze focused on hers.

"Thank you," she murmured, embarrassed at how she'd been behaving, mortified at insisting Damian was the father when she *knew* he might not be.

The doctor nodded and walked toward the door. "Feel free to use my office for a bit if you need to," he said and strode out, leaving Carole and Carter alone.

"I always thought I'd have a boy," Carter said, still in shock at all of Dr. Kernan's revelations. His kid. His baby girl.

"Are you disappointed?"

For the first time, Carter heard uncertainty in Carole's voice and fear underlying her words. "Not disappointed. Surprised. Excited. Anxious, too," he admitted.

"Yeah. Well I think we both are." She paused and glanced down. "It wasn't that I didn't want you to be the father."

"Yeah it was." But to his surprise, he wasn't bitter. "In an odd way I get it. Fuller has money and prestige and with him you wouldn't have to worry about anything."

She swallowed hard. "I was stupid. Up until the last second, I was an idiot. First of all, you should know that my job is a good one with decent benefits. We'll be okay."

"Babe, I have enough faith in myself for both of us. I'll go through arbitration and make good money. My stats this year have been phenomenal. My agent's sure things'll go well. By the time I'm up for free agency—"

She rose to her feet. "I can't count on you to support us. Baseball's uncertain. Look at Damian. He hasn't played in weeks. You can't know what's going to happen."

Carter knew her past and fear of living on welfare were behind her words, not a deliberate desire to hurt him. "I've learned that life doesn't come with guarantees. But I can promise to try and do my best by you both. And I will."

A tear dripped down her cheek. "You've become a really good guy. You deserve so much better than me."

"I'm the same guy who called the press about your pregnancy, remember? Don't go painting me with some angelic brush, okay? We're alike. We'll be fine."

"This baby could have been Damian's," she reminded him and turned away, obviously not wanting to face him.

He grabbed her arm gently and turned her around. "That was the past. We're looking to the future now. And I love you."

She shook her head. "You're the dad, Carter. Let's not push our luck and try to make ourselves into some big love story, okay? Neither one of us has done anything to deserve a happily-ever-after."

Rick cupped her cheek in his hand. "That's where you're wrong. We created this baby. That's the beginning of a new life. Hers...and ours."

But even as he spoke, Carter knew Carole was far from believing in him, in them or in their future.

NOT HIS KID. What had been the sole focus of Damian's life for weeks now suddenly had nothing to do with him. Damian wasn't sure how long he spent on the streets of Manhattan, dazed and confused by the news. Considering how fortunate he'd been in life up until now, he sure as hell hadn't expected to be sitting under a horseshoe when the test results had come in. He'd gotten lucky.

So why didn't he one hundred percent feel that way? Instead of the pure elation he should have been experiencing, Damian felt empty, almost as if a void existed where fear had once lived and breathed. Damned if he understood his reaction and he walked miles to sort through his emotions.

He glanced up at the familiar face of the building

he stood in front of. Somehow during his walking and reflecting, he found himself outside the Hot Zone offices. Micki had been ducking his calls since before the charity event and he'd deliberately given her space after. He hoped with the baby mess behind him, they could go back to being…what? Friends? Lovers? Damian shook his head. Like everything else right now, he figured the answers would come.

A glance at his watch told him Micki would be at work and he headed inside to share the news. He bypassed the receptionist and headed to her office, stopping at her secretary's desk.

"How's it going?" he asked the woman who'd come to know him pretty well from his visits.

"See for yourself." She gestured toward the partially open door.

He glanced inside but didn't let Micki know he was watching.

"Come." Micki pulled on the dog's leash but the pooch remained stubbornly committed to her current position.

The dog lay on her back, spread-eagle on the floor.

"You spoiled, pampered mutt!" Micki growled in frustration. "I will not rub your belly every time I want you to listen to me. It took me fifteen minutes of massaging just to get you out of the apartment to poop this morning and another twenty to get you to leave with me to go to work!"

Damian chuckled. "Isn't that just like a lady? Give a hand and next time she'll take the whole arm."

Micki glanced up, startled. Once the shock evaporated, a warm glow of appreciation spread across her face.

It was definitely a look that said *it's nice to see you,* Damian thought. The feeling was definitely mutual.

"Apparently Noodle's from the upper, spoiled class."

He chuckled. "Either that or she's just missing your uncle."

Micki raised an eyebrow in disbelief. "He's crotchety and cranky and that's on a good day. Oh and did I mention he lied? The dog is not trained to help people. She flunked doggy school."

"But she loves your uncle for who he is."

Micki laughed, a light, appealing and definitely arousing sound. He hadn't realized how much he needed to see her—see her happy and enjoying life—until right now.

"You've got a good point. And I'm going to ignore her until she starts doing things my way. Either that or I'll have to say to hell with the rules and deposit the dog at the rehab facility because I can't take much more of this." She walked back toward her desk, motioning for Damian to come inside. "So what are you doing in my neck of the woods?" she asked lightly.

Too lightly, Damian thought. In fact, for a woman who'd ducked out on him two weeks ago, she was acting awfully pleased to see him now. And that was the key word, Damian thought. *Acting.* The distance she'd been deliberately placing between them was more real than the smile on her face at the moment.

"I'm here to share some news." He lowered himself into a large chair across from her desk. He was disturbed that he didn't feel as emotionally free as he should and wished he understood the heaviness still in his heart.

Micki took in Damian's conflicted expression. "What's going on?" she asked, suddenly on guard.

Micki had been counting the days even if she wouldn't admit it aloud and she knew it was time. There'd only be one piece of news Damian could possibly want to share.

"The test results are in and…"

Micki leaned over her desk, her heart racing, her throat dry. "And?"

"It's not mine," he said, obviously still in shock. "All this time and energy, all this fear and anticipation and the baby isn't mine."

"That's fantastic!" she said, rising and coming around the desk before she could stop herself. "Damian, this is the best news!" She wrapped her arms around his neck, hugging him tight because not only did she think he needed the support and physical contact, but because she knew she needed it even more.

"Yeah, it is." His hugged her back, his face buried in her neck, his scruffy half beard rubbing her skin.

God, he turned her on, she thought, wishing they could act on the feelings instead of having the all important discussion that was necessary. The one they'd been destined to have once he finally received the test results.

She stepped back and leaned against her desk. "You know I had no doubt you'd have made a great father if it came to that."

His lips turned up in a grim smile. "That was probably the one thing that got me through. Your faith in me when I had none in myself."

She shrugged, embarrassed her feelings about him were so obvious. "I'm glad to have helped. I'm also glad it turned out the way you wanted it to."

"Yeah. Funny thing about that," he began.

"Wait, okay? There's something more I have to say."

He shifted in his seat, getting more comfortable. "Okay. Shoot."

Micki drew a deep breath. "First I just want to make sure you realize we need to schedule a press conference of sorts or release a statement and get your words out there first. We want this story to end with your spin on it, nobody else's."

He nodded. "That's fine. PR is your area. I'll do whatever you say."

"Good," she said. "Good." Easy clients were the

best ones. Now for the harder part. She reached back
and grabbed a pencil, grateful for something to hold
on to, and she rolled it between her palms. "When
you speak to reporters, whenever that is, they're going to ask about your future plans. You may think
they mean baseball, but they'll be talking about your
personal life."

Damian burst out laughing. "At this point, I have
nothing to hide."

"All you need to remember is that you learned
from the experience, you realize you are a role
model to your fans, you're sorry if you disappointed
anyone and you intend to go on from here."

"I'm sure I can handle that," he said soberly.

The situation with Carole had obviously scarred
him but Micki had no doubt his relief would give way
as he reacclimatized himself to his life. She vividly
remembered his words back on the island, a time that
felt so long ago, she might have been a different person. *You need to know that any partner I've ever been
with knows the score and agrees to play by my rules.*

Who knew his rules would hurt so much?

"One last thing."

He tipped his head to one side. "What would that
be?"

"When you resume your…umm…former life-
style, you should try to be discreet for a while. Don't
let the media catch you at clubs picking up women.

It'll look like you didn't mean it when you said you were sorry and you knew you'd dodged a bullet."

"Clubs and women?" he asked as if he'd never considered the notion.

He was probably too stunned by the test results to have had time to think, but she knew the inevitable would happen. Micki swallowed hard. Letting him go and meaning it were two different things.

She had to say the words out loud. "Come on, you're Damian Fuller. You made enjoying life and winning baseball legendary. The scandal's behind you. Don't tell me you haven't been itching to get back to living."

"Living, huh?"

She forced a laugh at the way he repeated her words. "You're definitely still in shock."

He shook his head hard. "You could say that. Speaking of living, want to get dinner tonight?"

"I'm sorry but once I catch up on work, it's my night to visit Uncle Yank."

He shrugged. "Okay, how about I go with you?"

"I'm not sure that's how you want to spend your first official night of freedom. Go celebrate," she urged him.

He might have gotten used to lying low, but she knew the time would come when he'd be ready to resume a normal life. It wouldn't do her any good to be around him more than necessary.

He blinked, staring off into space, as if he were

thinking things through. "Yeah, I guess you have a point. The sooner I get back to 'normal,' the sooner I'll feel like myself again."

Her smile actually hurt. "That's the spirit. So...do you want to go for a press conference or a press release to announce the results?"

"I vote for a release. I'm really not up to dealing with reporters right now."

She nodded in understanding. "They'll find you eventually but I think it's a smart move for the time being." She jotted some notes on the pad she always kept on her desk. "I'll take care of it," she promised.

It was probably the last thing she'd do in her capacity as publicist in charge of Damian Fuller, Micki thought. Once they wrapped up this issue, she intended to turn him over to Annabelle or Sophie, either of whom could easily coordinate with Uncle Yank and Spencer Atkins on Damian's professional future.

He rose to leave, pausing where she leaned against the desk. "Goodbye, Micki."

"Bye," she murmured. With him standing so near, she could inhale his sexy masculine scent and take in his scruffy beard and rugged features up close one last time. Her heartbeat kicked into high gear as she struggled to hold back her emotions.

His steady gaze met hers. For a man who'd just been given a reprieve, he didn't look relieved. But if she asked what was bothering him, she'd be investing herself in his life again and she'd struggled too hard to protect herself from those feelings.

If she didn't put up barriers first, he was bound to wake up and distance himself from her sooner or later.

Better she have enough self-respect to make it sooner.

DAMIAN WAS STINKING DRUNK and he still didn't feel a damn bit better. He'd headed to the bar after the 4:00 p.m. game where he'd suited up but hadn't played. Not even a Renegades win helped his mood.

"I'll have what he's having," Carter said to the bartender and slid into the seat next to Damian.

"Of all the bars in Manhattan you had to choose this one?" Damian asked.

The other man shrugged. "What can I say? The Blue Season seemed to fit my mood."

That surprised Damian. "Things didn't go well back at the doctor?"

"Depends what you mean. Is the baby mine? Yeah." And at the admission, a wide grin spread over Carter's face. "Is Carole thrilled with the fact? Couldn't tell you. She's not interested in some big love story. In fact she thinks I deserve better than her. How's that for a laugh? If you ask me, we're so damn alike we deserve each other." With that, he finished his scotch in a few healthy gulps.

Damian burst out laughing. "I couldn't have said

it better myself." But he felt for the guy. Damian gestured for another round.

"So what's with you?" Carter asked. "I thought you'd be celebrating your escape. Instead you look like a guy on a bender."

Damian stared into the golden liquid. "Go figure," he muttered. "Because I sure as hell can't."

"Don't tell me you're disappointed with the results." Carter sounded appalled at the notion.

With a shrug, Damian took another gulp of the fiery drink. "Like you said, depends on what you mean. Am I happy I'm not the father of Carole's kid? Hell, yeah." He shot a glance Carter's way. "No offense intended."

"None taken."

"But are you looking at a happy man right now? Hell, no. The thing of it is, I have no idea why I'm not celebrating."

"I'm younger than you and I've done my share of stupid things, but I can still look at you and answer that question. It just depends if you want to hear what I have to say."

"Why not? It's not like *I* have any answers." Damian leaned on one elbow and stared into the eyes of the rookie, the kid poised to take his place on the team.

Damian had accepted that now. He glanced down at his aching, braced wrist. He'd had no choice. "So what's your take on my life?"

"You're looking at the end of your career and you hate it," Carter said, shoving his chair back and himself out of Damian's reach as he spoke.

Damian chuckled. "I'm not going to hit you."

"I'm not taking any chances."

"Go on."

Carter paused for a drink first. "Maybe you got used to the idea of having a kid. In general, you know? Not Carole's kid but one of your own. Maybe you thought it'd fill the void when you weren't playing anymore."

"What the fuck are you, a shrink? I've never once considered the end of my career and I never thought about having kids."

"Not consciously but what about unconsciously?" Carter asked.

"You mean subconsciously."

The kid shrugged. "That, too."

Damian wiped a hand over his face and groaned. "I need air."

"What'd she say about you not being the father?" Carter asked, ignoring him.

"Who?"

Carter drew a deep breath and looked at Damian warily. "The hot little publicist, that's who."

Damian shot to his feet and pulled Carter up by his shirt at the same time. "You talk about her like that again and you're a dead man."

Carter held his hands up in front of him. "You said you wouldn't hit me."

"I changed my mind."

He shook his head. "Whoa, man. Who'd have thought a stab in the dark would pay off? Look, Captain, anyone with eyes can see she means something to you. Except maybe you." This time Carter actually ducked and headed for the door.

"Good reflexes," Damian called out to him, laughing despite himself.

"Youth," Carter called back from the doorway of the bar. "No offense."

"None taken."

If only Damian could dismiss the rookie's pop psychology as easily.

CHAPTER SIXTEEN

DAMIAN'S LIFE WAS A MESS. He needed fatherly advice and for the first time, he couldn't go to his own dad because his whole family was so thrilled about the baby being Carter's, they couldn't see past it to the deeper issues driving Damian insane. There was only one man Damian could trust with his emotions and that was the same man he'd entrusted with his career right from the beginning.

He strode into the rehab facility, an expensive establishment that Damian felt certain Yank must hate. The older man would despise feeling useless, needing help getting around, relying on other people. Man, Damian could relate.

At a large window, he asked where to find Yank Morgan's room and followed the instructions until he walked off the elevator on Yank's floor, then followed the arrows to his room. As usual, when it came to Yank, Damian was surprised by what greeted him there.

A yellow warning ribbon, reminiscent of police tape, had been wrapped across his door, blocking the entrance. A large sign had been taped to the door, which read Enter at Your Own Risk, Nasty PITA Inside.

Damian howled with laughter at the blatant description of Yank as a Pain In The Ass.

"Who's out there?" Yank called from inside his room.

Damian ducked beneath the tape and joined Yank by the chair in which he sat. "What'd you do to piss off the nurses?" Damian asked, still chuckling. "Hell, don't you know if you're sweet to these ladies they'll be sneaking you extra dessert?" He pulled up a seat, straddling it backward as he made himself comfortable.

"It's not their attention I want," Yank muttered.

Damian nodded in understanding. So Lola had bailed on him. "Why don't you just ask her to come see you?"

Yank shot him a scowl and pulled the blanket covering his legs up higher over his Burberry pajamas. Obviously his nieces had been spoiling him even if the nurses here hadn't been.

"She wants me to grovel. *I love you, Lola. I'm sorry, Lola,*" Yank said in a pretty damn good imitation of the woman.

Damian did his best not to laugh. "I don't see your pride taking good care of you right now, so why not go ahead and do what she wants? At least then you'll both be happy."

"For how long? How happy is she gonna be cutting my food when I can't see?"

Damian exhaled aloud. He understood now how frustrated Micki, Sophie and Annabelle must feel around the older man. "Why don't you let her make that decision?" Even as he asked, Damian knew the answer. "You're afraid after all these years, she'll turn you down. That's it, isn't it?"

Damian found himself staring into blue eyes similar to Micki's. Yank gave him a quick nod, then averted his gaze, obviously embarrassed.

"You can't end up any worse off than you are now, right?"

He waved a dismissive hand. "I'm tired of talking about me. What's going on with you?"

Damian knew that was the end of discussing Yank's personal life. He'd come here for fatherly advice and now was the time to spill. He glanced down at the floor, unsure of where to begin. "Since the time I was a kid, my whole life has centered around baseball. I've seen the end coming for a while now but I refused to admit it. I ignored all the signs. But rehab's not working, cortisone shots aren't helping the hand, and the team doesn't need me hanging on for selfish reasons when they could use another player on the roster."

Yank placed a hand on Damian's shoulder. "So what are you sayin'?"

"I met with Coach and told him I think I'm through. The doctors can't promise a return this season." The words were as painful now as they had been a few days ago.

"I'm proud of you for makin' the decision. If you're ready, I'll get working on the details of retirement and the contract issues."

Damian nodded. "What about the endorsements I already do?"

"I'll take care of everything. Don't you worry, okay?"

"Yeah. Thanks." He glanced up. "What the hell am I going to do now?"

Yank gestured around the room. "Come join me for a daily card game?"

"No thanks," Damian said wryly.

"You do realize we're alike, you and I."

Damian cocked his head to one side. "Other than a bum body that doesn't want to do what we tell it to do, how so?"

"Have you spoken to Micki lately?"

Damian's nerve endings went on instant alert. "She's not taking my calls at the moment. Since issuing that press release, she's declared our business relationship over and reassigned me. Apparently Annabelle's working part-time now and technically she's more familiar with the workings of the Renegades," he said, quoting Micki's secretary who'd been quoting her boss.

She'd handed him over to her sister like yesterday's news and if he thought ending his active career was painful, Micki's withdrawal hurt just as badly.

Yank glanced at him, tapping a finger against his bearded cheek. "My Micki did that?"

"She did."

"What'd you do?" Yank asked, suddenly angry and defensive.

Damian held up both hands. "I didn't do a damn thing. She just suddenly decided to treat me like dirt."

"Same thing Lola did to me. I told you we were alike."

His head hurt trying to keep up with Yank's way of thinking. "I'm lost."

"Okay let me spell it out for you. I lost Lola because first I was scared and then I was a jackass and now it's too late. Are you gonna risk losing the woman you love the same way I did?" Yank asked.

Love, Damian thought, dazed. "Is that what this is all about?" he asked, but even as he wondered aloud, he knew.

He loved Micki.

Even Carter had tried to tell him.

Suddenly all the recent disappointment and confusion made sense. The parties and women that had once defined his life no longer held appeal and when Micki had suggested he return to his old ways, he'd been repelled by the notion. Because he'd rather be with her.

"Looks to me like you didn't recognize a good thing when it was starin' you in the face," Yank said.

"Just like you."

Yank nodded. "So are you gonna wait till you can no longer see her looking back at you?"

Damian shivered at Yank's words. The thought of a life without Micki in it at all wasn't one he wanted to contemplate. Bad enough he was losing baseball. He refused to lose her, too.

He glanced at the older man he'd always admired. "Tell you what. I'll go after Micki if you swallow your damn pride and tell Lola what she wants to hear. It's not like you don't have the feelings for her, so get over yourself and let her know," Damian taunted. He had no choice but to push and prod his agent or else they could both lose.

"You're telling me my niece's happiness depends on whether I'm finally willing to pony up with Lola?"

Damian folded his arms across his chest. "That's exactly what I'm saying."

Not that he intended to stay away from Micki if Yank got stubborn, but it was a good threat and a decent negotiating point. The older man deserved his own share of happiness even if he was, as his nieces believed, too pigheaded to admit it.

Yank blew out a frustrated puff of air. "I've been alone a long time."

"And you hate it," Damian reminded him.

Yank shook his head. "Yeah, I do."

"So?" Damian asked the one-word question, then lapsed into silence.

He wanted to give Yank time to think. Would the other man finally see how much he needed Lola? Would he put his happiness and hers before his pride? From what Damian understood, it was a battle Micki and her sisters had been fighting for a long time. Yank and Lola together was a gift Damian would love to be able to bring to Micki.

"I don't even know if she wants me anymore. For all I know, she'll get me to open an artery just so she can wipe the floor with my blood."

Damian winced. "Nice analogy but somehow I don't think the woman's that cruel."

Yank snorted. "That's what you think."

"I'm still waiting for an answer," Damian prompted and tapped his foot against the linoleum hospital floor for good measure.

"Okay, okay," Yank said at last. "I'll go for it if you will."

A rush of adrenaline spiked through Damian's veins. "I don't know if Micki wants me either," he admitted, scared spitless at the possibility of her turning him down.

Yank shook his head. "Neither of us has any way of knowing how things'll turn out in the end. It's a big gamble."

"It'll be okay," Damian said with little conviction, though he hoped it was true.

Yank groaned. "Life's a bitch, huh? Especially for two men used to getting their own way."

Damian nodded and rose to his feet. If he had anything to say about it, that particular tradition would continue.

MICKI HAD TO BE at a photo shoot for one of her clients at 4:00 p.m. but until then, her schedule was free. Because Noodle had slept at Sophie's for the past two nights, Micki took pity on her sister and brought the dog along with her for a walk through Central Park.

The sun shone overhead and she let the heat warm her arms as she strode along the path. Joggers passed her and people sat on the grass, reading on the lawn. It was a perfect New York City day. She finally came to her favorite spot, a place she and her sisters often came to together for an escape from the office and stress.

She unhooked Noodle from her leash and let the dog run free, hoping that the exercise would calm her for the night ahead. Thank goodness Uncle Yank would soon be out of rehab and back in his own apartment with his spoiled dog.

She popped open a can of Dr. Brown's Cream Soda she'd brought with her and watched the dumb dog try to make friends with people only to run to the next person when they tried to pet her.

"Mind if I join you?" a familiar voice asked.

She glanced up, shading her eyes from the sun with her hand. She would swear her heart stopped beating when she saw Damian towering over her, looking delicious in his light blue shirt and dark jeans.

She patted the ground beside her. "How'd you find me?" she asked, surprised because nobody except her sisters knew about this spot. "Don't tell me. Sophie snitched," Micki muttered.

Damian remained tellingly silent.

"Well?"

"You said not to tell you." He grinned, making her forget about being angry at her sister.

"Okay then what brings you by?"

"Now that's a loaded question."

Between his serious tone and expression, Micki's stomach churned with pure agitation. She wondered what he wanted to say but first she glanced aside to make sure Noodle was still in calling distance.

When she saw the dog was hanging out with someone's leashed pet, she turned her attention back to Damian. "What's going on?"

"In the time we've spent together since the island, you've gotten to know me pretty well, wouldn't you say?"

"I suppose."

"I think you have. I think you know me better than anyone else in my life, short of my family, and that's

because they don't give up when they want answers."
As always, his eyes sparkled with warmth and humor
when he spoke of them. "But you know me in a different way."

"What do you mean?" She swallowed hard, unsure of where he was going with this.

"It's a gut feeling kind of thing. You seem to sense
when I need space and you sense when I could use
company. You understand the career thing and you
don't put pressure on me one way or another."

Without warning, laughter bubbled up from inside
her. "I came to your apartment and told you it was
time to grow up. You don't call that putting pressure
on you?" she asked in disbelief.

The corners of his mouth lifted in an endearing,
sexy grin. "See that's another thing. When you read
me the riot act, it doesn't sound like my family telling me what to do or your uncle guiding my career."

She glanced down at her sneakered feet. "What's
it sound like?"

"It sounds like you telling me what I know deep
down inside except I need to hear it out loud from
someone I trust. And that someone is you." He
reached out and lifted her chin so their gazes met and
she couldn't avoid him or their conversation.

This was getting very personal and intimate. She
wiped her damp palms beside her on the grass, suddenly nervous and frightened.

Since her parents had died and Micki had fallen into the habit of relying on Annabelle and Uncle Yank to bolster her emotionally, she was seldom scared. She rarely found a situation she wasn't ready to meet head-on. Damian presented that rare emotional challenge and, like when she'd come to Sophie for tips on how to be more of a girl, Micki again found herself at a loss.

"I'm not surprised we connected that way. I have a knack for understanding the athlete's psyche." She deliberately depersonalized what they shared, unwilling to put her heart on the line.

"Don't," he barked out, startling her and she jumped. "Don't put up the *one of the guys* front and definitely don't try and tell me that what's between us is no different than what you share with your other clients." His eyes flashed with anger and obvious hurt.

Micki sought for a way to explain when Noodle bounded toward them and landed squarely in Damian's lap. "She must have heard you yell," Micki said.

Damian clenched his jaw, his frustration with Micki unmatched by anything he'd ever felt before as blood pounded inside his head. "I didn't yell," he said in a tense but calmer tone.

"You raised your voice and the dog heard."

"And I didn't come here to talk about the dog or to let you use her as a buffer or an excuse to avoid a serious conversation."

She lifted her chin a notch. "Okay then, no more

beating around the bush. What did you come here to say?"

This was the Micki he knew, the one who refused to run from a confrontation or discussion. The one who'd stood by him even when he'd known how difficult that must have been.

He covered her hand with his, running his fingers over her smooth skin and gathering his courage at the same time. "I've never said this to anyone before," he said, speaking as quickly as the thoughts came to mind. "I've never even thought it about anyone before."

He glanced up to see her watching him. Her blue eyes were wide and clear, her fear as palpable as his own.

Well, Damian thought, at least they were in this together. "I love you, Micki Jordan."

She just stared at him for a moment and then murmured barely above a whisper, "I love you, too." She blinked and a tear fell. "But…"

With that one little word, his stomach cramped like crazy. "But *what?*"

"You're coming off a situation you can't even begin to have dealt with and when you do, you have a life waiting. A life by your own admission that you love. You don't want to be tied down. You don't need a woman who wants more from you than you're capable of giving. And I'm not going to put myself through the hell of letting you go twice." She jumped up from her cross-legged position and stood, unraveling Noodle's leash.

That she'd just up and leave panicked him because she seemed so serious, he didn't know if he'd ever get her back. "My own words coming back to bite me," he muttered. "I've changed. The situation with the baby? It made me reevaluate what I want out of life. What I want beyond baseball. I want you."

"You got used to having me around," she countered. "Big difference." She bent down and hooked the dog's leash to his collar, giving Damian a clear view down her shirt to her softly rounded cleavage.

His groin hardened at the sight. Micki tempted him like no other woman ever had and for the first time in his life he knew even forever wouldn't be enough time to spend with her. Or inside her.

Once she pulled the dog to her side, he rose beside her. "Don't you think I know the difference?"

"In time you will. Right now you're confused and I don't want to have invested more of myself only to have you finally come to see I was right." She scooped the dog into her arms where he happily settled in. "You don't need me anymore, so just go back to living your life. Enjoy your freedom. You got lucky, now act like it." She trembled, giving him hope that this mindset would change once she believed his words. Believed in him.

Maybe it was just too fast, Damian thought. Maybe she needed time. "Before you go, want to know what I felt when I discovered the baby wasn't mine? Once the reality set in?"

"What?" she whispered.

"Disappointed." Of course he'd had to have the reasons spelled out for him, but damned if he wasn't one hundred percent certain they made perfect sense.

Micki blinked. "You wanted Carole's baby to be yours?" she asked in disbelief.

He stepped closer. "I wanted a baby to be mine. I want *your* baby."

She opened her mouth, then closed it again, obviously at a loss for words.

But he wasn't. He still had plenty more to say. "So don't tell me I don't need you anymore. I do. But I've figured out where your head is at. You're not used to being needed in a non-professional way and that scares you."

"Meaning?" She squeezed the dog closer to her chest and she yelped. Micki loosened her grip.

"Birth order. We're both the spoiled youngest children. You're so used to being taken care of, you don't know how to handle us now. And I'm not a shrink but I'd guess there's something going on with you being one of the guys. It's always been an easy excuse for you to hide from being yourself."

She shook her head. "What do you know? Like you said, you aren't a shrink."

"Well maybe I should be because I have you pegged right. If you can consider yourself one of the guys, you have a perfect excuse if a relationship fails." He drew a deep breath, realizing how much was on the line right now and how easily he could blow things. "We won't fail, Micki. Unless you don't ever give us a try."

The sun beat down overhead, his heart hammered inside his chest and he broke into a sweat waiting for her to reply.

"It's yourself you need to know better," she tossed back. "As soon as you get over the letdown of building yourself up to be a father, you'll realize how lucky you are to be free. And you'll thank me for not throwing myself into your arms now." Tears flowed profusely down her face and she made no attempt to wipe them away.

He shoved his hands into his front jeans pockets because that was the only way he wouldn't reach out for her. "You're dead wrong. I've already looked inside myself and come to terms with my future, so if anyone needs to get to know themselves better, it's you." He started to walk away, then turned back to face her. "And by the way, I won't be thanking you for this anytime soon."

As defeat and loss settled on Damian's shoulders, he wondered if Yank would fare any better with Lola.

ONE WEEK LATER, Damian realized he'd been had. Yank had come home from rehab and begun short days at work. Damian knew because together they were planning his retirement announcement and future plans, but the older man had avoided any talk about his personal life at all.

Damian banged on Yank's office door and walked inside. "You screwed me, old man."

Yank scowled, looking completely affronted by the accusation. "I did no such thing."

Damian cocked his head to one side. "Are you telling me that you did lay your heart on the line for Lola?"

He glanced down. "Not yet."

"Mind telling me what you're waiting for? Because misery loves company and since Micki turned me down, I figure it's your turn. After all, we had a deal."

Yank coughed and looked away. "Did I tell you how good it is to be home?"

Rolling his eyes, Damian sat himself in the chair across from Yank's desk. "You're not overdoing it, are you?"

He shook his head. "The girls wouldn't let me."

"How about Lola?"

Yank groaned. "You aren't going to give this up, are you?"

"Nope."

"Micki's a stubborn one," Yank said. "Just like Lola."

"No kidding." Damian couldn't believe he'd bared his soul to the woman he loved and despite her claim that she felt the same way, she'd rejected him anyway. He'd barely slept since that day in the park. "I suppose I deserved the kick in the ass though. I mean all those years of being so arrogant with women. It was my way or no way. Sleep with me, no strings attached and be grateful or take a hike. It never mattered to me." He rose and strode to the window overlooking the city.

"It matters to you now," Yank said, stating the obvious.

Damian nodded. "With retirement looming, what I want out of life seems more important than ever." Every time he said the word *retirement*, dizziness assaulted him, but he had to admit, he was beginning to accept the inevitable.

"We've got some strong interest from cable and satellite stations in having you as commentator. I think I can get them into a bidding war with GMA."

Damian inhaled deeply, then slowly exhaled. "Funny thing is, I'm not as worried as I thought I'd be about that part of things. I trust you and I have enough faith in my ability to pull something off. Anything to keep myself busy," he said and forced a laugh. "It's not the professional stuff that's getting to me. It's the personal."

Suddenly Yank rose and slowly came up beside him, leaning heavily on his walker as he moved.

"I didn't realize you were walking so well," Damian said.

"If I wanted to get out of that hellhole, I had to work for it."

Damian nodded.

"Micki was always the lost one," Yank said, the topic of conversation catching Damian off guard.

But now that the older man had opened up, Damian wanted to know more and Yank seemed more than willing to talk.

"Annabelle was the oldest and she understood if I didn't take them, social services would split 'em up. So she became the peacemaker, the one who made sure her sisters behaved, not that they ever did," he said, chuckling at the memory. "But she took it on her little shoulders to try. She was serious and the little mother, following behind Lola and making sure everything was just so."

Damian smiled at the vision.

"Then there was Sophie. She was always hardest to figure out. She'd escape reality with her nose in a book all the time. In some ways it made her the easiest because she had all the answers even before I knew there were questions."

"And Micki?" Damian asked.

A smile curved the man's mouth into a smile. "Always had a soft spot for her 'cause she told it like it was and was never afraid of my bluster. She walked up to me that first day and called me a pig. Then she told me to call her Micki instead of Michelle. Didn't sit well with her sisters, that much I can tell you."

Damian met Yank's gaze. "I didn't realize her name was Michelle," he said, surprised.

"I don't believe anyone has called her that since the day I took the girls in. She just looked me in the eye and became my little Micki. But she missed out on the girlie stuff her sisters enjoyed and they never thought to include her since she seemed to like sports so much more."

With a groan, Damian leaned against the windowsill, exhausted from no sleep and overwhelmed with the desire to understand what he could do to fix things between himself and Micki. Assuming there was something left to fix.

"So she considered herself one of the guys?"

"And I never did anything to discourage it."

"I'm sure the guys she's dated have dispelled that notion," he said, his gut cramping at the thought of another man's hands anywhere on Micki's body, never mind another man actually making love to her. He knew he wasn't the first but he damn well wanted to be the last.

"Not too many guys that I know of. A jackass or two wanted an in with me. Another couple she dated but if you ask me they were pansies, not worthy of my niece." Yank shook his head. "I shouldn't be telling you any of this. It feels like I'm betraying her."

Damian laid a hand on the other man's shoulder. "You're giving me insight that might help. I'd slit my throat before I'd use it against her," he promised.

Yank nodded, seemingly satisfied. "End result is she's confident in business and one hell of an athlete, but her self-esteem in the female department leaves something to be desired. It wasn't till just recently that she started to make an effort to look more… womanly. Even a blind man like me could see she was tryin' hard."

"She never had to try with me. I knew from the first time we ki—I mean from the first time we met, that she was special," he said, watching his words this time. He opted for *special* over *hot number* since Damian didn't need Yank coming after him with his walker.

"I knew that. She saw the real you, too. She knew you were more than the idiot ladies' man you pretended to be." Yank ran a hand over his straggly beard. "But if I know my Micki, she's only thinking about the kind of women you spent time with before her and she thinks she can't compete."

"She can't," Damian said, slamming his good hand against the window.

"Watch it, wise guy. You bust the other hand and nobody's gonna help you wipe your—"

"I get the picture." Damian cut the older man off, suppressing a laugh. "But I'm serious. Micki can't compete against those women because she's head and shoulders above them."

Yank pulled him into a hug with one arm, hanging on to the walker with the other hand. "Good luck convincing her of that," Yank said. "Because the one thing Micki learned from me beside sports is stubbornness and once that girl makes up her mind, changing it is some kind of difficult."

Damian glanced heavenward. "Thank you for that advice," he said, sarcastically.

Yank grinned. "My pleasure. Oh and if it makes you feel any better, I didn't screw you. I just wanted to be livin' on my own again before I asked Lola to accept me and my problems back into her life."

Damian could respect and understand the man's position. "I hope you make out better than I did."

"You got a game plan for the future?" Yank asked him.

Damian spread his hands wide before him. "Completely open and in Micki's hands." Too bad she wasn't returning calls or e-mails, not even in the guise of business.

Micki found it too easy to ignore his overtures so Damian was now using the silent treatment. If she didn't mind being ignored, he was out of options and heading back to the island.

Alone this time.

CHAPTER SEVENTEEN

YANK HATED THE WALKER. He hated not being able to
see everything clearly. But he hated being without
Lola more. Maybe he'd had to be kicked in the butt
a ridiculous number of times and let decades go by
before he was ready to see what was in front of him
all along. "But dammit I'm seeing it now!"

"Excuse me, sir?" The new security guard who
rode the elevator in the Atkins building asked.

"Nothin'. Seventh floor, please," Yank said to the
man.

He'd been out of rehab for over a week and now
that he was managing to get along, thanks to his
driver and walker, he was out of excuses for avoiding his fate.

A series of consecutive beeps let Yank know when
he'd arrived on the right floor, as did the sound of the
doors sliding open.

"We're here," the guard said.

Yank maneuvered his way out, walker first. He
could make out shadows enough to see where he was

going and he also knew Spencer's office space well enough to manage on his own.

"Mr. Morgan!" The receptionist at the main desk jumped up from her seat. "We weren't expecting you."

"Good. I like the element of surprise. I want to see Lola."

"She's in her office. Should I tell her you're here or do you prefer the element of surprise there, too?"

"You can tell her I'm coming to talk to her and to clear anyone else out of there."

"Yes, sir." The woman picked up the phone while Yank slowly headed to Lola's small room off Spencer's office.

He knew by the familiar perfume that she was waiting for him in the doorway. She'd used the same scent or something similar since the day they'd met. He smelled it in his dreams, Yank thought.

"I can't believe you're up and around," Lola said.

"Yeah. Time flies when you're havin' fun."

"Well you certainly used the time to get yourself healthy."

He nodded. "I didn't have anything else to do except rehab and think."

"Come on in." She stepped back so he could walk into the office.

He had no choice except to allow her to help him into a chair. He ought to get used to it, he thought and clenched his jaw.

"So what brings you by?" She lowered herself into the seat next to him.

Surrounded by her scent, a warm familiar feeling and unmistakable arousal kicked in. "You're really gonna make me spell it out for you?" he asked, annoyed she couldn't understand that this visit was his way of making a major statement.

She jumped to her feet. "I'm too busy for games so if you have nothing to say, you can leave now."

Yank groaned. "Okay, okay, cool your jets and sit down. Please," he added, afraid she wouldn't even give him a chance.

He wasn't sure but he thought she narrowed her eyes and glared at him. He certainly could sense steely anger emanating from her in waves. Didn't the woman know how hard this was?

But then how hard had he made her life all this time? He'd thought about this long and hard and he hadn't come to her empty-handed.

Yank reached into his pocket and wrapped his hand around a jewelry box. He'd gone shopping alone, not wanting to involve the girls. He hadn't wanted to get their hopes up nor had he wanted to face their pity if Lola turned him down.

Lola slowly eased herself into a seat again, watching Yank warily. She'd known him too long to jump to any conclusions. Just because she'd given him an ultimatum again didn't mean he'd come around. Af-

ter all, she'd tried once before and she was still working with Spencer and not Yank.

Suddenly he pulled a small velvet box out of his
pocket. A jewelry box if she wasn't mistaken, and she
began to shake. Her palms grew damp. And despite
the evidence in front of her, she still refused to believe. Who knew what was inside? He could have
bought her a necklace or something.

"Well aren't you going to take it?" Yank asked.

She accepted the box. Hands shaking, she turned
it over and over again, almost afraid to open it.
"It's got teeth marks," she said, recognizing the in-
ane comment.

"I don't think the girls fed the dog too well while
I was in rehab. She's picked up some awful habits I'm
gonna have to break."

Lola laughed and ever so slowly opened the box.
Inside was a huge pink sapphire stone set in white
gold and surrounded by diamonds.

She sucked in a startled gasp. "It's… It's…" For
the first time in her life words failed her.

"It's five karats and each diamond is pretty damn
big. I can't remember the size. But I can get bigger.
Or green if you'd prefer an emerald. Or one large diamond. We can do that, too. Whatever you like, the
jeweler said he'd get it for you," Yank said, rambling.

Also a first, Lola thought. Tears streamed down
her cheeks and Yank reached out and wiped her face

with his hand. "How'd you know I was crying?" she asked, knowing he couldn't possibly see her tears.

"Because after all these years, I know you," he said in a gruff voice filled with more emotion than she'd ever heard from him before.

Lola swallowed hard. "So is this a friendship ring?" she joked for lack of knowing what else to say.

Yank had never been an eloquent speaker, and now he'd handed her a box with the most beautiful ring she'd ever seen inside. Yet he hadn't explained its significance. Just like the man, she thought with exasperation, the tears still flowing.

"Well here's the thing. I'm no bargain. I'm getting closer to being legally blind. I've got a bum hip and use a walker, though it'll soon be a cane."

She leaned forward, holding her breath.

"I'm grouchy on a good day and my dog craps and sleeps wherever she wants. You can blame the girls for that. I had Noodle trained."

"Somehow I doubt that," Lola said. "Now quit getting off the subject and go on."

He shook his head. "Right. Well I probably waited too damn long and I no longer look like the prize I once was—"

She snickered and he shot her a dirty look.

"And a part of me thinks you gave me this ultimatum so I'd say what you want to hear just so you can dump me on my good-for-nothing, arrogant—"

"Yank!"

"Yeah, yeah. Well I was wondering if you'd like to marry me. I'd say raise my kids but you already done that. I'd say for better but there isn't much of that these days. I can definitely offer you for worse and know you'd have that to look forward to—"

"Yes."

"What?" He blinked, obviously stunned by the one little word. "Yes what?"

"Yes, I'll marry you, you stupid fool. I'll take you half-blind and limping and obnoxious. I'll even accept your foolish dog just as long as you really want this, too," she said, unable to turn off the waterworks. She sniffed and reached for a tissue on the corner of her desk.

Yank grabbed for her hand. "I'd get down on one knee but I'd never get up again. I wasted years of our lives and I got no excuse for it. I can't believe you'd take me now."

Lola pulled him into an embrace. "Yank Morgan, you've always been mine and I've always been yours. It's just taken you longer than most to come around."

He chuckled. "What can I say? I'm special."

"That you are," she whispered. And she intended to spend the rest of her life making sure she took good care of him each and every day.

"You're no slouch yourself, Lola. I don't know

what I did to deserve you but I'm the luckiest man alive. Do you know how much I love you?"

She shook her head. "I don't think I do, but you can spend the rest of your life showing me."

He grinned. "You gonna put that ring on now?"

"No, you're going to do it for me." She placed the ring in his palm and held out her hand.

By sense of touch, he easily slid the ring onto her finger.

She raised her hand to admire the stone and the way the sun shining through the window highlighted all the perfect facets. "It fits!"

He chuckled. "I told you I know you."

And she knew him. He was a unique man, one who'd given up his bachelorhood and raised his three nieces. Lola had gone through periods of frustration and yet she'd never regretted devoting her life to Yank and his family. Not even after she'd decided the time had come to move on without him.

And now all of her dreams had come true.

MICKI BLEW OFF an afternoon PR function and had one of the staff pinch-hit for her, heading home to the comfort of her apartment instead. She took a hot shower and didn't even pay attention when Noodle licked the droplets of water off her legs. While using his walker, her uncle had nearly tripped over Noodle, who lacked the brains to get out of the way. So until Uncle Yank was more mobile, she'd agreed to keep the dog with her. Micki hated to admit it but Noodle was good company, especially since she was feeling lonely right now.

A few short weeks ago, Damian had offered her everything she'd dreamed of and she'd pushed him away. She'd never thought he'd actually say he loved her, but he had. Had he meant it or did he just believe it for now because she'd become his safety net? Those were the thoughts that haunted her day and night.

Along with thoughts of her own past and future. Thanks to her uncle and her sisters, Micki had always known love and security. They'd cushioned and protected her, too much at times. As a result, she was insecure when it came to trusting her instincts. Oh, she could handle herself professionally because there she'd been given free rein. But personally and emotionally, sometimes she felt ill-equipped to handle things.

Was it any wonder that at her age she'd had to turn to Sophie for advice on dressing and acting more femininely? Was it any wonder she couldn't bring herself to believe a sexy jock like Damian Fuller would really be in love with every guy's friend, Micki Jordan?

And really, those were the truths at the crux of her turning Damian away. It was easier to continue to pull back now than to take a chance with him only to have her heart broken when Damian finally realized his true feelings and walked out on her later.

She trembled and pulled the old afghan around her shoulders, cuddling up on her couch. Noodle lay at her feet, the dog's body heat warming Micki's toes from the air-conditioning blowing around her.

Tears fell freely and she wiped them with the knitted blanket, ignoring the knocking at the door, waiting for the person to go away. She shut her eyes, only to hear the rattling of a key chain and see the door open wide.

"Micki?" Sophie walked inside and slammed the door behind her. "As soon as I heard you bailed on your afternoon appointment, I knew something was wrong. What's going on?" Her sister walked over to the couch and knelt by Micki's side.

She didn't feel like talking about it so she remained silent.

"It's Damian, isn't it?" Sophie asked. "You've refused to talk about him ever since the day I sent him to find you in the park."

"It's Damian," she said, agreeing to the obvious.

Her sister nudged her in the side. "Come on, Mick. You're not going to feel better if you don't open up and talk about it."

Micki eyed Sophie knowingly. "You mean *you're* not going to feel better until I talk about it." Resigned, she pushed herself up against the armrest and faced her sister.

Sophie slid into the empty space on the sofa. "Same thing."

Even now, the words wouldn't come any easier. "Damian wanted to talk about us." She laid her chin on her bent knees and met Sophie's gaze. "He said he loves me."

Her sister's eyes opened wide. "That's wonderful! It's everything you dreamed of! So why have you been moping around like you lost your best friend?" Sophie leaned back and really looked at Micki for the first time. "And why are you crying now? I'm really confused. You love him, too, yes?"

"Yes." Micki nodded. "But I still sent him on his way."

"I thought it was something like that, but what I don't get is why?"

"I have my reasons." Micki went on to list the excuses she'd fed Damian. Some of them, like the relief he'd feel when the reality of not being a father set in, she truly believed. Others, like him being used to having her around, she didn't buy for a minute. Because she loved him, too, and it wasn't that she'd gotten used to having him by her side. She enjoyed it. She wanted it forever.

But she didn't believe it would last.

Sophie rose to her feet and planted her hands on

the hips of her expensive suit jacket. "I could kill you! Who pushes away a good, kind, decent, sexy man with a bunch of bullshit excuses?"

From her tone and uncharacteristic use of foul language, Micki knew her sister's rant was just beginning and she hoped to head it off. "I guess the obvious answer is, I do. Now will you please respect my decision and leave me alone?"

"Let me ask you something."

"It's not like I have a choice, is it?"

Sophie shot her a scowl. "You came to me and asked if I'd help you make yourself over. I did. You specifically hoped to land Damian Fuller. You did. And now that you have him exactly where you want him, you push him away. I simply don't understand, so you're going to have to explain it to me." She waved her arms in a dramatic gesture that had Micki ducking to avoid being whacked in the head.

She rubbed her burning eyes and groaned. There was no way she'd get her sister to go away and leave her in peace without a long-winded talk.

"Millions of women would kill to have Damian say he loved them—" Sophie continued.

"Do you really want to know why I pushed him away?" Micki cut in. "Fine, I'll tell you. It's exactly what you said. It's because there's no way Damian Fuller wants a woman like me when he could have any woman just by snapping his fingers," she yelled, her cheeks hot at the embarrassing admission.

Sophie pulled her into a tight, sisterly hug. "Oh, Micki. You are so wrong about yourself. So wrong."

Micki's throat grew tight. "Have you seen the women he usually dates?"

"The ones like Carole with fake boobs and no morals? The ones who'd try and pass a kid off as his when she knew there was a fifty percent chance he wasn't the father? That kind of woman? Yeah, I can see why Damian would choose someone like that over you," Sophie said wryly. She grabbed Micki's hands. "He'd be lucky to have you. Why can't you see that?"

"Because I'm scared."

"Then get un-scared and do it fast. Otherwise you'll make the same mistake Uncle Yank did."

Micki glanced at her sister. "It's not that easy."

"No, it isn't. But what good is your makeover if you're still the same insecure person on the inside?" Sophie shook her head. "And that's not you. You're the woman who can handle a locker room full of men with a shrill whistle. You can run a huge PR event and have everyone in the room kissing your ass. Come on! You're going to let the best thing that ever happened to you walk away because you're afraid to take a chance?"

Micki drew a deep breath and sought to explain. "I've never had to take a real chance before. I always had Uncle Yank and Annabelle to lean on. Lately you've had my back. With Damian it's like walking a tightrope with nobody to catch me," she said, expressing her greatest fear.

"Well then jump and trust in *him*," Sophie said, frustrated.

"Easy for you to say."

Sophie shrugged. "Maybe you'll get the opportunity to throw my advice back at me one day. In the meantime, you're my sister, I love you and I'd hate to see you miss a once-in-a-lifetime opportunity."

Micki rubbed her bare arms and wondered if she had the faith in herself Sophie thought she should have.

Her phone rang and she picked it up. "Hello?" She listened to her uncle and then Lola and pure happiness filled her at the news.

She hung up and turned to her sister. "Uncle Yank and Lola are engaged," she said amazed.

"Wow. Hell hath officially frozen over!"

Micki laughed. "Yeah. What do you know?"

Sophie shook her head, a wide smile on her face. "I know I've just seen one miracle. Now it's time for another."

"I need time, Sophie." Time to sort through her emotions and make sure she could handle any possibility where Damian was concerned. Time to be sure she could believe in her ability to hold on to Damian.

"Well don't take too long. Now that he's announcing his retirement, he'll have more free time on his hands than he knows what to do with. And a guy like Damian Fuller won't stay unattached forever."

DAMIAN WAITED UNTIL A DAY OFF to clean out his locker. A travel day when nobody would be around. The day after he announced his retirement to the world. With Sophie acting as his publicist, and Yank, his coach and the Renegades owners by his side, Damian had held a press conference at the stadium. The timing had been perfect. Coming right after the game when the Renegades clinched a place in the postseason, Damian Fuller announced his permanent leave from the game he loved.

The Renegades retired his number, twenty-two, which would hang on a stadium wall in honor of his career. He was proud, he was sad, and though he had a broadcasting job waiting for him beginning with the play-offs, he still felt at loose ends. A trip to the island was just what he needed to get his head back on straight, Damian thought.

Outside it rained, a torrential summer soaking that darkened the sky and matched his mood as he began pulling mementos out of his locker. From a distance, he heard the familiar sound of the creaking locker-room doors swinging open wide. Annoyance shot through him. He'd asked the equipment manager to make sure nobody bothered him so he could take the time to empty his locker in peace.

If they'd let a reporter in… He shook his head and returned to his job, removing one thing at a time, from baseballs to old jocks, to sunscreen and bubble gum that'd turned hard a long time ago. He'd collected a lot of crap, Damian thought.

"I thought I'd find you here."

"Micki?" At the sound of her voice, Damian turned around fast.

"Surprise," she said somewhat sheepishly.

"It sure is." He hadn't seen her in weeks nor had he heard from her since she'd turned him down back in Central Park.

He'd spent the past few weeks not only arranging his future but trying to put Micki in his past. Now she was here on the second most difficult day of his life and, though a part of him welcomed her, another part immediately erected barriers a mile high. No way would he let her slice his heart out again.

He leaned against the metal bank of lockers and stared. He wasn't about to make this easy for her— no matter how good she looked in a short pink skirt and tie-dyed tank under a white top that fell over her shoulders in the old *Flashdance* style. Her cheeks were flushed and her hair spread over her shoulders in a tangled mass of curls. She was more appealing than she had a right to be, all things considered.

"So what brings you by the locker room? Looking for a jock to represent now that you have a free slot in your schedule? You ought to know the team's on the road." He winced at his callous tone and deliberate sarcasm. Obviously he was more hurt and angry than he'd wanted to admit, even to himself.

Her eyes flashed with hurt. "That was mean."

He cleared his throat. "Yeah."

"But not entirely uncalled for." She pursed her lips in a thin line. "I came here to talk."

She piqued his curiosity. "It's not the most comfortable place but have a seat." He gestured to the wooden bench he'd spent years using to lace his shoes. She lowered herself to the bench and he joined her.

"I caught the press conference yesterday," she said. "I'm not sure what to say first. I'm sorry it happened so soon and at the same time I was really proud of the way you handled yourself with the media. I know it wasn't easy."

Her soft, approving gaze warmed his heart. "It wasn't. Want to know why I was able to do it?"

She nodded.

"Because you told me I could handle it. Just like you told me I could handle being a father. When you say it, I'm able to believe."

"I'm glad. At least I've been good for something other than ego bashing," she said wryly. She folded one leg beneath her. "Seriously, watching you was impressive. You faced the very thing you feared most. You stood up to your fear of losing baseball and you answered every reporter's question without flinching."

He shrugged. "Years of training, I guess."

"Did you hear that Uncle Yank and Lola got engaged?" she asked, an excited grin lighting up her face.

"I sure did." He didn't see any point in mentioning he and Yank had agreed to go for it at the same time. "I'm glad he hit a home run."

She laughed. "Love the baseball analogy. To me, he's an example of another person facing his fears."

Damian wasn't in a talkative mood and he had a lot on his mind. Small talk with a woman he wanted and couldn't have wasn't his idea of a good time.

He met her gaze with a serious one of his own. "Micki, what do you want from me?"

"I want to do what you and Uncle Yank did. I want to face my fears." She paused. "When you and I got together that first time, I knew the rules. I did. I admit at the time I hoped I'd be that one woman who caused you to change your mind, the one you'd fall in love with, you know? I knew it was a ridiculous wish. I mean how many women in your life thought the same thing?"

Damian didn't speak. He didn't move, he didn't breathe, afraid that somehow he'd mess up and she'd walk out and he'd never hear what else she had to say. He didn't know how this was going to end, but he didn't want to miss a second of what came before it did. Because she *had* been the one special woman who'd changed his mind and then she'd bolted on him anyway.

Micki drew a steadying breath. "I guess I never thought my fantasy had much of a chance of becoming reality because when it did, I panicked."

"You ran."

She nodded. "Afraid to face my fears."

She was on the edge, Damian realized. She could still explain and refuse to take a chance on them or she could jump off that cliff and see if he would catch her. He needed her to believe he'd be waiting when she made the leap.

He reached out and grasped her hand, ignoring the slight pain in his wrist and focusing solely on Micki. On keeping her right here with him and convincing her that this was where she belonged.

"What exactly are you afraid of?" he asked. "Because God knows if anyone has experience in avoiding commitment and relationships and being afraid of putting himself out there, it's me."

She gave him her bravest smile. "But you have a lifetime's experience of going out there every day in front of a crowd and facing possible defeat. It may have taken a pregnancy scare to show you what you really wanted in life, but once you realized, you went after it the same way you went after your career. With your whole heart. And I broke it in return." She glanced away.

"Hey." He turned her face towards him. "Something tells me you're not finished."

She shook her head. "It's just not easy, baring your soul."

"Not easy but worth it in the end, I hope."

"This whole girlie thing." She lifted the edge of her skirt and let it flutter around her thighs. "It's all new to me. And I look at the women you dated and I look at myself and I think, how can I even hope to hang on to you?"

Listening to her gut-wrenching honesty nearly took Damian's breath away. He understood how she was raised and the influence her uncle had had upon her and yet that's what made her unique. "Honey, when I look at you, you're right, I don't see anything similar to those other women."

She tried to pull her hand away but he held on tight.

"But don't you see? That's what makes you so special. That's why I love you. That's why until you, I never once thought about spending the rest of my life with anyone I'd been with. They never captured my interest the way you do. I'd never had to worry about being distracted during a game because of anything a woman did or said to me. Then you showed up and I couldn't stop thinking about you. In the field, at bat, when I was facing the possibility of having fathered Carole's baby, all I could think about was you."

Micki swallowed hard but the lump in her throat

was too large and the tears she'd been holding back began to trickle down her cheeks. As if admitting her inferiority complex wasn't embarrassing enough, now she had to turn into a crybaby.

She swiped at the tears with the back of her hand. "You're not going to get bored one day?" she asked.

He shook his head and laughed. "Not in a million years. Unfortunately you're going to have to take my word for it." He cupped his hand around her cheek. "Can you do that?"

"If you can have patience. I'm actually not used to this insecure part of me. It seems to rear its ugly head only around you."

His other hand followed the first, so he cradled her face, making her feel warm, secure and completely needed. In his gaze, she viewed a depth of feeling she'd never seen before.

"Around me you're not going to have any reason to think or feel insecure."

She bit down on her lower lip. "I was hoping you'd say that. Because I decided if you're still interested, I'm ready to go after what I want."

"And I was hoping you'd say that," he echoed with a grin.

Micki decided then and there to shed her insecurities and keep them at bay. She knew that she'd slip at times. She also knew she'd have Damian there to catch her if she fell.

She rose to her feet, straddling the bench as she stood. "I love you, Damian."

"I love you, too. But you said that before and you sent me away, so what's different this time?"

"I am. I'm ready to give not just my heart but my trust, too." She meant it but she didn't know what he wanted any longer. "You said you imagined having my baby." For weeks she'd tried not to remember those words because she'd been running from her fear.

His dark eyes raked over her in an invisible caress. Her body trembled and her nipples puckered beneath her clothes. He noticed and she saw a shudder run through him as well.

"Do you still feel that way?" she asked.

"You know I do," he said in a voice rough with desire.

"Well, I thought maybe I'd give you a present to remember this locker room by." As she spoke, she pulled her T-shirt up and over her head. Her tank came next, followed by her barely there strapless bra.

In the time it took her to blink, he'd tossed his shirt aside and pulled her against him. Her aching breasts pressed against his hair-roughened chest, sensations of warmth rushing through her. Liquid heat trickled between her legs, a welcome feeling after ignoring her desire for Damian for so long.

And then his lips came down hard on hers and

Micki knew this was meant to last forever. His tongue swirled inside her mouth as she feverishly worked at the button on his jeans. Her heart pounded hard in her chest, pure joy and ecstasy bubbling inside her.

He lifted his head, staring into her eyes for a long, sweet time. "I definitely don't have protection here."

Micki swallowed hard. "I definitely don't want you to use any."

With a low growl, he stepped back long enough to unbutton and pull off his jeans himself, while she, too, undressed. He made love to her standing up, no condom. The sensation of Damian, every hard, smooth velvety ridge of him was like nothing she'd experienced before.

So real, so honest, so very very emotional, Micki thought, as her imminent climax built higher and higher, his pace ever more frenzied until he came inside her. He thrust upward one last time, taking her along with him, calling her name on a low groan that vibrated through her entire body.

"I love you," he said, his arms still wrapped tightly around her.

She smiled. "I love you, too."

He looked into her eyes and she knew she saw his soul there. "Marry me," Damian said, his body still touching hers, their skin still damp from making love.

Micki could only nod and then she laid her head

against his chest, listening to his heart beat, knowing how lucky she was.

How lucky they both were.

EPILOGUE

DAMIAN'S NORMALLY QUIET island home was filled
with guests. His parents, his sisters, their husbands
and all their children, Sophie, Annabelle and Vaughn,
Yank and Lola, and all Annabelle's and Yank's animals
gathered in his house for a long weekend. And a wedding.

Lola and Yank had eloped the week before. Yank
had refused to be a spectacle, walking down the aisle
with his poor excuse for a Seeing Eye dog leading the
way, stopping to sniff every flower and person. Lola
hadn't wanted a wedding, she only wanted Yank, and
so they'd sprung the news on the girls at the first formal staff meeting of the still-unnamed merged firms
of Atkins Associates and the Hot Zone. As usual, the
men couldn't agree on whose name or initial should
go first on the letterhead.

With business and her uncle's personal life settled, Micki and Damian had set their own date, one
they'd decided to push up after discovering that their

locker room rendezvous had actually resulted in Micki getting pregnant.

"Are you ready?" Sophie entered the room where Micki had just finished changing into her ivory dress.

She smoothed the long train behind her and nodded. "Nervous but ready."

Sophie, the picture of perfection in her soft pink gown and French braid, walked over and kissed Micki's cheek. "You can't be nervous about marrying Damian."

"Of course not!" Micki had never been more certain of anything in her life. "But I am nervous about facing Uncle Yank for the first time since he discovered I'm pregnant and unwed."

Sophie laughed. "Oh, Lola will keep him calm."

"Want to bet?" Annabelle asked, joining them.

Like Sophie, she was also dressed in light pink, except hers was maternity wear and she was very pregnant. "He's downstairs threatening to nail Damian to the backstop by his... Well you get the drift."

Micki cringed. "Let's get this wedding over with before he neuters the groom."

"Good idea, especially if you two are really looking to load the field with your own baseball team."

Micki felt herself pale. "No way am I doing this nine times. I'm too nauseous even to contemplate a repeat performance."

"They say you forget the bad parts of pregnancy

as well as the pain of childbirth," Sophie said helpfully. "I figure it must be true or nobody would have more than one kid."

Micki shot Annabelle a knowing grin. "This from the only one in the room who's still single."

"The bleachers are filled with athletes for her to choose from right now," Annabelle said.

Micki and Damian had decided to marry on his beloved field of dreams. The guests filled the bleachers. Completely apropos as far as Micki was concerned.

"You both know I prefer not to date athletes. They use their bodies more than their brains. Present company's husbands and soon-to-be husbands excepted of course." Sophie grinned.

Micki walked over to her middle sister. "Trust me when I tell you, love finds you when you least expect it."

"And don't know what to do with it," Annabelle added.

Sophie planted her hands on her hips. "Spoken like two women head over heels. Thank God I'm the sister with the most common sense."

Micki and Annabelle rolled their eyes.

"Until your Mr. Right comes along," Annabelle said.

"I can't wait to be a fly on the wall when that day comes." Micki lifted the front of her dress as she stepped forward. "Now we have a wedding to pull off."

The New York Post
The Renegades Postseason Update

Ex-center fielder Damian Fuller married his publicist, Micki Jordan, in a private ceremony on an island off the coast of Florida. Fuller will become a permanent fixture on television as he joins the Renegades' new cable channel as one of the official announcers for all of the team's home games.

Fuller's replacement, Rick Carter, agreed via arbitration to a multimillion-dollar deal rumored to be worth ten million a year plus incentives. Carter and his live-in girlfriend are expecting their first child in a few months. The baby was the subject of a paternity claim naming Damian Fuller as the baby's father. The claim turned out to be false. According to Carter, marriage isn't out of the question. His girlfriend denies the possibility but the two are inseparable, though according to neighbors in their new high-rise apartment in Manhattan, they are also prone to loud bickering.

In other news, the sports agencies of the Hot Zone and Atkins Associates have merged into a new firm called Athletes Only. The Hot Zone will continue on solely as a PR firm run by the Jordan sisters.

Annabelle Jordan Vaughn is currently married to football great Brandon Vaughn and recently gave birth to their first child, a girl named Sydney. Micki Jordan Fuller is also expecting. The father, when reached for comment, said the sonogram indicates the baby is a girl. Sophie Jordan, the third partner in the highly respected firm for elite athletes, is unattached as of this publication. But with her uncle and sisters settled down, can marriage be far behind for the last Jordan sister?

Sophie Jordan couldn't be reached for comment.

* * * * *

Eligible bachelors. New York City is full of them. Sexy men. Caring men. Men who aren't afraid to step up and do what is right. Men who'e be the perfect catch if only the right woman came along. Don't miss the first two books of Carly Phillips's newest series

MOST ELIGIBLE BACHELOR

KISS ME IF YOU CAN
August 2010
&
LOVE ME IF YOU DARE
September 2010

REQUEST YOUR FREE BOOKS!

2 FREE NOVELS
FROM THE ROMANCE COLLECTION
PLUS 2 FREE GIFTS!

YES! Please send me 2 FREE novels from the Romance Collection and my 2 FREE gifts (gifts are worth about $10). After receiving them, if I don't wish to receive any more books, I can return the shipping statement marked "cancel." If I don't cancel, I will receive 4 brand-new novels every month and be billed just $5.74 per book in the U.S. or $6.24 per book in Canada. That's a saving of at least 28% off the cover price. It's quite a bargain! Shipping and handling is just 50¢ per book in the U.S. and 75¢ per book in Canada.* I understand that accepting the 2 free books and gifts places me under no obligation to buy anything. I can always return a shipment and cancel at any time. Even if I never buy another book, the two free books and gifts are mine to keep forever.

194 MDN E4LY   394 MDN E4MC

Name _____

(PLEASE PRINT)

Address _____ Apt. #

City _____ State/Prov. _____ Zip/Postal Code

Signature (if under 18, a parent or guardian must sign)

Mail to **The Reader Service:**
IN U.S.A.: P.O. Box 1867, Buffalo, NY 14240-1867
IN CANADA: P.O. Box 609, Fort Erie, Ontario L2A 5X3

Not valid for current subscribers to the Romance Collection
or the Romance/Suspense Collection.

Want to try two free books from another line?
Call 1-800-873-8635 or visit www.morefreebooks.com.

* Terms and prices subject to change without notice. Prices do not include applicable taxes. N.Y. residents add applicable sales tax. Canadian residents will be charged applicable provincial taxes and GST. Offer not valid in Quebec. This offer is limited to one order per household. All orders subject to approval. Credit or debit balances in a customer's account(s) may be offset by any other outstanding balance owed by or to the customer. Please allow 4 to 6 weeks for delivery. Offer available while quantities last.

Your Privacy: Harlequin Books is committed to protecting your privacy. Our Privacy Policy is available online at www.eHarlequin.com or upon request from the Reader Service. From time to time we make our lists of customers available to reputable third parties who may have a product or service of interest to you. If you would prefer we not share your name and address, please check here. ☐

Help us get it right—We strive for accurate, respectful and relevant communications. To clarify or modify your communication preferences, visit us at www.ReaderService.com/consumerchoice.

carly phillips

77432	HOT STUFF	___ $7.99 U.S.	___ $9.99 CAN.
77401	LUCKY BREAK	___ $7.99 U.S.	___ $8.99 CAN.
77375	LUCKY STREAK	___ $7.99 U.S.	___ $8.99 CAN.
77331	LUCKY CHARM	___ $7.99 U.S.	___ $7.99 CAN.
77351	SECRET FANTASY	___ $7.99 U.S.	___ $7.99 CAN.
77326	SEDUCE ME	___ $7.99 U.S.	___ $9.50 CAN.
77110	SUMMER LOVIN'	___ $7.99 U.S.	___ $9.50 CAN.

(limited quantities available)

TOTAL AMOUNT	$ _____
POSTAGE & HANDLING	$ _____
($1.00 FOR 1 BOOK, 50¢ for each additional)	
APPLICABLE TAXES*	$ _____
TOTAL PAYABLE	$ _____

(check or money order—please do not send cash)

To order, complete this form and send it, along with a check or money order for the total above, payable to HQN Books, to: **In the U.S.:** 3010 Walden Avenue, P.O. Box 9077, Buffalo, NY 14269-9077; **In Canada:** P.O. Box 636, Fort Erie, Ontario, L2A 5X3.

Name: _____

Address: _____ City: _____

State/Prov.: _____ Zip/Postal Code: _____

Account Number (if applicable): _____

075 CSAS

*New York residents remit applicable sales taxes.
*Canadian residents remit applicable GST and provincial taxes.

HQN™

We *are* romance™

www.HQNBooks.com